Cats in the Belfry

A Klepto Cat Mystery

Patricia Fry

Matilija Press
147 N. Encinal Ave.
Ojai, CA 93023
www.KleptoCatMysteries.com

Cats in the Belfry

A Klepto Cat Mystery
by Patricia Fry

copyright © 2017 Patricia Fry
ISBN 978-0-9985356-5-4

This novel is a work of fiction. The characters, names, incidents, dialogue are the products of the author's imagination or are used fictitiously. Any resemblance to actual persons, companies or events is purely coincidental.

Cover Art: Bernadette E. Kazmarski
Cover layout: Dennis Mullican
Page layout: Dennis Mullican

Printed in U.S.A. by: Create Space

Other Novels by Patricia Fry

Catnapped
Cat-Eye Witness
Sleight of Paw
Undercover Cat
The Colony Cat Caper
Celebrity Cat Caper
The Corral Cat Caper
The Gallery Cat Caper
Mansion of Meows
PAWtners in Crime
PAWsitively Sinister
The Purrfect Lie

A Picture-Purrfect Christmas
Meow for the Money
Claws for a Cause
Cabin FURvor
A MEOWvelous Witness
Cats in Cahoots
The Amazing CATventure
By Cat or By Crook
Merriment, Mayhem, and Meows
A Christmas to Purr About
Cattywampus Travels

Cats in the Belfry
A Klepto Cat Mystery

Book 24

"Be careful, Vannie," Margaret said as the two of them made their way slowly up the old bell tower stairway with Savannah's cat. She chuckled when she saw Rags tugging against his leash. "He sure seems eager to get to the top." Before taking another step, she asked, "Hey, want me to take him?"

Savannah hesitated, then nodded. "Yes. Maybe you should. I'm a little off balance already with this baby bump, and Rags isn't helping."

"Okay. Here, you hold the light and hand me the leash." But as the women attempted to make the exchange, somehow they lost their grip on the flashlight and it tumbled down the spiral staircase with a clang and a clatter. "Damn!"

"Oh no."

"I thought you had it," Margaret complained.

Savannah let out a sigh. "Now what?"

"I guess I'd better go back down and get it. Or," she hesitated before saying, "we could scrap this witch hunt."

"So it's become a witch hunt, has it?" Savannah snarked.

"What would you call it?"

More quietly, Savannah said, "I guess that's what we were going to find out today. Yeah, it's getting late. Let's go back down and regroup."

"Okay," Margaret agreed. "Hold onto that railing and step carefully. It's pretty dark up here."

"I will. You hold onto Rags."

"Huh?"

Savannah stopped in mid-step. "Rags," she hissed. "Auntie, you have him, don't you?"

"No. You didn't hand him over."

"Yes, I did," Savannah insisted." You took the leash before you dropped the flashlight."

"No, I didn't. And I didn't drop the flashlight, either. I handed it to you and you dropped it."

"Are you delusional?" Savannah spat.

Margaret tried to focus on her niece in the near-darkness. "Are you saying you don't have hold of the leash?"

"No, I don't!"

"Good God," Margaret murmured. "What just happened?"

Savannah suddenly felt a familiar knot in the pit of her stomach. "Rags!" she called. "Here kitty-kitty. Where are you, Rags? Come on, boy."

Margaret tried her hand at enticing the cat. "Here kitty-kitty-kitty," she trilled. "Rags! Here kitty-kitty-kitty."

Still holding tightly to the railing, Savannah leaned over and felt around for the cat on the steps. "Where is he, Auntie? Which way do you suppose he went?"

"I don't know. I'd better go get that light and see if we can figure it out. Maybe he went back down these stairs. At least, let's hope he did. Otherwise…"

"Otherwise what?" Savannah asked, not wanting to hear her aunt's response.

"Otherwise he went up and we don't know what in the heck is up there."

"Rags!" Savannah called more loudly. "Rags! Kitty-kitty-kitty."

Margaret sighed. "Come on, let's go back down. Now step carefully, Vannie. In fact, let me go first in case you stumble."

But before they could make any headway, they heard an ear-piercing screech. Margaret grabbed for Savannah. "What in the hell was that?"

Too shaky now to stand, Savannah lowered herself and perched on one of the narrow steps, muttering, "Oh my gosh. Oh my gosh. Rags…"

"Didn't sound like a cat to me," Margaret said. "Where'd that weird noise come from, anyway?"

Savannah pointed toward the bell tower. "Up there, I think." She pulled herself to her feet, using the railing. "Let's go." More quietly, she said, "Please be downstairs, Rags. Please, please, please."

Just then Margaret screamed. She slapped frantically around her head.

"What's wrong?" Savannah shouted.

"Something just attacked me—a damn bird or a bat, maybe."

"Are you okay?" Savannah shrieked.

"Yes. Let's just get out of here." As Margaret began taking the steps more quickly, she turned and instructed, "Now, you take it slow." She reached the bottom of the stairs first, picked up the flashlight, and directed it at the few steps Savannah had left to descend.

"Do you see Rags?" Savannah asked.

Once her niece was on solid flooring, Margaret shined the light around the spiral staircase, then into the hallway. "Oh my God!"

"What?" Savannah could feel her heart pounding hard in her chest.

"Your cat! That black bird's got him!" She shuddered. "It looks like he's attacked Rags!"

Savannah gasped. "A bird? Is he okay?" she asked, her view obstructed by her aunt, who was now running toward where the cat lay.

"Shoo!" Margaret shouted. "Get off him! Get off him!"

The large black bird unfolded its wings and flew over her head up toward the bell tower emitting a shrill call as it disappeared in the darkness above them.

"Rags," Savannah said, kneeling next to the large grey-and-white cat. She ran her hand over his body. When he didn't move, she quickly checked his vitals. "He's breathing. His heart rate's a little slow." She shook him and called his name. "Rag. Rags."

Just then, the cat opened his eyes and lifted his head. When he saw Savannah and Margaret he quickly stood up, stretched, and yawned.

"Oh Rags, you're okay," Savannah said, hugging him to her.

Margaret looked around cautiously. "That bird must have knocked him out or something."

Savannah ran her hands over the cat, checking for injuries. She gazed toward the spiral staircase and said, as if thinking out loud, "Or he was hypnotized or drugged, maybe." She enveloped him in her hands and kissed the top of his head. Then, lifting him into her arms, she said, "Auntie, I'd like to take him outside."

"Yes," Margaret whispered. "Let's get the heck out of here."

4

As the two women and the cat slowly descended the wide staircase to the ground floor, Savannah thought back to the day they first discussed coming out to this eerie place and the reason they'd thought it was important to do so.

***

It was one week earlier when June Balcomb ushered Savannah and Margaret into her home at the Ragsdale Cat Ranch. "It's wonderful to see you both," June said, extending her hand to each of the them. "I hear you're back from quite a lengthy vacation."

"We sure are," Margaret said. "It was a good trip, but I don't want to do that again anytime soon."

Savannah nodded. "It was exhausting, but such a lot of fun." She focused on the elderly woman. "How are you, June? You look well."

"Thank you." June glanced down toward Savannah's feet and smiled. "I see you brought him. Good. Mazie Mae will be glad to see him. Some of the others will too. Come in, come in," she invited as she led the two women and Rags into what she referred to as the cat room.

"So you still keep your cats separate from the rescue cats?" Savannah asked upon entering the room, which was equipped with several cat trees, kitty perches, and cozy beds, and occupied by a number of cats of various colors and sizes.

"Yes. They were accustomed to this space and their private outdoor playpen long before we added the area for the rescues. I didn't want to uproot them. I could see no reason for it."

"Of course not," Margaret said. She chuckled. "Oh, look. I think Rags remembers his friends."

The women watched as the curious cat expressed an interest in a Himalayan that stared at him through clear blue eyes.

"Remove that apparatus, Savannah, and let him mingle, will you?" June instructed.

Once he was free of his harness, Rags joined Mazie Mae at the top of the kitty jungle gym and they spent several seconds sniffing one another. "She remembers her hero," June said, smiling. She gestured toward the conversation area. "Please sit down wherever there isn't a cat." She chuckled. "They do take over."

"Well, I'll just put this one on my lap," Margaret said, picking up an orange tabby from the seat of a wingback chair and sitting down with her.

June smiled. "She'd love it. By the way, Maggie, that's Marmalade Jam."

Savannah sat on a satin Victorian sofa next to a tabby cat. "Tabitha, right?" she asked, petting her.

June nodded, then pointed at Savannah. "You don't have much room on your lap for a cat these days, do you?"

She caressed her bulging stomach. "So true."

"When do you expect your new little one?" June asked.

"Around May twentieth."

"So how are things going here at the cat ranch?" Margaret asked.

June looked at Rags as he continued to greet her cats and explore their play area. "Very well. I'm living my lifelong dream of helping cats. And to think it all started with Ragsdale. After he so gallantly saved my Mazie Mae from freezing that night when she was snatched from our home, I knew I would celebrate his legacy in some wonderful and important way." Her eyes lit up when she said, "And then, you brought me Nola and Luke." When Savannah started to protest, June put up a hand to stop her. "Yes, you did. You both are responsible even if somewhat indirectly." She gazed into Savannah's eyes, then Margaret's. "Maggie, if I hadn't attended your Hammond Cat Alliance meeting, I would not have learned about Nola." She focused on Savannah. "And you, Savannah, you and Dr. Mike had the grand insight to introduce me to Luke."

Savannah smiled. "It sounds as though they're working out well for you. I'm sure glad to hear it."

"Yes," Margaret said, "it's not easy to find good—I mean *good* help for an operation like yours."

June tilted her head. "Well, I do believe that Nola and Luke brought just the magic I needed to start and run this rescue and feral cat shelter." She folded her hands under her chin. "They are a godsend, those two. Without them, I would never have fulfilled my dream to help some of the world's more helpless cats." She looked Savannah in the eyes. "If I didn't have this wonderful shelter—Ragsdale's Cat Ranch—I probably would have faded away into obscurity by now."

"You'd think all the work would wear you out," Margaret said.

"Oh no. Just the opposite," June protested. "It invigorates me." She leaned forward, a twinkle in her eye. "Of course *they* do all the work. I'm just along for the ride." She rolled her eyes for emphasis. "And what a ride it's been."

Savannah smiled. "That's wonderful, June. I'm glad it's a joy for you and not a burden. As Auntie said, it can be a lot of work."

"But the rewards make it all worthwhile." June faced Margaret. "Maggie, do you remember those feral cats you brought to me from the Lander place?"

Margaret nodded.

"Luke has managed to release the fear from most of them so they can be successfully adopted. In fact, I believe a couple of them are enjoying life in loving homes as we speak. Isn't it wonderful?"

"It sure is," Margaret agreed.

Savannah giggled. "I love kitty-cat happy-ending stories." In a more serious tone, she asked, "So, June, Luke seems to have found his niche here, huh?"

"Goodness gracious, yes. He's a marvel, that young man. I bless the day he came to me."

"And to think it was just a little over a year ago when we found him—or he found us," Savannah reminisced.

Margaret smirked. "Yeah, living homeless and pilfering from neighbors to survive."

"And selling his flutes," Savannah added. "June, is he still making flutes?"

She nodded. "Yes, in his spare time."

"And Nola—didn't I hear she has a beau?"

June shook her head. "Oh no, that broke up months ago. No, she's single again and I like it that way." She grinned sheepishly. "Selfish, I know. But I don't have to worry about her running off to get married and leaving me and the cats."

"Well, she is young and attractive," Savannah reminded her. "That's bound to happen at some point—

at least the getting married part. But maybe she won't leave the cat ranch. Anyway, didn't you make her a partner in the enterprise?"

"Yes. You're right. For better or for worse, all this will be hers when I cross over. And I'm confident that she will carry on as I wish." Suddenly June glanced up and acknowledged the young woman who had entered the room with a serving tray. "Nola dear. Thank you." With a twinkle in her eye, she addressed the others, "Not only is she wonderful with the cats and the business end of the shelter, she's the hostess with the mostest."

Nola smiled at June, then said, "Good morning Savannah, Maggie. Would you like a cup of tea?"

Margaret smiled. "Sounds good. Thank you."

"Savannah?" she offered.

"Yes, please." Savannah chuckled and asked, "You aren't the cook and chief bottle washer too, are you?"

"Heavens no," Nola said. "June still employs some of her longtime kitchen staff. I asked if I could serve the tea and greet our guests today." She gazed at Margaret, then Savannah. "I hear you two are embarking on an interesting project—the cat colony out at the old seminary, right?"

"That's what my aunt tells me," Savannah quipped.

Margaret winced. "It should be challenging."

"Challenging?" Savannah questioned, her eyes wide.

"Well…" Margaret started.

June interrupted. "Do you have any idea why no one has tackled that colony before?"

"Yeah, Auntie," Savannah prompted, "why is that?"

Margaret shook her head. "I don't really know, other than the fact that the place is pretty run-down, off the beaten path, and I guess the cat population there is kind of out of control."

June winked. "You probably won't find a rodent problem."

"That's one thing to be thankful for," Margaret said.

"Do you have permission to go in there?" Nola asked.

Margaret nodded. "Yes, the out-of-state owner plans to take down the building and he wants the cats removed before they start the demolition. That isn't scheduled for several months, so we can take our time with the project. I want to survey the situation and consider the best way to approach it. We may decide to get the cats stabilized where they are before moving them. A move can stress them."

June was quiet for a moment, then she asked, "Do you think you'll be safe out there?"

This piqued Savannah's interest. "Why? What do you know that we don't know?"

"That place was in the news a lot during the eighties and nineties. As I hear it told, there's a lot of negativity around it. You might sprinkle salt or burn sage before getting involved."

Savannah stared at June, then asked, "Isn't that for cleansing bad vibes, removing bad spirits, or something? Do you think we'll encounter evil forces out there?"

"Well, I'm not completely sure. All I know is that there must be a lot of negative energy around there after some of the activity that's been reported over the years."

"Hogwash," Margaret muttered. When the others looked at her, she said, "Some people just have big imaginations and nothing better to do than spread rumors."

Nola studied the three women for a moment. "June, how do you know so much about that place?"

She hesitated, petted the cat in her lap, and revealed, "I knew the owner. We were in a couple of civic groups together." She glanced at the others. "He bought the old seminary decades ago from the religious or spiritual organization that previously owned it."

"What did your friend do with the property?" Nola asked.

"He planned to create a business development there—offices, you see. He didn't have a lot of capital, so he hired some...um...shall we say less desirables, and let them board there. That faction attracted others. Soon he'd lost control of the goings-on and he walked away from the project."

"Was his name Crandall?" Margaret asked.

"No," June said. She thought for a moment. "I think it was more like Montgomery...Montague, that's it."

"Oh, well, he must have sold it. From what I understand," Margaret said, "the current owner bought it about fifteen years ago and he plans to put up a shopping center. There are new housing tracts going in out that way and I guess he and his investors believe we need another place to shop." She shrugged. "They're probably right."

"I'm all for it," Nola said. "Anything would be better than what that place has become."

"So, Nola, you've been out there?" Savannah asked.

The younger woman nodded. "I was with a group of friends one night maybe five years ago. Actually they were friends of a friend of a friend. It turned out to be one of those situations that, once I was involved, I couldn't back out of. I was riding in someone else's car and all that." She continued, "We ended up out at the seminary late at night and boy, was that a spooky experience." She looked at Savannah, then Margaret. "You two are courageous to take on that colony."

Wide-eyed, Margaret asked, "What did you see out there? What happened?"

"Well, it was what we heard, mostly. Some sort of...um...I guess you'd call it chanting. It sort of echoed through the building real eerie-like." She laughed. "I was scared from the get-go, but you should have seen some of the instigators—those who made fun of us for being frightened. When that chanting sound started getting really loud, they were the first ones out of the building." She snickered. "The big brave driver almost left without us, he was so eager to get away."

"Wow!" Savannah exclaimed. "Sounds scary, all right. But we probably don't have any reason to go inside the place." She looked at Margaret. "The cats are outside, aren't they?"

Before Margaret could answer, June asked, "How did you two get involved, anyway?"

12

Margaret took a deep breath. "Max knows the caretaker. Andy came to us just before we left on our trip and asked if we knew anything about relocating cats." She addressed Savannah. "Yeah, you're right, we won't be going inside. Andy said the place is locked up and all the cats are outside. Piece of cake."

"What's your time frame, Maggie?" June asked.

"He has given us a month to work our magic." She faced June, then glanced at Nola. "We wanted to find out if you have room, in case we need a place for some of the cats—in particular the least socialized ones."

"Do you know how many you're dealing with?" Nola asked.

Margaret shook her head. "From what Andy said, maybe as many as twenty-five." She winced. "But, as you know, it's kitten season and we could find a dozen or so more."

"Yes," June said, "we can accommodate all that you want to bring us."

Margaret smiled. "Thank you. Only I hope we won't have to overwhelm you. We should be able take maybe ten or twelve, plus any nursing kittens, but it's hard to tell what the need will be at a shelter like ours from one day to the next."

"So true," Nola said. "However, we're in pretty good shape here, so no worries. You two ladies go rescue those sweet kitties and between us, we'll make sure they have a happy and healthy rest of their nine lives."

Margaret smiled. "Thank you."

"Yes," Savannah said, "it makes our job less stressful knowing that you're here. So you have room in the feral cat enclosure?"

June's face lit up. "Yes. Nola, show them what we've done out there." She turned to Savannah and Margaret. "We've enlarged it and Nola and Luke have begun a more stringent socialization program with some of the most recent wild ones in hopes that we can place more of them in forever homes." She smiled at Nola. "Those two really make things happen around here. Aren't they wonderful?"

"They sure are," Savannah agreed.

"And to think I found her in a jail cell." June grinned at Nola, then glanced at the others. "… all because of her passion for helping cats. What a beautiful day it was when I met Nola."

The younger woman smiled sweetly at June, then issued an invitation to the others. "Come on, I'll show you what we've been doing." She started to step out of the room, then turned and said, "Luke's out here. He'll want to see you too."

"So he's doing okay?" Savannah asked as she walked along next to Nola. "Did he finish school?"

Nola nodded. "Oh yes. June made sure of that."

"And his grandmother's okay with him living here and working with the cats?" Savannah added. "As I recall, he and his brothers lived with their grandmother."

"That's right." Nola laughed. "Yes, she's here a couple of times a week helping out, herself. She says if she wants a relationship with her youngest grandson, she'd better become a cat lady. She has convinced Luke to take business classes at the community college and he seems to be enjoying that, actually. Yeah, he's doing okay."

"And you?" Savannah asked. "Is it working out well for you? You should be out..."

Nola turned to face Savannah. "Out what?" she challenged. "Partying, shopping, focusing on my makeup? Naw, that's not me. I'm doing just what I want to be doing at this point in my life. I'll always cherish the day I met June Balcomb. Not only is she the best mentor I've ever met, she's the grandmother I never had. We're a great team and I just adore being here." She chuckled. "You know, my mother loves cats too, and she also volunteers here. It's strange for me and Luke to be bossing our parents around."

"Well, you're young," Margaret said, "don't forget to have fun and enjoy the benefits of your youth. Don't make it all about your work."

Nola stared at Margaret for a moment. "I appreciate you reminding me of that. Yeah, I owe it to myself and friends and family to be more well-rounded." Her smile brightened when she explained, "I've joined the recreation department and they sponsor activities for adults. We hike somewhere or bicycle and even horseback ride just about twice a month."

"Good girl," Savannah said.

"Oh, there's Luke." Nola waved. "Luke, we have visitors!"

"Hi, Ms. Savannah, Ms. Maggie," Luke greeted, removing a glove in order to shake hands with them.

"Working hard?" Savannah asked.

He nodded.

"Good for you."

"And good for the cats," Margaret added, smiling at the array of cats she could see in the feral cat pen. "They sure look healthy and happy."

"They should be," Luke said. "Ms. June feeds them the best and Dr. Mike keeps a close eye on them." He tilted his head. "So what brings you out here?"

"They're managing a colony of a couple of dozen cats," Nola explained.

"Where?" he asked, furrowing his brow.

"The old seminary," Margaret responded. When he looked confused, she explained, "It's that abandoned building out where they're constructing those new tract homes."

He shook his head. "I guess I'm not familiar with it. I'm kind of new to this area, having grown up in Mason."

Margaret winced. "We're not all that familiar with what's going on out there, either. We plan to take inventory today. Just wanted to make sure we have a place to bring the overflow of cats and kittens. Oh, and Luke, we may need your help with the trapping." She nodded toward Savannah. "She can't be doing any heavy lifting—you know, like of traps full of cats."

"Sure. Just let me know when. I'll be glad to help."

Margaret put her hand on Savannah's arm. "Well, we should get out there and see what we're dealing with."

Savannah let out a sigh. "Okay, let's go."

Nola smiled. "Well, good luck. I hope it's a trouble-free transition for all the kitties. Let me know if I can help, will you?"

"Sure," Margaret said.

Savannah waved. "Thanks. We'll be in touch."

***

Later that Thursday morning in early March, Savannah and her Aunt Margaret took Rags home, then set out on their mission.

"It sure is run-down." Savannah noticed as they drove through the gate onto the seminary property. "Looks like it was abandoned an awfully long time ago."

"Yeah, by people, anyway." Margaret looked around. "But I imagine there are a lot of spiders and other crawly things all over this place."

"And cats," Savannah added. "You say around two dozen of them? Where do you suppose they all came from?"

"Most likely when the seminary was still operating, they brought in a few cats for rodent control and…"

"Let me guess," Savannah interrupted, "they allowed the poor cats to breed indiscriminately." She asked, "Do you know if they're being fed?"

Margaret nodded. "Andy has been feeding them for years. But in recent months, it's been only sporadically—you know, now and then."

Savannah frowned. "From the looks of that feeding station over there, it's been a while since they were served a fresh meal." She gazed at the structure. "Does the caretaker live here?"

"He did up until a year or so ago, when he began to have some health issues. Andy's now in an assisted living facility and he relies on others to bring him out here whenever he feels well enough. The investor has authorized Andy to relocate the cats. Of course, he isn't up to doing the trapping himself and that's why he came to Max for help." She looked at her niece. "You know the rest of the story."

"Yeah, the gullible duo jump in with both feet," Savannah said, laughing.

"Pretty much." Margaret squinted toward Savannah. "What does Michael say about your involvement in this?"

"He's not convinced it's the best use of my time right now."

"What would he prefer you be doing? I mean, saving cats is certainly a noble cause."

Savanna nodded. "I know, but he'd rather see me safe at home, embroidering or standing over a hot stove canning fruit."

"Your orchard isn't ready to pick, is it?"

"Not quite. Unfortunately, most of the canning will take place in the heat of the summer, when I have two little ones to chase after instead of just one."

Margaret grinned. "The baby will be running around by then?"

"Oh, you know what I mean. He'll have his demands." She snickered. "He is a male, after all." Savannah faced her aunt. "Since Rob suggested I write Rags's...um...memoirs, Michael would really rather see me working on that. And I am, in my spare time."

"So Rob is more than a producer of documentaries and children's books? He also produces books for adults?" Margaret asked.

Savannah shrugged. "I guess he moves in whatever direction seems to have the most potential.

Don't forget he gets a cut of the profit from the documentaries and books featuring Rags."

"Well, tell me about the book you're writing." Margaret grinned impishly. "Will it be in first-person... er...first-cat, an as-told-to, or will you write a full-blown biography?" Before Savannah could respond, Margaret added, "You'd better promote it as fiction, 'cause no one's going to believe the things your cat does."

"No, Auntie. There actually is an audience for true animal stories. From what Rob tells me, these books are quite popular." She nudged Margaret. "He thinks I could become a female James Herriot."

"Pshaw, Vannie, the only thing you have in common with Herriot is your veterinary credential."

Ignoring her aunt, Savannah twisted her hair into a loose knot on top of her head. "I think I'll write it chronologically. Right now, I'm just jotting down the things I can remember about Rags's adoption and my first days with him and some of the things he's done over the years. I'll interview people who knew him when we lived in Los Angeles. I'd like to interview you and Max too."

Margaret looked at her niece and shook her head, then took a breath and muttered, "Okay, where to start; where to start? Vannie, this is probably the largest colony I've dealt with in my career—that is my volunteer career." She winced. "Two dozen cats and counting." She added, "I've been involved with larger cat-hoarding situations, but that's another animal altogether."

"And counting?" Savannah repeated.

"Yes. As you can imagine, some of the cats out here are already loaded with their spring litter of kittens. And Andy believes that more cats have joined these in recent years, presumably from that older housing tract across the way. He told Max that the homes have become rather ramshackle and many of them are rentals. You know how that is—people come and go. Rentals can attract a rather nomadic group. He says some of the renters, when they move out, leave their cats behind. Naturally, those cats find their way over here." She pointed. "Then there's that new tract up on the hillside. Those residents are evidently complaining about the seminary cats."

Savannah glanced around the property. "They must be going outside of this compound to find food."

"Yes. I'm sure the cats took care of the rodent problem here long ago, and with Andy feeding only when he's well enough, they're out hunting and foraging elsewhere." She grinned. "If I were one of these cats, I'd sure be looking for handouts at that upscale development." She let out a sigh. "Okay, let's walk around and see what we have here, okay?"

Savannah looked at her watch. "Let's do it. I have an hour."

"What happens in an hour, do you turn into a pumpkin?" Margaret laughed. "Actually, you already look like a pumpkin with that belly of yours."

Savannah rubbed her baby bump. "Yeah, I'm getting pretty round, but not as big as I was with Lily, do you think? I seem to be carrying this one differently. At least I'm not waddling yet. I don't feel so awkward."

"You have what—two months to go?" Margaret asked as she pulled a clipboard out of the car.

"Eleven weeks. Closer to three months."

Margaret stared at her niece for a moment, then hugged the clipboard to herself and said, "Let's start over there, where it looks like Andy was feeding them." She called over her shoulder, "Got your gloves?"

Savannah nodded and followed after her. When she noticed her aunt stop at the feeding station, she said, "You've done a lot of these, haven't you—I mean colony evaluations."

Margaret made a note on her pad, then responded. "Yes, and hoarding situations, abandoned cats—you name it—and I've seen it just in these past five or six years that I've been working with Max." She shook her head disgustedly. "I just don't know why some people won't take responsibility for the cats they adopt or purchase or even happen to find. If you decide you no longer want a cat or you know of one that seems to be homeless, step up and take responsibility. Make sure the cat has a warm place to sleep, food in its tummy, and someone to love it. It's the least we can do. But there seem to be two types of people—no three: those who love and take care of their cats, those who create problems for cats, and those who must scramble to help the cats. Know what I mean?"

"Yes." Savannah chuckled. "Auntie, what would you do with yourself if there were no needy cats?"

Margaret frowned at her. "Huh? What would I do? There are many things I could be doing instead of scavenging around a filthy old building surrounded by ancient machinery and other debris, trying to round up cats."

"Name one thing," Savannah challenged.

Margaret stopped and thought for a moment before saying, "Oh Vannie that's silly. I don't have time to daydream right now. Come on, let's get to work."

"Yeah, just as I thought," Savannah said, grinning.

"Okay, let's pick up these crusty, rusted-out dishes." Margaret pointed. "There's a trash bin over there. I'll place a few clean bowls here to mark the spot." She stooped and peered into a crawl hole under the large building. "Then we'll see if we can spot any cats."

"There's one!" Savannah said.

"Where?"

"A dirty white one. It went under that wheelbarrow over there."

"One dirty white cat," Margaret repeated, writing it down on her notepad. "Adult?" she asked.

"Yes." Savannah then said, "Oh, there are some cats peeking out from behind those shrubs." She crouched and tried to entice them. "Here kitty-kitty." She rattled a small bag of cat treats. "Want a treat? Come and get it."

"Hmmm," Margaret muttered, "they look interested. We actually might be able to get our hands on those tiger kitties."

"That would be nice."

"Let's continue around the building," Margaret suggested. "Then we'll put down some food and water and observe them for a while. If we can make friends with any of them today, we'll go ahead and take them to our shelter."

"Oh, there's a bi-color adult—looks like a young adult. Uh-oh, I believe she's with kittens."

Margaret cringed. "Now, that one we really want. Be on the lookout for the pregnant or lactating ones. We definitely want to rescue them—and any kittens—first."

"And sick ones."

"That's the program," Margaret said.

Once the women had walked the perimeter of the building, they pulled two folding chairs out of the car and discretely prepared a few cat carriers.

"So how many did you count, Auntie?" Savannah asked while unfolding her lawn chair and placing it in a sunny spot near where they'd noticed the greatest cat activity.

Margaret referred to her pad. "Eight adults, including two intact males and two probably-pregnant females. We saw three teenagers—you know, around six or seven months old. They're most likely from a fall litter."

"And many of them seem to be skittish—curious, but skittish," Savannah observed. "We may be able to make friends with some of them. What do you think?"

"Well, before we feed them, let's see if we can lure some of them with those treats you brought. Go ahead and sprinkle a few in this clean bowl." Margaret took a deep breath and faced her niece. "We may need to come out here after dark. Cats are nocturnal as you know—ferals, even more so."

"Yeah, I figured as much. Michael's not going to be thrilled."

"Why?"

"Well, he says this place has been a den of iniquity over the years."

Margaret squinted in Savannah's direction. "What?"

"He says evil takes place out here."

"It was a seminary and a church, for heaven's sake."

Savannah looked confused. "You mean this wasn't a biker-gang hangout and black market headquarters? You never heard any of that? I mean, June also sort of alluded to the fact that there was bad stuff going on out here."

"Maybe a long time ago." Margaret shrugged. "…or not. I don't recall hearing or reading anything concrete, just fleeting rumors, mostly." She shivered with excitement. "As Nola indicated, it's supposed to be haunted."

"She indicated that?"

"Well, yes. What do you think scared her and her friends away that night she told us about?"

"Sounds," Savannah said. "She just mentioned some sort of odd sound."

"Ghostly sounds," Margaret said.

"And you still want to come out here at night?"

After thinking about it for a moment, Margaret said, "Look around. Do you see anything frightening here?"

"Yeah, seems completely abandoned. There sure doesn't appear to be anything weird going on. It's just a refuge for cats. That's all." Suddenly, she jumped a little in her chair and whispered, "Hey, look."

Margaret turned in time to see the white cat eating the few treats they'd poured into a bowl. Once the cat had finished, she gazed at the two women and Savannah promptly offered her more of the treats.

"Oh goodie, here she comes," Margaret said under her breath.

It took some coaxing, but Savannah was finally able to get her hands on the cat and she put her into a carrier. "I do believe she's with kittens," she said. "Her tummy's pretty lumpy."

"Bummer," Margaret said. "Well, one down. Let's see if we can find those other pregnant females we saw."

"One was under the building, wasn't she? Didn't we see her in the crawlspace?" Savannah asked, standing up. "She actually seemed pretty calm. Gosh, I hope we can get all of the pregnant females to a safe place. The babies would be so vulnerable out here." She started to walk toward the crawl hole when suddenly she stopped and cocked her head. "Did you hear that?"

"What?" Margaret asked.

"Kittens. I think I hear kittens." Savannah walked in the direction of the sound. As she approached a large, mostly dead shrub, she was startled by a tiger-striped cat that leaped out of hiding and ran off. Savannah walked closer. "Here they are," she said, lifting a piece of cardboard that lay across the top of the shrub. "Look at this, their momma made a little nest for them. Let's see, there are three…no, four kittens about maybe three-and-a-half-weeks old. Do you want to take them?"

"Sure do," Margaret said. "But we need to get the mom too. We'll put this little family in foster care until the kittens are old enough to adopt."

"Okay," Savannah said, picking up two of the kittens with her glove-protected hands.

Margaret snatched the other two and noticed that the mother cat was crouched just inside the crawl hole watching fretfully. Once the kittens were safely, although not happily, placed in a large carrier, the women began pursuing the mother cat. While she was definitely interested in the treats Savannah offered, she seemed frightened and unsure.

"Hey, let's show her the kittens," Savannah suggested. "Maybe she'll come closer if we bring the kittens out here."

"Good thinking, Vannie." When Savannah started to head toward the car, Margaret followed after her. "Hey, I'll get them. You don't need to be carrying that bulky carrier."

The two women patiently worked with the mother cat for several minutes until Margaret was finally able to get her hands on her. With Savannah's help, she put her into the large carrier with the kittens.

"There's another pregnant female," Savannah said when she saw a tortoiseshell cat with a bulging tummy walk cautiously up to the food dish, where Savannah had sprinkled more kitty treats. As Margaret took the carrier back to the car, Savannah moved closer to the tortie, shaking the treat bag in an attempt to get her attention. "Come on, girl," she crooned from a distance. "Let us help you and your babies." When the cat seemed mildly curious, Savannah perched on a low wall near the feeding station, poured a few kitty treats into her hand, and held it toward the cat. She tossed a kibble closer to the tortie and watched her gobble it down. She lobbed another treat closer to herself and the cat moved cautiously forward, all the while keeping her eyes on Savannah. It wasn't long before the cat was

26

eating out of Savannah's hand and she was able to pick up the tortoiseshell cat and slip her into a carrier.

"Wow!" Margaret said. "This was one successful day. It appears that we have all of the kittens and the mothers with kittens imminent. And this is only our first day."

"Are you sure we found all of the litters? I think we should walk the grounds again and see if there are any still hiding," Savannah suggested.

"Good idea." Margaret motioned. "Why don't you go that way? I'll take the high road."

Savannah had walked almost halfway around the building, checking dense brush areas, debris piles, inside and around a few abandoned cars and among machinery that she couldn't identify, when something skittered across her path. *A rat?* she thought. *Maybe a squirrel or a rabbit.* She chuckled. *Probably not, with so many cats living out here.* Curiosity got the best of her and she decided to investigate. *Heck, I just saw it out the corner of my eye and there's a breeze. It could have been a leaf blowing across the ground.* However, after searching the area for a few moments, she saw a pair of round blue eyes peering at her through the spokes of an old bicycle. "Well, hello there," Savannah cooed. "Wanna come out and play?" She reached among the spiderwebs and weeds and, to her delight, retrieved an adorable eight-week-old buff-and-brown pointed kitten. She scoured the area, hoping to spot others or maybe a mother cat, but saw nothing. So she continued around the building to meet up with her aunt and was surprised to see Margaret cradling a black-and-white kitten of about the same age. "Aha," Savannah said, "siblings, I presume."

"Probably," Margaret agreed. "Where'd you find that one?"

"Just around the corner there. And you?"

"Up against the building, behind an old crate. Do you think we should look for more?"

Savannah nodded. "It would be a good idea. Let's put these wiggle worms into a carrier, shall we?" She crooned to the kitten she held, "It may seem scary now, little one, but I think you'll be much happier and definitely much safer in a loving home than out here in this desolate no-man's land."

"Amen," Margaret said. She scrutinized the two kittens. "A bath, a medical exam, and some good food, and you two will be prime candidates for adoption."

"Don't forget their little snip-snip," Savannah reminded her.

"Shhh," Margaret said. "Don't say that in front of them. You'll scare them."

"Like they aren't already scared." Savannah held the kitten close. "But they're not aggressive. Yes, I think they're quite adoptable. Lucky kitties."

After managing to nab a few more rather docile cats, the women agreed that they'd better fill the bowls with food and water and be on their way with the kittens, the moms, and the moms-to-be.

"Same time tomorrow?" Margaret asked.

"Yes. Helena will be doing some light housecleaning for me in the morning and she likes to have Lily keep her company." She focused on her aunt. "What's the plan? Will you start trapping tomorrow?"

"Possibly. I'd like to get more information from Andy about the cats that are still out here. I also want to observe how much the cats eat and drink overnight.

That will give us an idea of how many are actually here. Then we need to isolate the tame ones from the more frightened ones and identify those that may need medical attention. I'd like to take any sick ones first. Once we start trapping, you never know which ones you'll end up with. And I prefer the hands-on approach as much as possible. Trapping, while of course doesn't harm the cats, is kind of…what would you say…?"

"Well, it's probably rather frightening and insulting to the cats. So you think we should spend more time observing them, right?"

Margaret nodded. "Want to call your husband and see if he can come by our place on his way home and check all these guys out?"

Savannah removed her cell phone from her pocket. "Sure." Into the phone, she said, "Hi, hon. I'm surprised you answered. Are you on a break?"

"Just finishing up some paperwork. The next patient is scheduled for after lunch, around one. How are you?"

"Good. We have some patients for you. Can you stop by Max's and Auntie's on your way home this afternoon?"

"Tame ones, huh?" he asked.

"Yeah, some are a little feisty. They're obviously not used to being loved on, but they don't seem aggressive. We have six kittens, a couple of teenagers, one mother cat, and three that are about ready to burst with kittens probably anytime, and…" she thought for a moment. "Oh yes, one intact male adult."

"Hey, that's quite a haul on your first visit out there. Good job."

"Yup, we're on a roll. I just hope the rest of the project goes as smoothly."

***

Late that afternoon as Savannah tossed a salad for supper, Michael stepped in through the side kitchen door. "Hi, hon," he greeted, kissing her.

"Daddy," their two-year-old called, pushing away from her small table where she'd been playing with a musical puzzle.

Hi, punkin." He picked her up and hugged her. "How's my girl?"

"Airplane, Daddy!" Lily shouted excitedly. "Airplane!"

"Okay," he agreed, spinning around with Lily in his arms. When he put her on the floor a few minutes later, she ran toward the living room. "Daddy's shoes! I get Daddy's shoes!" She returned carrying his flip-flops and placed them on the floor next to him.

Michael smiled. "Thank you, punkin." Before he could slip into them, Rags walked up, sniffed the flip-flops, and stretched out across the top of them.

"No, Rags!" Lily screeched. "No! Daddy's shoes."

The couple laughed when Lily sat down behind Rags and tried to push him off the flip-flops. When the two-year-old began to cry in frustration, Savannah lifted the cat and snuggled with him. Lily wiped her tears, picked up the shoes, and handed them to Michael. "Sit, Daddy," Lily insisted. "Put on shoes."

"Okay, if you say so," he teased.

Savannah chuckled upon releasing Rags, saying to Michael, "Hon, I think you've become too predictable."

He looked up from the kitchen chair. "What do you mean?"

"She knows that as soon as you come in from work, you change into your flip-flops. Next, she'll be handing you your phone so you can check for a text from Keith."

"Huh?"

"That's the second thing you do every evening—check for a text from Keith or a call from Aggie."

He smiled slyly. "I guess I do, don't I? Well, my brother and I have a lot to catch up on—over thirty-five years of memories we didn't get to share."

"I know," she said tenderly, bending down and kissing him. She patted his face playfully. "And you and Aggie seem to have a lot to talk about too."

He nodded. "I never knew a grandmother could be so cool." He looked at Lily. "I'm so glad she has your mom and your aunt, who's kind of like a grandmother to her. And soon she'll have a chance to get to know her great grandmother Aggie."

"Oh?" Savannah said, sounding surprised. "Does she know when she's coming here?"

"Probably around the time the baby's due, if that's okay with you."

"I'd welcome her. She's a delight."

Before she could turn away, he grabbed her hand and kissed her palm. "I sure do love you."

She winked at him. "Me too." She gazed at their toddler, who was engaged in her puzzle again, then poured a glass of iced tea and set it in front of Michael.

"Thanks, hon." He took a sip of the tea, then studied the glass. "Gosh, I guess I *am* becoming predictable." He tilted his head and looked at her as she returned to the kitchen counter. "Is that a bad thing?"

"Not as far as I'm concerned. What would I do if I couldn't count on you to come home to us every evening?"

He smiled. "Well, good. I like my routine." He took another swig, then said, "I saw the products of your work today."

"Huh?"

"The cats and kittens from the seminary. They're actually in pretty good shape, from what I can tell. We have to wait for the test results, but they seem pretty clean and healthy…well, except for the white one." He chuckled. "Looks like she lost a tug-of-war over a mud puddle. But she'll clean up. Those are some nice batches of kittens. Let's hope they all find good homes." After taking another sip from his glass, Michael focused on Lily. "Are you having a tea party? Finished with your puzzle?"

She pointed at his glass. "Daddy tea."

"Yes. Daddy has tea. Are you serving your dolly tea?"

"Kitty," she said. "Rags kitty."

"Is Rags coming to your tea party?"

Lily nodded. She looked under her little table and demanded, "Rags, drink tea."

"Where is Rags?" Michael asked.

Lily peered under the table again and pointed.

When Michael leaned over, he could see the lanky cat lying behind one of the small chairs next to a plastic cup and saucer from Lily's tea set.

"Oh, I see the kitty's having tea with you, isn't he?"

Lily nodded and proceeded to stir the imaginary tea in one of her little cups.

"How're you coming on his memoir?" Michael asked Savannah.

"Okay, I guess. But I'm sure rusty. I haven't written anything of any magnitude since college." She sat down across from him at the table. "I'm thinking about signing up for a creative writing course. There are a couple at the community college, but I'm kind of drawn to the one at the art center. It sounds more intimate—more in line with what I need."

"Don't you think a writing course might confuse you?"

"Confuse me?"

"I mean, you have your own style. You don't want someone trying to teach you a different style of writing. Your stories won't come across as sincere, will they?"

"Oh, I hadn't thought of that." Savannah chuckled. "But I don't know that I have a style."

"Sure you do," Michael insisted. "You have a style of walking, talking, and I'm sure you also have a specific style in your writing."

"I suppose. So you don't think a writing brush-up course would help me?"

He leaned back in his chair. "It could be that you just need a confidence boost. And yeah, you might get that from a class. If that's what you want to do, you should do it."

"Yes, I think I'll sign up. The first class starts Wednesday night."

"At night?"

She nodded. "At seven. Only…"

"Only what?" he asked.

"Well, I stopped by the art center to ask a few questions and happened to meet the instructor. Her curriculum sounds pretty much in alignment with what I'm looking for, but…"

"But what?"

"Well…" Savannah swallowed hard, "she seemed a little…um…odd."

"In what way?" He laughed. "You know it's not unusual for an artist to be odd."

"Yeah, I guess so. For some, their oddness is their charm." She crinkled her nose. "Oddness. Is that a word?" She shook her head. "See, I need help with my word choices and I hope to learn how to string my words together to make the story interesting."

Michael punched the air with his fist, asserting, "Confidence, that's what you need."

"Maybe."

"So tell me about the teacher. What struck you as odd?"

"Well, she's probably in her fifties and kind of on the plump side." Savannah squinted and added, "She knows how to dress for her size and she has a sort of flamboyance about her."

"Flamboyance?" he questioned.

"Yeah, she has crazy hair. I don't know if I can learn much from someone with blue and purple spiky hair. How can I take her seriously?"

Michael grinned at his wife. "It's the style some people choose these days."

"Yeah, celebrities, motorcycle chicks, hippies, and young women seeking their own identity. But I don't expect to see that among teachers and other

34

professionals." Savannah thought for a moment before saying, "Actually, she isn't a bono-fide teacher. She's self-taught. She sort of came up by the seat of her pants, which is one thing that attracted me to her class in the beginning." She frowned when adding, "…until I saw her."

"Savannah, are you prejudiced? Do you judge a book by its cover?"

"No!" She paused. "At least I don't think so. Do I?" When Michael didn't respond, she explained, "It isn't just her hair and her overdone makeup and her tattoos…"

"Oh, tattoos too, huh?"

"Yes," Savannah said adamantly. "Does she know what those tattoos will look like as she ages? That soaring eagle on her arm will become a wrinkled old pigeon when she's eighty!"

"Does she care?" he asked, playing devil's advocate.

"I suppose not." She smiled. "I actually find her kind of interesting. She seems knowledgeable, but…"

"But what? What is it that has you concerned?"

"She seems a little stand-offish—unfriendly— like detached."

"I think you've been hanging around Rochelle for too long," Michael suggested. "You're starting to read things into people and situations that maybe aren't there."

She wrinkled her brow. "Like what?"

"Like when you said that Peter isn't the marrying kind and he'd never get married. I think you said the same thing about Harrison. And now both Peter and Harrison are married."

She tilted her head. "Oh that's right, Peter and Rochelle got married."

He nodded. "Yup. I talked to Peter a couple of days ago. They're now Mr. and Mrs. Peter Whitcomb."

"Wow! I'll have to pick up something to send them." She sat in contemplation for a moment. "Well, I guess if the timing's right and the perfect person comes along…"

He interrupted her. "And what about Marci?"

She frowned. "What about her?"

"You told me just recently that you sense she's hiding something from her husband and the world at large. Marci and Eric seem happy. Don't you think so?"

She shook her head. "Oh, Michael, I still think there's something lurking there. I just hope she can come to terms with her demons before something awful happens."

He squinted in her direction. "Where do you get this stuff?"

"I don't know. I guess I'm just observant."

He grinned. "And you have a big imagination."

When he noticed her rather absentmindedly rubbing her wrist, he asked, "Something wrong with your arm? It's not swelling, is it?" He looked down at her legs. "Are your ankles swelling? You had that water-retention problem toward the end of your pregnancy with Lily."

She shook her head. "No, I was just thinking about my charm bracelet." She cringed. "The one you gave me last year for Mother's Day."

"What about it?" he asked.

Just then, Lily ran to Michael. She leaned against his knee while looking at Savannah. "Mommy's bracelet all gone."

Savannah chuckled. "Yes, we've looked everywhere for it, haven't we, sweetie?"

Lily nodded, then walked to the kitchen door and tried to open it.

"No, honey bun, we're not going outside to look for it now. It's going to be dark soon, and dinner's just about ready."

"What happened to it?" Michael asked. "How did you lose it? Did it fall off?" He frowned. "That clasp wasn't faulty, was it? The price I paid for it, it shouldn't be."

"No. I wore it this afternoon when I took Lily on a playdate with Alicia and Crissy. You know, Lily likes me to tell the stories behind the charms, so I took it off later while the two of us sat on the porch soaking up the last of the afternoon sunshine. And we were talking about each of the charms."

"Did you drop it through the slats on the porch?" he asked.

She shook her head. "I don't think so. When Lily got tired of the stories, I set the bracelet on that small mosaic table and we took a walk around the yard." Savannah giggled. "She likes to count the fruit on the trees in the orchard." She ran her hand over the toddler's hair. "We had to go check the corral."

"Horsie all gone," Lily said, a worried look on her little face.

"Yeah, she misses Peaches too." Savannah smiled. "But Bonnie says she's doing great there at the stables. Bonnie's riding her a lot." She paused. "Anyway, when we came back to the porch…"

"It was gone, huh?" Michael said. "Did you check Rags's stash?"

"No. Rags didn't go out with us. I purposely left him inside. I was ready for a break from him; he was kind of naughty this afternoon. Anyway, yeah, when we were ready to come back inside, I started to pick up the bracelet, but it was gone."

He cocked his head. "Are you sure Rags didn't somehow get out there and take it?"

She shook her head. "No. He watched us from his window perch, complaining the whole time. I could see his mouth going…*meow, meow*." She chuckled. "But, no. It wasn't Rags this time. I guess it could have fallen off the table or Lily dropped it on the porch, but we looked all over that deck. Michael, it would be a real long shot if it fell between the boards, because those spaces are so narrow." She grimaced. "No Michael, that bracelet has flat disappeared. I just can't imagine what could have happened to it, unless a squirrel squirreled it away."

"Well, I don't know what to tell you. Let's hope it shows up."

"Mommy's bunny all gone," Lily said, looking down at her shoes.

"Mommy's bunny?" Michael asked.

"That's her favorite charm—a little bunny my aunt gave me," Savannah explained.

Lily nodded, then said, "Mommy's blue birdie all gone."

Savannah picked up Lily and put her on her lap. "Yes, and the little heart Daddy gave me, the Christmas

tree, the baby booties…it's all gone. But we'll find it."
She stood with Lily in her arms. "How about let's get
you washed up for supper, shall we?"

Once the couple and their daughter were
seated around the table eating the meal Savannah had
prepared, Michael asked, "So you think the teacher is
snobbish…unapproachable?"

"Yes, kind of."

"Do you think that will hamper your ability to
learn from her?"

After some thought, Savannah said, "I don't
think so. At least I hope not. I'm rather eager to go back
to school, actually. I think it will be a good experience
for me." She giggled. "I just hope I can keep a straight
face during Char's lectures."

"Char?"

"Yes, Char Lorraine, the tattooed, purple haired,
aloof teacher."

Michael laughed. "It sounds like your rendition
of her would make a good story. You could write it for
one of your class assignments."

Grinning, Savannah said, "Yeah, right! That
would leave a good impression." She shook her head.
"Naw, I'd better stick to my original plan and work on
Rags's memoirs. It'll be challenging enough trying to
capture his personality in words and make his crazy
exploits interesting to read about."

Chapter 2

The following morning as she climbed into Margaret's Jeep Liberty, Savannah smiled and asked, "How are your new boarders, Auntie?"

"Doing well. Michael agreed with us that the cats are in pretty good shape, considering. We plan to bathe them this afternoon. Then we'll wait for the test results to come back. One litter is almost old enough to move on and some of the volunteers want to put little bows on their heads and promote them for Easter."

"Cute." Savannah narrowed her eyes. "But you'll maintain your strict adoption policy, won't you? And you'll have them spayed and neutered before you adopt them out. I mean, you won't let them go to people who just want a cute Easter gift for their child, will you?"

"Of course not." Margaret glanced at her niece. "Michael said we should have two more litters by midweek. And all of the momma cats seem to be calm enough to adopt out. So far so good with the seminary colony."

"Let's don't count our kittens before they're hatched." Savannah giggled. "Or something like that." She changed the subject. "Did I tell you I'm going back to school?"

"No," Margaret said. "Why?"

"I'm taking a writing class to help me write Rags's memoirs."

Margaret laughed. "I still can't believe you're going to do that."

"Yes I am. But it's sure taxing my memory. I'm eager to start talking to people who can help me recall some of the incidents I've forgotten about. So far, I just have a whole bunch of notes and I'm not sure where to begin."

"Maybe from the beginning," she offered. When Savannah didn't respond, Margaret suggested, "Once upon a time a kitten was born. Not just any kitten, but a kitten that would become one of the world's most disobedient, mischievous, impish…"

"Now, Auntie," Savannah scolded. She thought for a moment and said, "But yeah, something like that might work. Good idea."

"So how much are you paying the teacher?"

"It's one-fifty for a four-week course."

Margaret held out her hand, palm up. "You can give me fifty dollars for my great advice and scratch the class."

Savannah smirked playfully at her aunt.

"Got your gloves?" Margaret asked as she parked the car inside the ramshackle construction fence that surrounded the seminary.

"Yup. So what will we do today?"

Margaret looked out through the windshield. "Well, I'd like to take a count again and see if we spot any cats we didn't see yesterday." She lurched forward. "Look, there are some cats. I'm sure there are some in that group we haven't seen." She picked up her clipboard and pen. "A long-haired pointed cat— probably the dad to the two older kittens we rescued yesterday—a couple of orange tabbies, a solid grey, and a larger black-and-white cat. Right, Vannie? The black-and-white we logged yesterday was smaller, wasn't it?"

"I think so. Yes. Did you write them all down?"

"Uh-huh. Oops," Margaret said, staring toward the building. "Most of them just ran into the crawl hole.

That seems to be their safe place." She grimaced. "I just hope there are no kittens under there. We'll never get them out."

"We have time. I mean, demolition is several months away. We can probably trap them."

"Yeah, unless they're too little to crawl out. Vannie, I don't want to leave any cat or kitten behind."

"Of course not. We can bring Rags out here—you know, to ferret out any that we may have missed or that can't come out by themselves." She paused. "And since they're going to demolish the place anyway, it's probably okay if we cut holes in the floor to rescue them if we have to."

Margaret nodded. "Yeah, that's right."

Savannah faced her aunt. "See, you rely on Rags too. Maybe you'd better not be using your snarky tone about him anymore," she teased.

Margaret ignored the remark, stepped out of the car, and studied the crawl hole. "And maybe we can get Luke to go in there and shine a light around before we end this project, just to make sure we've found them all."

Savannah nodded as she climbed out of the car and the two of them moved toward the feeding station. "Food's all gone."

"Yeah, they were hungry."

"And they dumped their water," Savannah said. "We'd better invest in some sturdier water bowls—like those straight-sided pottery bowls they use in rabbit cages."

"Oh, I don't think so," Margaret said. "I prefer something larger—you know, wider, so their whiskers don't get scrunched while they're eating and drinking.

Did you read that article I sent you the other day about whisker relief bowls?"

"Yes. It's something I hadn't thought of before. Had you ever heard of whisker fatigue?"

"No. But I guess it's a reality. Some cats just have sensitive whiskers."

"I've already changed out the plastic bowls we once used, because Walter was starting to get chin acne."

"I've heard of cats with that problem," Margaret said. "Who knew that cats had so many issues with their food and water bowls?"

"Well, it's not really natural for cats to eat off of fine china," Savannah reminded her. "Their wild ancestors certainly didn't have that luxury—or that complication."

Margaret nodded, then said, "Okay, I'll put bowls on the list."

"Oh, look." Savannah pointed toward the building.

"What?" Margaret asked.

"I thought I saw a pair of eyes peeking out at us." When Margaret looked confused, she said, "Through that boarded-up window. See the spaces between the wood pieces? Look just to the right."

Margaret squinted toward the window. "I don't see anything. Must have been your imagination."

"No," Savannah argued. "I saw it. I'm sure it was a cat face—at least I'm pretty sure. Auntie, I believe there's a cat in the building."

"Can't be. Max's friend said the place is locked up and all the cats are outside."

"I'm sorry, Auntie, but I beg to differ. There's at least one cat inside and I think we'd better let it out. If he's locked in there, he could starve to death."

Margaret stared at the window again, then finally said, "Well, I vote no. I didn't see a cat. Vannie, I think it was a figment of your imagination."

"*We* vote to go check it out," Savannah said defiantly.

"We?" Margaret asked, frowning.

Savannah rubbed her baby bump. "Yes, *we*. I have two votes." Suddenly she hissed, "There it is again. Look, Auntie. A black cat. You can see it clearly when the sun catches his eyes. Did you see that?"

"Well, I caught a glimpse of what could have been something. Black, huh? We don't have any black cats on our inventory list. Maybe we ought to go inside and check it out."

Savannah stood with her hands on her hips and scoured the building. "But you don't think there's a way in, huh?"

"From what I understand, there isn't. But if there's a cat in there, I guess that information is wrong."

"They could be getting in from underneath," Savannah suggested, "like they were out at the old Fischer building. Remember that?"

Margaret rolled her eyes. "Oh, don't remind me. Gads, let's hope this rescue operation goes more smoothly than that one did." She looped her arm in her niece's. "Well, come on. Let's go find out if there's a way inside, shall we?"

"Yeah, without having to go through the crawl hole."

44

The women had walked more than halfway around the building, trying every door and testing the boards across every ground-floor window, when they noticed a small entrance directly below the bell tower, almost hidden by a massive vine.

"Now that's odd." Margaret felt some of the tendrils that wove through the lattice partition. "It's alive—a living plant." She glanced around at the mostly dead shrubs growing here and there, then examined the foot of the green plant. "Someone must be watering this thing."

"Probably your friend, Andy," Savannah said. "Maybe this was the entrance to his room when he was staying here. He wanted it to look nice."

Margaret huffed. "It's more like he—or someone else—wanted to hide this doorway. Well, we found it. Let's see if it's open." She added over her shoulder, "If not, we may have to break it down." Margaret grasped the old worn knob, turned it, and tugged until the door creaked wide open. "Oh, good. Let's go see if we can find that cat."

"Do you suppose this is how he got in here?" Savannah asked, stepping inside.

"I doubt it. It was closed. If he found his way in on his own, it had to be from under the building, like you said. We'll have to search for a hole in the floorboards." Margaret looked around. "This must have been the laundry room and furnace room—a sort of basement, but on the ground floor."

Savannah nodded. She glanced in all directions. "Shall we go see if we can find the cat?"

"Yeah. Got the flashlight?"

"Yes. Got the inventory sheet?"

"Check," Margaret said.

The women had walked through nearly the entire lower floor of the structure when they finally saw a cat.

"There she is!" Savannah exclaimed. "That's the black cat I saw; and it appears she has kittens. Yeah, good place for them—inside out of the cold." She spoke to the cat, which stood across the room, looking suspiciously at the intruders. "We're not going to hurt your babies. Where are they?" She gazed around the room. "In that box of straw?"

"Kittens in a manger," Margaret said, chuckling.

The two women moved closer to the cardboard box and Savannah continued to croon, "We just want to see your babies, pretty kitty." But before they reached the makeshift manger, the cat jumped up into it and began to hiss.

"Vannie, stand back. Let me see if I can get closer," Margaret said. "She might be less frightened with just one of us coming toward her."

"Makes sense," Savannah said, retreating into the shadows while shining the light for her aunt.

As Margaret drew nearer to the litter, the black cat leaped out of the box, sat on the floor below it, and continued to hiss. "Awww, aren't they cute? They're about five weeks old, I'd guess." She made notes on her inventory sheet. "They're all black. That's odd. Three all-black kittens." She glanced around, then looked down at the mother cat. "Are there more of your kind in here?"

"Well, there must be—she didn't get pregnant all by herself," Savannah said. She lighted the area around her. "This must have been the registration area for students."

"Yes." Margaret agreed. She pointed. "There are the kitchen and dining room."

"Classrooms must be upstairs."

"Classrooms?" Margaret questioned.

"Yes. Isn't a seminary a school—a religious school? They would have classrooms, wouldn't they? And maybe living quarters." Savannah shined the light to the left. "That's where we see all those small windows from outside. I'll bet the boarders' rooms are down that long hallway. Have you ever been in here, Auntie—I mean when it was up and running?"

She shook her head. "No, but Iris's mother was a cook out here. She used to tell some interesting stories about this place." Margaret faced her niece. "We'll have to ask Iris what she remembers." She then suggested, "Well, while we're in here, let's look around, shall we?"

"Okay." Savannah walked into the hallway. "I want to see what the students' rooms were like." Upon entering the first room, she said, "Oh, that's disappointing. This room's empty. I wanted to see the old furniture." The women soon discovered that all dozen of the small rooms along the west hallway were empty.

"Not even a shoe, a hanky, or a hanger left in the closets," Margaret remarked, opening one of the accordion doors.

"And some of the closets don't even have doors," Savannah noticed. She then suggested, "Let's take the stairs and see what we can find up there. I definitely want to check for more cats."

Once they'd started to ascend the staircase, Margaret warned, "Be careful, Vannie. Some of the steps are kind of rickety. In fact, why don't you go ahead of me, since you have the light?"

When Savannah stepped onto the second-floor landing, she yelped and pointed. "Black cats—two of them."

"Where?" Margaret asked, joining her on the landing.

"At the end of the hall. I don't see them now; they must have darted into one of the rooms." She began walking faster. "Let's go." Several seconds later, Savannah stood in the middle of a small room, shining the flashlight around.

"Are you sure you saw them?" Margaret asked. "It's pretty dark up here."

"Yes, I happened to catch them in the light. I saw them for sure." She scratched her head. "But I can't imagine where they went." After opening the closet door and checking inside twice, Savannah walked toward the hallway. "Let's take a look in some of the other rooms."

They checked all of the upstairs rooms, then Margaret shook her head in disbelief. "How could we have missed them, Vannie—I mean, if they actually went into one of these rooms? There's no furniture—no place for cats to hide." She patted her niece's shoulder. "I think your eyes were playing tricks on you, or maybe it's your imagination." She grinned playfully. "Yeah, that's it; now that you think you're a writer, you're making up stories."

Savannah tightened her lips. "No I'm not, Auntie."

Margaret contemplated the situation, then took a deep breath. "Well, let's go pack up that litter of kittens downstairs. Then I'd like to walk around the grounds again and see if we spot any more black cats." Before the two women had reached the staircase, however, they heard a loud noise behind them. Margaret grasped Savannah's arm and quickly turned. "What was that?"

"Probably one of those cats," Savannah said, shining the light into the hallway. She held the flashlight steady and peered into the distance. "Hey, look. There's one of them. See it? It's about halfway down the hallway."

"Yes. That's a black cat, all right," Margaret agreed. She then muttered, "Is it a new one, or is it the mother cat we saw downstairs? See if you can get closer to it, Vannie," she instructed.

As Savannah edged toward the cat, a second black cat appeared and sat down next to the first one. They both stared at the light as Savannah slowly approached them. When she was about six feet away she crouched, laid the flashlight on the floor next to her, and poured a few of the kitty treats into her hand. "Here, kitty," she cooed, reaching her hand toward the cats. They didn't seem at all interested in the kibbles, and without warning they disappeared into a room at the end of the hall. "Come on, Auntie, I saw which room they went into for sure this time."

"Yes, so did I," Margaret said, moving swiftly and quietly toward the doorway. Once inside, she clenched her teeth and said, "This is just too spooky. They've vanished again. How? I mean, how can they just disappear like that?"

"Yeah, like my bracelet," Savannah said quietly.

"You lost a bracelet out here?"

"No. I lost it at home. Just like those cats, it simply vanished."

Margaret gazed at her niece for a moment, then looked around. "It's a puzzle to me. There's no furniture in here, no shelving…this room doesn't even have closet doors. There's no place for those cats to hide, yet they're nowhere to be seen." Margaret opened her eyes wide. "Ghost cats, that's what they are."

Savannah chuckled. "Aren't ghosts white?"

"Evidently not in this case." Margaret shook her head slowly. "I mean, what other explanation could there be?"

Savannah stared at her aunt for a moment, then asked, "So we haven't documented any black cats yet, right? I mean, except for the momma cat we just saw downstairs and her kittens."

"No, we haven't seen any solid black cats outside." Margaret looked around. "I wonder what they're doing in here." Under her breath, she added, "If they really are here at all. If they're real, why haven't we seen them outside with the other cats?"

Just then Savannah let out a shriek and ducked. "Look out!"

"What was that?" Margaret asked, once she'd recovered from the shock of it.

"A crow, I think," Savannah said from where she now sat on the floor. "What in the heck is he doing in here? How did he get in?"

"Vannie," Margaret said quietly, "black cats…a crow…are you thinking what I'm thinking?"

"Probably not. What are you thinking?" she asked, lifting herself to a standing position with her aunt's help.

"Voodoo, witchcraft—that's what." Margaret raced into the hallway, pulling Savannah along. "Let's get the heck out of here."

"Wait," Savannah insisted as she was virtually yanked out of the room. "I want to check once more across the hall. Maybe…just maybe they…"

But before the women could make a move, a voice sounded behind them. "Hello."

Savannah gasped and quickly turned. She shined the light in the direction of the greeting and saw a man and a woman standing in the hallway peering suspiciously at them. "Oh, hello," she said, panting just a little while she tried to catch her breath. She glanced at her aunt, who held tightly to her arm, her eyes wide. "You startled us."

"What are you doing here?" the man asked rather abruptly.

Savannah noticed that he was probably in his early seventies, on the short side, and thick around the middle. "Um…"

Margaret let go of Savannah's arm and cleared her throat. "We're from the Hammond Cat Alliance and we're managing the cat colony that has formed here."

The woman adjusted her designer eyeglasses. "Good! Will you be taking them away? They've been a real nuisance." Before Margaret could answer, the woman motioned to the south. "We moved into that new tract several months ago and these cats are trying to take over—they dig in our flowerbeds, sleep on our lawn furniture."

"Yes, they've been out here for a long time," Margaret explained. "This is their home."

"And we're the encroachers," the woman said, laughing. "They must resent us something awful."

"They're probably coming around your place hoping to find food," Savannah suggested. "It doesn't look like anyone's been feeding them on a regular basis."

"So what will you do with them?" the woman asked, pulling her lightweight sweater around her thin frame.

"We've started a feeding program," Margaret said. "Once we've fed them and observed them for a week or so, we'll determine the best situation for each cat and kitten. June Balcomb, at Ragsdale Cat Ranch, will probably take most of them, some will be placed in foster care, some in permanent homes. Those that are too frightened to be adopted and aren't able to even work as a barn cat, they'll spend the rest of their days in the feral enclosure at the cat ranch."

The woman let out a sigh of relief. "Oh, that's wonderful. Just wonderful. I adore cats—we have one of our own. While we don't want the cats from over here tearing up our garden, scattering our trash, and scaring our kitty, we sure don't want to see them harmed." She spoke more quietly. "I've been concerned that less-aware neighbors will hurt them or trap them and maybe release them out to the hills. That's one of the solutions we've heard neighbors speak of. So I'm awfully glad you're here to help. I'll definitely spread the word." She tilted her head. "What are your names?"

"I'm Maggie Sheridan. This is Savannah Ivey."

"Ivey, Ivey," the woman repeated. "Do you know Dr. Mike at the Ivey Veterinary Clinic?"

Savannah smiled. "Yes, he's my husband."

"Oh, what a small world! Well, I know these cats are in good hands if Dr. Mike's involved." She reached out to shake hands with Savannah, then Margaret. "By the way, I'm Lauren Ward. This is my husband, Karl." She looked around. "We walk past here a lot, but this is my first time inside. We saw your car and wondered…" She shook her head and cringed. "Believe me, I'd never come over here at night, that's for sure. Not with what I see going on at this place."

"Oh, Lauren," Karl said, "you read too many of those mystery books."

"You stay up past eight one night, Karl," she spat, "and you'll see what I'm talking about."

"Dare I ask what you see?" Margaret asked hesitantly.

Lauren looked at Margaret, then Savannah before speaking. "I don't rightly know." She addressed her husband when saying, "But it's real and it's spooky!" She turned to leave and said, "Just don't come out here after dark and you'll probably be fine."

Just then they heard a clattering sound and they all looked in time to see something crashing down the staircase. "What was that?" Lauren hissed, grabbing her husband's arm.

Savannah and Margaret recoiled.

When Savannah shined the flashlight in that direction, Karl said, "Looks like one of the hand railings gave way, that's all."

"Maybe that crow did it," Margaret said quietly.

Lauren frowned. "Crow?"

53

"Yeah, we think it was a crow that flew over our heads a while ago."

"Hmmm," Lauren said, "are you sure it wasn't a raven? I've seen a couple of ravens out here. They're larger than crows, you know."

"It was big all right," Savannah confirmed. "But it flew past us so fast, I didn't get a good look at it. Did you, Auntie?"

She shook her head. "It's hard to see a black bird or a black cat in here, as dim as it is." She shivered a little. "Well, shall we get out of here? I don't see those cats anymore." Margaret took another look into the hallway. "I'm still confused as to where they could be."

This piqued Lauren's interest. "Vanishing cats?" she said, laughing nervously.

Margaret nodded. "Yes. We saw them go into that room, but when we followed after them, we couldn't find them. As far as we could tell, there's only one way in and out of that room."

"I believe it." Lauren leaned toward the other women. "I think this place has been taken over by something of another world."

"Now, Lauren," Karl warned, "you don't know that. No sense in scaring them." He turned to leave. "We have work to do and so do they. Let's get out of their way, shall we?"

"Okay." Lauren started to follow him, then changed her mind. "You ladies be careful out here, will ya?"

Savannah nodded. "We will." She then called out, "Thanks for coming by."

"Oh, wait," Margaret said, digging into one of her pockets and pulling out a business card. "Here's my number. Would you call me if you see anything strange going on out here?"

Lauren looked at the card, then at Margaret. "Sure," she said, stuffing it into her pocket.

Once the couple had left, the two women made their way down the wide staircase. "Let's take the kittens," Margaret suggested.

Savannah stopped and glanced around the large reception area. "You know, they look so good, I wonder if we should leave them alone for now—maybe until we find out more about the other black cats. It could be that someone's taking care of them."

"Who?" Margaret challenged.

"I don't know. Maybe someone from that tract, or a transient is crashing here and feeding them. Maybe it's actually someone your friend Andy knows. Why don't we leave them alone until you've talked to him?"

After thinking about it, Margaret agreed. "Yeah, you're right. Good thinking, Vannie." Once the two women had stepped outside, Margaret pulled the small door firmly shut. "I wonder if we should leave this open for the black cat or cats."

"If they're even going in and out," Savannah said under her breath. She raised a finger in the air. "Hey, this door was closed, wasn't it? If they're going out at all, they probably have an escape route through the floor and under the building."

Margaret thought for a moment. "Yeah, I had my eye peeled for something like that—you know, floorboards missing, perhaps. Didn't see anything." She scratched her head. "But I still can't figure out why we've seen no black cats out here." Margaret winced, then said, "Okay, let's finish our inventory and feeding and call it a day."

"Do we have extra bowls we can leave inside for the black cats?" When her aunt looked at her, she explained, "You know, in case no one is feeding them."

"Yeah, let's do that," Margaret agreed. "Just in case."

***

That evening over dinner, Michael asked, "Well, how did it go today? Everything okay?"

Savannah nodded while serving Lily a small plate of meatloaf, mashed potatoes, and peas. "Pretty well, I guess. You'll be busy in a few weeks when we start bringing the cats in for their little snip-snips."

"How many are there?"

"Would you believe we've counted thirty-one so far, including the kittens?" She joined him at the table. "We found some cats and kittens hiding inside the place today. All of them black. It's strange because the only black ones on the property are those we found inside." She raised her eyebrows. "And two of them seem to be little Houdinis or magicians."

"How's that?" he asked.

"Well, they keep disappearing."

Michael peered at his wife over his glass of iced tea. "They disappeared? Where?"

"We don't know. We'd see them—or we'd think we saw them—and when we followed them, they weren't there."

He stared at her for a moment, then asked, "Do you think you've found all of the new litters?"

"Well, we hope we've found all the kittens and pregnant females." She let out a sigh. "But there's a lot of debris around. I suppose we could have missed some."

"Take Rags out there. He'll find them."

"Yeah, I guess we may have to."

"You sound reluctant."

"And you wonder why? Michael, I'd think you'd be the last one to want Rags involved."

He chuckled. "Yes, that's true. But in this case, he just might be helpful."

"Oh, we met some of your clients—Lauren and Karl Ward. They said they bring their kitty to you."

"Oh yes. They have a Maine coon. Nice cat." He frowned. "Where did you meet them?"

"They live in that new tract near the old seminary and they came in to ask what we were doing there."

"Peas, Mommy," Lily chirped. "Peas, Mommy."

"Eat your potatoes and meat, punkin," she said.

"Peas!" Lily shouted.

"You already ate your peas. Eat some of your potatoes and I'll give you more peas," she bargained. "Come on, you like smashed potatoes and meatloaf."

"No like!" Lily said, throwing her spoon.

"Uh-oh. Are we going to have a temper tantrum?" Savannah asked.

"Peas!" Lily demanded.

"Just mix some peas with her potatoes and meat," Michael suggested.

Savannah stared at him. "Oh, you mean that then she'll have to eat some of the meat and potatoes?"

He nodded.

Savannah gave him a sideways glance. "I don't know, Michael. She doesn't like her food mixed like that."

"Here, try it," he urged, taking Lily's plate and spooning some peas over her potatoes and meat. "There you are. More peas."

"What do you say, Lily?" Savannah prompted.

The toddler smiled sweetly at Michael. "Thank you, Daddy."

He picked up her spoon, wiped it off, and handed it to her. "You're welcome, punkin. Now eat up." He winked across the table at Savannah. "Problem solved."

"One can only hope. That little mind of hers gets stronger every day." She watched as Lily carefully picked the peas out of her mashed potatoes with her fingers and ate them one by one. She grinned, then said to Michael, "Lauren Ward says she sees strange things at that place at night."

"She does? Like what?"

"I don't know. That's all she said."

"Well, you won't be going out there at night, will you?"

"Um…"

"Savannah?"

"Well, we may go out once to see if we can catch sight of cats we don't see in the daylight. You know how feral cats are—more nocturnal than a house cat."

Michael chuckled. "Who could be more nocturnal than Walter? But he sleeps *all* the time, doesn't he?"

"Pretty much. He doesn't leave his chair very often, that's for sure. But sometimes he's awake in his chair—simply having a bath or sitting there watching Lily or Lexie. He loves to watch Lexie."

"Yes, they were the best of friends at one time. When we acquired you and Rags, things changed."

Savannah laughed, "Acquired us?" she repeated.

He nodded, then continued with his thoughts on their black cat. "It's like Walter suddenly became old. As you know, he does have some health issues and I think he's just aging faster than normal or he's depressed."

"He seems to be doing better on his new diet. I think he's had more energy these last few days."

"It could help. I hope it does. It doesn't seem like much of a life, just sleeping, eating, and sleeping some more." Michael looked down and smiled. "Well, Walter, speak of the devil. What are you up to, old boy?" He scratched the cat alongside his neck and Walter pushed against Michael's hand, asking for more.

When Lexie saw the black cat, she rushed to him and poked her nose against Walter.

"Look at this, hon," Michael said. "Walter's actually playing with Lexie. When's the last time you saw that?"

"It's been a while, that's for sure," Savannah agreed. "Awww, how cute. Now don't get too rough, Lexie," she cautioned the Afghan-hound mix. "Be gentle."

"No!" Lily shouted when she saw the two animals playing. "No, Lexie! No hurt kitty."

"Awww. It's okay, punkin," Michael soothed. "They're just playing. Walter's okay. Lexie likes Walter."

Lily leaned over and watched the animals until Walter trotted under a kitchen chair, where he sat down and proceeded to watch the dog from a safer place.

"Are we having our family-and-friends meal after church Sunday?" Michael asked.

"Yes, at the inn. Iris has asked Mattie to prepare lunch for us." Savannah shivered in excitement. "It will be neat seeing everyone. It's been a long time."

"What do you mean?" he challenged. "I see Bud every day at the clinic and you see your aunt almost every day. We traveled with Maggie and Max and Iris and Craig just a couple of weeks ago, didn't we? And we all got together last Sunday."

"Right—but I haven't seen Colbi or Iris or my sister to really visit with. I miss them when I don't see them for a long time." She lurched forward a little. "Oh, that reminds me. I want to ask Iris what she remembers about the old seminary. My aunt says her mother used to work there and that she'd come home with some stories of strange happenings."

Michael set his gaze on Savannah. "Really? I wonder what kind of stories?"

"I'm eager to find out." Savannah glanced at him and cringed. "At least I think I am."

***

Two days later the regular after-church lunch group began to gather at the Kaiser Bed-and-Breakfast Inn.

"The place looks grand," Savannah said when Iris greeted her, Michael, and Lily in the foyer.

"Well, you've seen it at its finest—you know, when we had the grand opening party. What's different?" Iris asked.

After looking around, Savannah said, "Well, not much, I guess. It's just so lovely and it's nice to see it's staying that way. You must have a great staff."

"Indeed, I do," Iris said, smiling. "The cleaning staff keeps the vases filled with fresh flowers. And they clean every inch of this place weekly, if not daily. There's a lot of upkeep. But Melody left a large dowry when she died."

"Dowry?" Michael questioned. "It sounds like you took a bride rather than having inherited a bed-and-breakfast."

Iris laughed. "It's like taking a bride—it's a lot of responsibility, and I appreciate having the money to invest in it." She leaned toward the couple. "It's paying its way. Can you believe it? We're actually making a profit."

"That's wonderful, Iris," Savannah said, hugging her.

"You must have the right combination of staff and ideas," Max said as he entered with Margaret and joined in on the conversation.

"I think that's the key," Iris said. "How else would I have been able to get away for our amazing trip last month?"

"I know how nerve-racking it can be to leave your business to someone else," Michael said. "So the place ran smoothly while you were gone?"

Iris nodded. "As far as I can tell."

"It just shows how little she does around here," Margaret teased. "Ever feel like you aren't needed?"

"Now, Maggie," Michael reprimanded, it's actually a sign of good leadership when you can leave your business and the wheels keep turning in the right direction."

"And good employees," Bud said when he and Brianna joined the others.

Michael put his arm across Bud's shoulders. "Yeah, that's right."

"So where are your weekend guests?" Savannah asked.

"I didn't book guests for this evening," she said, smiling. "You're our guests." Iris glanced around at the others and gestured. "Well come in, everyone and prepare to feast. Mattie and Rupert are cooking up a fantastic gourmet luncheon for us."

"Rupert is a cook too?" Max asked.

"Well, he knows how to barbecue and he's grilling the beef tenderloin."

Just then, Craig emitted a very definite, "Ahem."

When Iris heard this, she grabbed his arm and announced, "Oh yes, and Craig helped."

"Yeah, what did he do," Margaret asked, "hold Rupert's beer?"

"It so happens," Craig said, "that I know my way around a grill. I gave Rupert a few pointers."

Iris grinned at her husband, then she noticed her manager emerge from the kitchen with a large platter.

"Almost ready," Ruth announced.

When she disappeared through the doorway again, Savannah said, "Looks like Ruth's helping her sister in the kitchen. How are the three of them working out? I know you're happy with Mattie. Are Ruth and Rupert doing okay?"

"Oh, yes," Iris gushed. "I'm so pleased with them. Mattie may have come with a less-than-desirable past and Ruth and Rupert may not actually have manager experience, but I have to say, they're all doing excellent work. Oh yes, we have a good thing going on here."

"So what's Mattie fixing?" Brianna wanted to know.

"Shrimp cocktail, mashed yams, roasted Brussels sprouts, and a raspberry tiramisu trifle for dessert."

"Oh my gosh," Margaret said, "you'll have to roll me out of here after a meal like that." She swooned. "Sounds wonderful."

Brianna rubbed her hands together. "Can't wait."

"Well, you don't have to," Craig said. "Let's get this eating-fest started."

As the couples walked toward the dining room, Margaret removed her lightweight jacket, and Iris reached out for Margaret's arm.

"New bracelet? I don't see you wear bracelets often." Iris studied it briefly. "I like it. Looks nice on you."

"Oh no, it's not mine," Margaret said. She called out to her niece. "Vannie, Vannie, I want you to take a look at something."

"What?" Savannah asked, doubling back to walk with her aunt.

Margaret held out her arm. "Look what I found this morning."

"Oh my gosh! It's my charm bracelet! Where did you find it? I've been looking for it for days."

"I know. It was in that big pot with the palm next to our front porch."

"Huh? How in the world did it get there?" Savannah asked.

"I figured you must have worn it to my house and it fell off your wrist as you walked up the stairs or something."

"No, Auntie. I'm sure I left it on our porch that day Lily and I were looking at it. I know that's the last time I saw it."

Overhearing the conversation, Brianna leaned toward her sister and her aunt. "Are you gals into levitation these days?"

Savannah creased her brow. "What do you mean?"

"Well, maybe you levitated it over to Aunt Marg's place or she levitated it from your porch to hers."

"Oh, you and your woo-woo stuff," Margaret grumbled good-naturedly. She unfastened the bracelet and handed it to Savannah. "It's a puzzle to me. But anyway, here it is. Now keep a closer eye on it, will you?"

Savannah hugged the bracelet to herself and smiled. "Thank you, Auntie."

When Lily saw Savannah fasten the bracelet around her wrist, she squealed, "Mommy's heart. Mommy's bunny."

Savannah lowered her arm so Lily could see the bracelet. "Yes, honey bun. Auntie found Mommy's bracelet."

64

"Oh, you found it, hon?" Michael asked. "Where?"

Savannah shook her head in disbelief. "Auntie said it was in one of the pots on her porch, but we haven't the slightest idea how it got there."

"Better ask your cat," Craig suggested.

"Yeah," Savannah agreed, "normally I would, but I can't imagine any way possible that he had a thing to do with this."

Brianna chuckled. "Maybe *he's* into levitation."

Once the meal had been served and the initial compliments had been shared, Savannah addressed Iris, who sat next to her. "Hey, my aunt says you know something about the old seminary. Your mother used to work there?"

Iris looked up from her meal. "Yeah, why?"

"Auntie and I are managing a cat colony out there and I was wondering about the history of the place. I don't remember it as a child." She grinned. "But then, I was a child. What do you recall? Was it like a school for students who wanted to go into the clergy or something?" When Savannah noticed Iris staring at her, she frowned. "What? You look like you've seen a ghost."

"Well," she said, raising her eyebrows dramatically, "you might say that. Gosh, I haven't thought about that place in forever." She tilted her head. "You found cats living there? I wonder how that happened."

"Yes," Margaret said from across the table, "that's all that lives out there now."

"I wouldn't be too sure about that," Iris said, sounding mysterious.

Savannah faced her. "What do you mean?"

When Iris noticed that others were waiting to hear her response as well, she brushed a red ringlet from alongside her face and said, "I guess nothing, really." She shook her head. "It's been closed for a long time. I'm sure everyone's gone by now."

"Are you talking about the old building with the bell tower east of town?" Brianna asked.

Savannah nodded, then squinted at her sister. "How do you know? You're younger than I am and I don't remember noticing it when we still lived here in Hammond."

Brianna rolled her eyes. "Oma took me out there a few months ago. She has some stories about it if you'd like to hear them sometime."

"Oh, Bud's grandmother?" Savannah asked. She glanced briefly at Margaret. "Yeah, we might actually want to hear her stories." She returned her attention to Iris. "So what went on out there that you recall?"

"As you said, it was a school—a religious school. Children of all ages studied theology along with a regular school curriculum, and many of them boarded."

"Yeah, we saw the big kitchen. And your mother used to cook there?"

Iris nodded.

Having overheard this, Max said, "I didn't know you came from a line of chefs, Iris."

Her face lit up. "Oh yes, Mom and I had some of our best times together in our kitchen." She frowned before saying, "But I sure didn't like going to the kitchen at that place where she worked."

"You went to work with her?" Savannah asked.

"What else was she going to do with me during the summer months? I couldn't stay home by myself until I turned eleven or twelve. Yes, it was twelve. I remember on my twelfth birthday telling Mom, in no uncertain terms, that I was not going to work with her anymore." Iris chuckled. "Know what she said? She told me that was okay, but if I stayed home, I had to clean house and prepare our dinner. Mom usually cooked the morning and noon meals at the seminary. But I was in charge of our dinner meal after that and that's when I had my first experience cooking by myself."

"Didn't you almost burn your kitchen down once?" Margaret asked.

"Yeah," Iris said, sloughing her off. "That's another story for another time." She leaned toward Margaret and glanced at Savannah. "But you want to know what went on in the seminary. Well, I was never exactly sure, but thinking back on it from an adult point of view, I wonder now if they weren't involved in some sort of black magic." She shook her head. "Something odd was going on there. I'll never forget the day I stumbled upon..." She paused and looked around the table at the others.

"What?" Savannah, Margaret, and Brianna asked. Most of the others were engaged in their own conversations—Michael and Max were discussing a health issue involving one of Max's shelter cats, Colbi and Damon were telling Ruth about something baby Rosemary had done that morning, and Bud was discussing grilling with Craig and Rupert.

"Well, there were actually two incidents," Iris said quietly. "There was one when I was a child and another when I was a rather wild twenty-something." She sat in contemplation before saying, "I always thought they were related, but I'm actually not sure they were."

"What?" Margaret asked impatiently.

"Well, one day when I was there playing with some of the other children…"

"What other children?" Brianna asked. "Students?"

"Yes, students and other kids who went to work with their parents like I did. I sometimes went to classes there—you know, in the summer."

Margaret huffed. "You, at a religious school?"

"They had regular classes, too; it wasn't all religious stuff." Iris winced. "There was a lot of praying going on, though—in class, before meals, and at the end of the day. Anyway, I guess they figured as long as I was there, I might as well be learning something." She grinned. "Maybe they hoped to recruit me." When she noticed some of the others now listening to her, she continued, "But it wasn't in the classroom that I had the first encounter."

"Encounter with what?" Colbi asked, now interested in what the women at the other end of the table were discussing.

"We're about to find out," Margaret said. She noticed that Ruth was also listening.

Iris stared into space for a moment.

"What was it?" Margaret asked. "You never told me about any encounters out there."

Iris looked down at her plate. "I never told anyone. It was too weird." She began speaking more quietly, as if remembering the details as she went along.

"I was only about nine or ten, maybe. The other kids went to class and I stayed behind playing with my Slinky on the steps of that sunken patio thing out back where the fountain is." She looked across at Margaret, then at Savannah. "Is that still there?"

Savannah shook her head. "No. Well, part of it is. I saw a cement slab behind the building and broken pieces of what could have been a fountain scattered here and there."

Margaret added, "Yeah, and there are cement body parts along the fence in a pile of junk."

Iris pointed a finger in the air, her eyes wide. "Yes, there were figures on it—cement figures of angels. I sometimes sat on the steps staring at those angels and imagining what they would do or say if they were actually alive." She swallowed hard. "Well, one day while I was playing with my Slinky, I saw a lizard on the edge of the fountain and I decided to give him a push." She flashed a sly grin. "I wanted to watch him swim. So I started to push him into the water. But before I could do it..." she glanced at the others, then continued, "...one of the figures spoke to me."

"A cement angel spoke to you?" Margaret asked in a cynical tone.

"Yes," Iris insisted. "As clear as day."

"What did he say?" Savannah asked, struggling to keep a straight face.

"Well, first a dove landed on the angel's wing. That was an interesting phenomenon on its own, but then I heard this voice."

Margaret giggled. "Are you sure it wasn't the dove speaking?"

Brianna nudged Margaret with her shoulder. "Good one."

Iris sat up straighter and cranked, "If you're going to make fun of my story, I'm not going to tell it."

"I want to hear it," Savannah said. "Don't pay any attention to them." She asked more quietly, "What did the angel say, Iris?"

"Well, I don't remember all if it, but basically he told me that I should be kind to all creatures and bring happiness to others—something like that." She made eye contact with the women around the table. "And then he said, 'believe or die.' That's the part I'll never forget."

"Yeah," Margaret said, "sounds like a message from that dove to me."

Margaret and Brianna snickered.

Colbi glanced rather disgustedly at the two of them, and asked, "Iris, are you sure there wasn't someone hiding behind the fountain? Maybe they were sitting out of sight praying out loud."

"No!" Iris said emphatically. "I thought so too, so I walked around the fountain and I saw no one but that dove and those cement figures."

"Wow! That must have creeped you out," Savannah said.

"Kinda. I was certainly afraid of dying and I didn't know what I was supposed to believe in order to keep from dying. I spent a lot of time trying to figure out that riddle. When I didn't die, I eventually forgot about it—well, I quit obsessing about it, anyway, until…"

"Until what?" Margaret asked.

"Well…" she hesitated. "This is almost too bizarre to even talk about."

"What?" Brianna and Colbi asked eagerly.

Iris took a shallow breath. "Not too long after that, another kid and I were playing out near the pond."

"The fountain?" Savannah asked.

"No, it's a natural pond out beyond the building, where you see all those trees." She chuckled. "To Timmy and me, it was a gigantic forest full of wild animals and adventures just waiting to happen." She smiled. "We had quite the imagination. But what we saw that day wasn't an imaginary tiger or lion or bear we could slay with our plastic swords. It was real and boy, was it scary."

"What?" Margaret asked. "Tell us."

"We'd been playing around the edge of the pond for a little while when we heard a strange sound—like a hum, sort of—coming from the forest. Of course, we wanted to see what it was. So we headed into the trees toward the sound. As we got closer and closer, it got louder and louder. We thought maybe it was a swarm of bees and we almost turned back, when all of a sudden we heard something else. It sounded like a man shouting 'Kill her! Kill her now!'" Iris glanced around the table at the others. "The humming got louder and louder and we started getting a little scared. But neither of us wanted to admit it, so we trudged on, not knowing what in the heck we would encounter."

"What was it, Iris?" Colbi asked.

"Yeah, was it that serial killer that was running loose around here when we were kids?" Margaret asked. "I remember hearing about him. Mama used to tell us stories about him to scare us into staying close to home. Was it him out there in that forest?"

"No, I don't think so," Iris said.

"Let her tell the story," Savannah prompted. "So what happened, Iris?"

"Well, we kept walking toward the sound and the deeper we went into the trees, the darker it got. It was winter and close to supper time as I recall and it was starting to get dark. When we finally saw them, we weren't too sure what we were seeing, but it looked like a group of people all dressed in black robes with hoods and…" she hesitated, "…they were chanting." She looked up. "Of course, we didn't know what that was or what to call it at the time. But now I know the humming sound we heard was people chanting." She lowered her voice. "They were leaning over something on the ground. To this day, I don't know if it was a person or an animal or what. But I swear those people had either killed it or were about to."

"Gads," Margaret said. "Were they Ku Klux Klan?"

"I don't think so," Iris said. "First, I think it was the wrong era and I've never heard of them in California, have you?" Before anyone could respond, she continued, "No. They looked more like monks, actually, but they each wore something shiny and shimmery around the waist of their cloak. I remember being struck by the shimmer coming from their robes. It almost looked like a string of lights or something. Maybe it was just the way the light from their fire caught the silver or whatever it was."

"They lit a fire out in those trees?" Brianna asked. She chuckled. "Maybe they were roasting marshmallows."

Margaret raised her hand for a high five with Brianna and both women laughed.

Savannah smirked at them, then asked Iris. "What happened? Did you ever find out what they were doing?"

"No. Timmy and I finally admitted to one another that we were scared and we agreed to hotfoot it out of there. I don't think we ever spoke of it again. And I never heard of anyone being killed." She looked off into space for a moment, then said, "But one of the students never returned to class after that."

"What?" some of the women shrieked.

"Yeah, no one ever talked about it that I know of and maybe it was all something very innocent. But I sure noticed Imogene's absence. She just seemed to disappear into thin air. She never attended a class again. In fact, I remember a few days later, seeing some men go into her room and pack all of her belongings into boxes. I always wondered…"

Colbi gulped. "Oh my gosh! Did they kill her?"

"Yeah, was she a sacrifice or something?" Brianna asked.

"I don't know. To this day, I just don't know."

"Did you ever see those people in robes again?" Savannah asked.

"Actually yes," Iris said. "I'd spent the night at the seminary with my friend, Greta. She was a boarder from some other country, as I recall. The bathroom was down the hall from the dorm rooms and I got up one night to visit the bathroom. When I opened the door to our room, I heard something and I peeked into the hallway." She glanced around at the others. "I saw someone in one of those robes with the shiny belt thing walking toward the staircase with a black cat in his or her arms. When I saw that, I almost peed my pants."

"So no one at the seminary wore robes—they didn't have rituals where they wore robes at all?"

Iris shook her head. "Not that Timmy or I ever saw. And I asked Greta about it. She said she'd never seen anyone wearing a robe. No, it was as if some weird cult worked behind the scenes or underground or something. Of course, I didn't come to that conclusion until I thought about it from an adult perspective. And years later, I became even more convinced of that."

After a few moments of silence, Savannah asked, "How's that, Iris? What happened later?"

"I was about thirteen or fourteen when the seminary closed. Mom was out of a job—well, for a while. She eventually went to work at a local restaurant. Turns out it was better pay, but it meant she worked a lot of nights. Anyway, the teachers and students all left the seminary."

"Yeah, Margaret said, "and it remained vacant for what…thirty-five years?"

"No," Iris said, her face drawn, "it hasn't been vacant for that long. It may not be vacant to this day."

"What are you talking about?" Savannah asked. "The cats? It's certainly occupied by cats."

"No. I'm not aware of the cats, but I know for a fact that at least a dozen years after it was boarded up, it was occupied. By whom or what, I don't know—but it was something more human than cats…and possibly more animal than human."

Margaret frowned suspiciously. "What are you talking about, Iris?"

"Yeah, now this is really getting interesting," Brianna said, bouncing in her chair. "What happened, Iris?"

"Well, I was in my early twenties and dating a guy with a motorcycle. A small group of us ended up out there at the seminary one night. I thought I'd show them around the place where I'd spent so much time as a child." She chuckled. "Jokester that I was, I sort of played it up as if the place was haunted."

"So you're the one who started that rumor," Margaret teased. She nodded. "Yeah, I could see you doing something like that. So what happened? Did you encounter ghosts?"

"I don't know what it was. We didn't stick around to find out. But I can tell you there was something stranger than strange out there and it scared the bejeebers out of us."

"What was it?" Brianna wanted to know. "Did you see what it was? What did it do?"

"Well, first we heard it. There was the most ghastly sound coming from the bell tower. Everyone heard it and we all hunkered down together, trying to maintain our bravado."

"What did it sound like?" Savannah asked.

Looking off into space, Iris said, "A cross between a wolf and a monster from the deep."

"What? What were you smoking that night?" Margaret insisted.

Iris smirked at her, then continued. "It was some sort of flying creature. It flew from the bell tower. It was the most grotesque thing I've ever seen, with its large green wings, pointed tail, and fiery eyes."

"Fiery?" Colbi questioned.

"Yes, they were glowing, like embers," Iris explained. "We took one look at that thing as it soared overhead, then we jumped on our bikes and shot the hell out of there. I was sure it would follow us and attack with its evil-looking talons. But we got away." She glanced around at the others before saying, "And we never went back, either."

The women sat silently for a few moments, assimilating what they'd heard. The only sound in the room was the drone of the men in conversation a short distance away. Suddenly, there was a shrill squeal and several of the women nearly jumped out of their chairs, grabbing at the nearest person for protection.

Colbi burst out laughing. "What's wrong, you guys? That was just baby Rosemary waking up and wanting to be fed."

Iris patted her chest. "Oh, poor timing, little one. You about gave Grandma a heart attack."

Margaret took a couple of deep breaths.

Brianna laughed nervously.

"Did you ever find out what it was?" Savannah asked.

Iris shook her head. "No. But if I were you, I'd be careful out there."

"Pshaw!" Margaret said. "I'm not afraid of figments of your imagination."

Brianna bumped Margaret playfully. "Have enough figments of your own, right Aunt Marg?"

Margaret laughed. "Something like that."

"I'm telling you," Iris insisted, "there's something out there—always was and maybe always will be. I'd be darn careful, you guys."

Chapter 3

"You're quiet," Michael said as he drove his family home later that afternoon. "Anything wrong?"

Savannah shook her head, then faced him. "That was a nice gathering. I enjoy our Sunday afternoons, don't you?"

"Yeah. Only it doesn't give me much time to do my puttering around the house. I may have to take some vacation days to finish up those projects I've started."

"That would be nice," she said, smiling. "Hey, what was it I heard you guys talking about? Are you going to a meeting or something?"

"Oh," he said, perking up, "Clem's Hardware is offering some do-it-yourself classes for home repair and remodeling. Damon wants to go and I thought I'd go with him. Max might like to get in on it too—not sure about Craig." Michael chuckled. "He's afraid that if he learns how to do things around the house, he'll have to do things around the house."

"That sounds like our Craig," she said, smiling. "When are the classes?"

"Mondays. The first one starts tomorrow night."

***

The following evening around seven thirty, Savannah was reading Lily a bedtime story when her cell phone rang. "Hi, Auntie. What's up?"

"Remember that couple who came out to the seminary when we were there?"

"Yes, Lauren and…um…what's-his-name."

"Yes. Lauren called me just now and said there's some sort of activity happening out there. She thought we'd want to know. She sees a light coming from the bell tower. Now that's odd. I mean, there's no electricity out there."

"No, but if someone's inside, they could be using lanterns or candles."

"Want to go check it out?"

"Um…well, I don't really want to take Lily out and, as you know, the guys are at that class. Did Max end up going?"

"Yes." Margaret hesitated. "Can you get Helena or Esperanza to come over for an hour or so?"

"Possibly. Let me make a call." Savannah added, "We've been wanting to go out at night and see if we can spot more cats. I guess this is a good opportunity to do that. Bring your inventory sheet and a few carriers, just in case." She added, "Do you have another light you can use? I'll bring our big flashlight."

"We have a camping lantern we use on the patio. I'll bring that. there's a flashlight in my car too."

Twenty minutes later, the two women drove onto the seminary property. They'd been sitting in the car looking around for a few minutes when Savannah asked, "Do you see anything?"

Margaret shook her head. "Lauren said the light was coming from the bell tower. Let's park here and walk over that way."

After a few moments, Savannah said, "I think I see a glow coming from up there."

Margaret looked around. "It could be a reflection from the moon."

"Reflecting off of what?" Savannah asked. "There's no glass around that bell tower. It looks all open." She turned to her aunt. "So, what do you want to do, go inside?"

"After the stories Iris told us, I'm not so sure," Margaret admitted. "What do you think?"

Savannah laughed quietly. "You believe in large green birds with glowing eyes, do you?"

"I thought you bought Iris's story," Margaret challenged.

"I did—I do. I believe she saw something, but that doesn't mean it was real," Savannah explained.

"Well, yeah, let's go in and see what's going on. If there's someone in there, we really should run them off. I don't think the owners want squatters here. And we don't want anyone hurting the cats."

Using the lantern and the flashlight, the two women walked to where they'd found the unlocked door a few days earlier. They entered, moved slowly and cautiously toward the wide staircase, and began to ascend it. As they reached the second-floor landing, Margaret motioned, indicating that they should walk to the end of the hallway. Once there, Savannah followed her aunt into the room on the right, then into the room at the left. When they returned to the hallway, Margaret mumbled, "I get the feeling we're standing just about underneath it, but how in the heck do you get up there?"

Savannah looked in the direction her aunt gazed. "Up where?" she asked, not sure she wanted to hear the answer.

"The bell tower, of course."

"Maybe there is no way up there."

"Then why would we see light coming from the tower?" Margaret reasoned.

Savannah shrugged. "That is a mystery."

Suddenly, they heard a shrill screech. Margaret grabbed Savannah, knocking her off balance, and she fell against a wall. She was able to catch herself, but not before the wall gave way. "Oh my gosh," she whispered, "I broke something."

"No," Margaret hissed. "No, you didn't. Look, the wall has opened up into another room. Now isn't that odd? How did you do that, anyway?"

"Heck if I know." Savannah glanced around, then took a quick breath and turned toward the hallway. "Okay, we've seen it, let's go."

"What," Margaret complained, "just when we're getting somewhere?" She grabbed her niece's arm and pulled her into the room which seemed to magically open up to them.

"Where?" Savannah challenged, once they were inside the secret room. "Where are we? Look up. Do you see the bell tower above us? Do you see any way up there?" She leaned closer to her aunt. "By the way, did you hear that screech? Come on, it appears that we're on a wild goose chase. And I don't want to catch the goose or ghost or whatever it is."

Just then Margaret let out a shriek.

"Ouch!" Savannah yelped. "It pulled my hair. What was that?"

"That crow or raven," Margaret hissed, staring nervously around the room. "Where did he go?"

"I don't know," Savannah said, still rubbing her head.

Margaret pointed. "Look! It appears that there's only one way in and out of here, through that secret door you found. So, whoever's in here is probably still here. Come on, let's snoop around and see if we can find him or her." Her voice sounded pinched when she added, "...or it."

"It?" Savannah questioned, grimacing.

"Yeah, like a big green bird. It could fly right out through one of those windows up there," she joked. More seriously, she said, "In fact, that's probably how that annoying raven got in here." She looked around and spoke more quietly. "But how did he get access to this room?"

"Maybe through that secret door," Savannah suggested. She let out a sigh and began moving around the room. Using her flashlight, she looked more carefully at the walls, hoping to find another secret panel. "You're right, Auntie," she said. "Look, someone's definitely been up here. Do you see how clean the floor is? It's not as dusty as the rest of the place. Oh," she yelped, "a black cat. Hi there, kitty. Where did you come from?" She observed the cat for a moment, then continued to move around the room, pushing on sections of the wall in search of access to another secret compartment. Margaret joined her in her pursuit. But before they could make any headway, they heard a chilling scream.

Margaret grabbed the back of Savannah's jacket. "Good God, let's get out of here."

"Good idea," Savannah said, backing out through the opening in the wall. Once they were in the hall, they moved as quickly as they dared toward the staircase.

"Hold onto the railing, Vannie," Margaret urged. "…or what railing is left."

"Yeah, I will. Let go of my jacket, would you? You'll make me fall." Once they'd descended the staircase, run through the reception area, and pushed through the small door into the night air, Savannah asked, her voice quivering, "What do you think that was?"

"Hell if I know." Margaret said, glancing up at the bell tower. She took hold of Savannah's arm and pulled her toward the car. Out of breath now, she said, "It sounded almost human, didn't it?"

"I don't know. The way it echoed through that place, it was hard to tell." Savannah shivered. "Gads, it was eerie." Once she'd entered the car and fastened her seatbelt, Savannah stared up at the bell tower. "Look, there's a light flickering up there again. Now that's weird. There are no cars out here—if someone's in there, how'd they get here?"

"And how'd they get up there?" Margaret pondered. "As far as I could tell, there's no way up into that bell tower."

Savannah tightened her lips, then said quietly, "There has to be a way. There just has to be."

"Not if what's up there is something from... um...you know, like from the other side." Margaret's voice sounded pinched. "Vannie, you know what? I'm beginning to believe in ghosts."

Savannah stared at her aunt in the near darkness. "Really? Are you serious?"

"Yes," she said, lowering her voice. "Vannie, we're dealing with something stranger than fiction here. I think we're going to need some sort of intervention in order to get our work done with the cats."

"Intervention?"

Margaret started the car and drove toward the main road as she explained. "Yeah, like from your friend, Rochelle, maybe."

83

After thinking about it, Savannah said, "You really think there's something…um…from the spirit world going on here?"

"I don't know. Can spirits light candles? Do they need light in order to do—you know—whatever they do?" She glanced at Savannah as she drove. "All I know is that something bizarre is going on out here and the cats might be in danger. Yes, I think we should call Rochelle and at least tell her what we've encountered."

"Which is what?" Savannah challenged.

"Good question. And a good reason to call her. It's unexplainable, and that's right up her alley."

***

Mid-morning the following day, Margaret knocked on the side kitchen door of the Ivey home.

"Hi, Auntie," Savannah greeted, upon unlocking the door. "Want a cup of coffee? I haven't cleaned the pot yet."

"You're not drinking coffee, are you?"

"No. Michael has a cup and a half before work—always a cup and a half. I usually make four cups just in case you or Craig pop in. I'll sit down with you and have a cup of tea."

"Okay." Margaret looked around. "Where's the princess?"

"Shhh. Napping. I can still convince her to take a nap most days—sometimes two naps. But she doesn't usually sleep for very long."

Margaret smiled, then leaned toward her niece in anticipation. "Did you call Rochelle?"

Savannah nodded. "Yes, she was intrigued, but she doesn't think that what we've encountered at the seminary is connected to anything from the spirit world.

She said it sounds more to her like a—what did she say?—a manufactured presence or a wannabe mystic or simply someone who doesn't want us there for some reason."

"Huh?"

"Rochelle doesn't think we're dealing with anything dangerous, just maybe a little crazy."

Margaret's eyes widened as she pulled a folded newspaper section from her jacket pocket. "Not dangerous, huh? Did you see the paper this morning?"

"No. Why? Did something happen out there?"

"It sure did. Check this out." As Savannah scoured the page, Margaret gave her commentary. "They found a dead body in a pond on the seminary grounds early this morning. A couple—maybe Lauren and what's-his-name—found it on their morning walk. In fact, the paper was late today, so I think they held up the presses to include the story."

Savannah looked across the table at her aunt. "Oh my gosh. The scream we heard. Do you suppose…?"

"Could have been," Margaret said. "We need to get those cats out of there and fast, before…"

"Before what?"

"Well, before we get tossed into that pond." Margaret squinted. "Where is it, anyway? Did you see a pond out there?"

Savannah shook her head. "It's probably out in that area where we haven't ventured yet." After thinking about it, she added, "Iris mentioned a pond and a forest."

"Yeah, over the years they've taken down most of the trees to build housing tracts. They were sort of southeast of the seminary, as I remember it. But according to this, there's still a pond somewhere on the property."

Savannah studied the article. "It says it's the body of an older man and that he may have been homeless and just stumbled into the pond in the dark. They found an empty alcohol bottle nearby. Evidently, there's no sign of foul play."

"Then who was that screaming last night and why?" Margaret asked.

"Maybe someone was just trying to scare us away." She grinned sheepishly. "It worked."

Margaret ignored her niece's attempt at humor. "Well, we need to set traps for the remaining cats and finish with our job pronto quick."

"That includes the black cats?" Savannah asked. Before Margaret could respond, she added, "I've been thinking about them. They seem well-fed and not skittish like those outside. And they're clean. I wonder if they live inside with…"

"With what? Or with whom?" Margaret asked.

"Well, with whoever lights the candles, I guess."

"And drowns people in the pond," Margaret added breathlessly.

Savannah thought for a moment, then said, "Would you feel better if Rochelle checked things out for us?"

Margaret's face lit up. "Yeah, would she do that?"

"She said she would. She has a jewelry show not too far from here weekend after next and I invited her to stay with us. I'm pretty sure she'll agree to go out there with us."

"Weekend after next? We could be finished with the trapping by then," Margaret complained.

"Oh, I don't think so," Savannah said.

Margaret let out a deep sigh. "Okay. But in the meantime, let's forget about what's going on in the bell tower; let's just concentrate on trapping those cats we can get. I want to quickly go in, set the traps, and get outta there. I'll see if Luke's available to help us."

"Good idea. Thanks. I'm taking Lily to Barbara's day care tomorrow. Want to set the traps then?"

"Okay."

Savannah reached out and touched her aunt's arm. "Oh, Auntie, we're missing something else." She chuckled. "I wonder if it might have shown up at your place."

"Huh?"

"You know, like my bracelet did." When Margaret didn't respond, Savannah explained, "Some of Michael's tools have gone missing."

"What kind of tools—hammer, saw?"

"Actually some small things—what are they called?—sockets—I think. They come in a set of different sizes."

Margaret pondered this for a moment. "You know, I thought he was really meticulous with his tools. I've never heard of him losing any." She grinned. "You, I can imagine losing things, but not Michael— especially his beloved tools."

Savannah smirked playfully at her aunt, then said, "Well, he was working on something out near the corral and he went to the tool shed to get some different size nails or screws and, when he went back to his project, a socket thingy was missing. He said he looked all over the place for it. He finally figured he must have carried it with him to the shed. He went back there and still couldn't find it. And get this—when he returned to his project another one of the sockets was missing."

"Gads, girl," Margaret said, "it sounds like you're in some sort of vortex that's sucking up your belongings."

"Yeah, and dropping them over at your house."

Margaret thought for a moment before saying, "Well, I'll keep an eye out for those socket things. But I doubt I'll find them."

"Why?"

"Because it's probably your cat's doings. Have you looked in his stash, lately?"

Savannah gazed at Rags, who was sound asleep in one of Buffy's pink canopy beds.

**

The following day after leaving Lily at Barbara's day care, Savannah and Margaret drove out to the seminary. "It looks rather benign in the daytime." Margaret said.

"Benign?"

"Yeah, like peaceful and non-threatening," she explained.

"I guess so," Savannah said, eyeing the place suspiciously. "Well, shall we get to work? Those traps aren't going to set themselves." Suddenly she shouted. "Oh no!"

Margaret jumped nervously. "What?"

"Looks like we missed a pregnant female."

"Where?"

"I just saw her run into that pile of junk over there. She's looks sort of like Rags. Let's see if we can get our hands on her." She turned to look into the back of the car. "Did we bring a carrier?"

Margaret nodded. "I think I saw one back there when I loaded the traps."

"Well, come on; I want to catch that cat."

Margaret handed Savannah a pair of gloves. "Don't forget these."

"Yeah, I'd rather work without them," Savannah complained, "but I guess it's important for the baby that I wear them."

"Now, which junk pile did you see her go into?" Margaret asked.

"Over here," she said, leading the way. Once they drew closer, Savannah exclaimed, "Oh!" She put her hands up against her chest and took a couple of steps back.

"What?" Margaret asked.

Savannah pointed. "That is just plain spooky."

"What is?" Margaret asked, impatiently. "I don't see anything."

Savannah moved an old weathered candle holder, a plastic five-gallon bucket, a set of venetian blinds, and an empty crate to reveal a dusty piece of bright green plastic. "There," she said, pointing.

Margaret frowned. "What is that?"

Hands on hips, Savannah announced, "Well, it could be part of a big, scary bird."

"A big, scary bird?" Margaret repeated. Suddenly she looked knowingly at Savannah. "Do you mean as in the one Iris saw flying out of the bell tower?"

Savannah nodded. "That's what I'm thinking." The women began moving more of the debris until they were able to pull the thing free. "It looks like it could have been a part of what Iris saw." She smirked at her aunt. "Plastic. It was just some old plastic thing someone built or found in a toy store to use…"

Margaret finished her niece's thought, "…to use to scare people?"

Savannah nodded. "I guess so." She chuckled. "We'll have to tell Iris about this." Giggling, she suggested, "Shall we take it and show it to her?"

"I guess you could," Margaret agreed. "However…" she hesitated. When she noticed Savannah waiting to hear more, she grinned. "…sometimes we prefer holding onto the original memory. It might crush her to find out it was a cruel stunt." She pointed and began laughing. "Oh no, look at that."

"What?" Savannah asked as she tossed the piece of plastic aside.

"A little flashlight with a red shield over the bulb. I'll bet this was one of that green monster's eyes."

"Probably was," Savannah said. She took a deep breath and began scouring the area. "Now, where did that cat go?"

"You probably scared her away with all that chatter about the green thing." Suddenly Margaret whispered, "Oh, wait. I see her." She reached into a space under a pile of wooden slats. "Gotcha, sweet kitty," she crooned, pulling back with the grey-and-white cat in her arms.

"I'll get the carrier," Savannah said.

Once they had the pregnant female in the carrier, Margaret unloaded the traps and the two women went about setting them.

"Is that female on your inventory sheet, Auntie?" Savannah asked.

"I don't think so." Margaret stood and glanced around. "I just wonder how many cats there actually are out here."

Savannah chuckled. "It seems as though this place manufactures them."

Margaret nodded, then went back to preparing the traps. Once they'd finished, she stood and stared at the building.

"What are you thinking?" Savannah asked.

"Just wondering if we should take the litter from inside."

"We don't have another carrier, do we?"

Margaret shook her head. "No. But we could go get one and come back. What do you think?"

"Or bring one when we come for the traps," Savannah suggested.

"Yes. Let's do that." Margaret started to turn toward the car, but stopped and peered up at the bell tower, then took a few steps back, hissing, "Vannie, did you see that?"

"What?" Savannah asked, shading her eyes and looking up. "What? I don't see anything."

"I don't know. It looked like a woman. Who do you suppose it is?"

Savannah shrugged. "Good question. Maybe the ghoul who's been making all the noise and feeding those black cats…"

"…and drowning people in the pond," Margaret added with a shudder.

"Now Auntie, the newspaper article said that was probably an accident."

Margaret shook her head slowly. "I don't think so, Vannie." She kept her eye on the bell tower. "I think there's something else going on out here." She tilted her head. "If she's real, how do you suppose she got up there, anyway?"

"If who's real?" Savannah asked.

"That woman up there," Margaret said impatiently. "I sure didn't see any stairs to the bell tower, did you?"

"No, as a matter of fact." Savannah laughed rather nervously. "But then I guess hallucinations don't need stairs."

"Think about it, Vannie, a bell tower has to have stairs—how else can someone take care of the bells?"

"What bells? I don't see any bells."

"Well, there probably were bells at one time, don't you think so?" When Savannah didn't respond, Margaret said, "Let's ask Iris. I'm going to call her." She pulled out her phone and touched the screen. "Iris, it's Maggie. Hey, we're out here at the seminary and I'm just wondering…"

"You're still going out there, are you?" Iris asked.

"Yes, we have cats to rescue. There are a lot of cats out here. But what I wanted to ask you is…"

"So have you encountered anything weird yet?"

"As a matter of fact…"

"Any green flying monsters?"

"Yes," Margaret said. When Iris remained silent, she explained, "We found your big green bird in a pile of junk—well parts of it, anyway."

"What?" Iris exclaimed.

"Yes, a piece of bright-green plastic and some little flashlights that were probably used for the eyes. I think someone was just trying to scare you."

"Well, undoubtedly." Iris was quiet for a moment, then said, "So it wasn't real, huh?"

Margaret chuckled. "What we're wondering is, did you ever see the stairs up to the bell tower?" After a brief silence, she said, "Iris?"

"Yes, I'm here. Actually, I did once."

"Where are they?" Margaret asked. "We were in the vicinity of the bell tower, but we couldn't find any stairs. We couldn't even see up into the bell tower from right underneath it."

"Maybe they've dismantled them," Iris offered. "Could be they're in that junk pile you talked about with the statues."

"I don't think so." Her voice pinched, she added, "Iris, we saw someone up in the bell tower just now."

"You did? Oh, my gosh. What did they look like?"

"I don't know. I just caught a glimpse of a sort of mauve scarf or filmy dress or something. We're wondering how she or he or whatever got up there."

"Oh. Well, as I recall, the stairs are a really tight spiral and they're off to the left side—that would be east. But you had to go into a door to get to them. They used to keep that door locked. Once, the janitor's kid sneaked the key from his dad and a bunch of us planned to go up the stairs just for fun. I was one of only a few who made it all the way to the top. There's a platform—you know, a floor up there that puts you right level with the bells."

"There are no bells, Iris. The bells are gone. And I guess that's why we couldn't see the bell tower windows from inside the other night, because of the platform. Interesting. So someone could get up into those windows and look out and be seen?"

"Yeah, if that staircase is still there."

"Thanks, Iris."

"Sure." She hesitated, then asked, "Maggie, you aren't going up there, are you?"

Margaret stared up at the bell tower, then said quietly, "Probably not."

"Oh. Well, be careful out there, will you?"

"Yes. Bye, Iris."

After ending the call, Margaret glanced up at the bell tower again.

"No!" Savannah said.

"What?" Margaret asked innocently.

"I'm not going up there," she asserted. "So forget it. Come on, let's get this cat settled. I need to pick up Lily."

Margaret took one last look at the tower, then followed Savannah to the car.

"You kitties eat up that stinky food now. Yum, yum," Savannah called out before stepping into the car.

***

On their way to meet Luke at the seminary later that afternoon, Margaret addressed her niece. "Vannie, I didn't think you'd come with us, since you have your class tonight."

Savannah glanced at her toddler in the backseat. "Oh, Lily was restless and I wanted to get her out of the house for a while. Besides, I want to see which cats we caught today."

Once she'd parked the car, Margaret looked down at Rags as Savannah eased herself out of the car holding his leash. "Maybe he can tell us if there are any litters hiding out somewhere."

"That's what I thought." Savannah handed Rags's leash to her aunt. "Here, want to hold him while I get Lily's stroller out? I'd rather she not run around out here." Once Savannah had placed Lily in her stroller with a juice box, she looked up and noticed a van approaching. "Here comes Luke."

Both women waved at him.

"Looks like you made a pretty good catch," he said as he climbed out of the van.

"Yes, trapping can be a slow process, but it's our only choice when the cats aren't cooperative."

"So true," Luke said. He moved closer to the traps. "You caught two in this one." He chuckled. "That's unusual. They must have come in at the same time."

Margaret laughed. "Or one of them held the door open for the other." She yelped and said impatiently, "Here, Vannie, take your cat. He's pulling my arm off."

Savannah took his leash. "Let's see where he wants to go. Find the kitties, Rags," she chirped. "Auntie, keep an eye on Lily, will you?"

Margaret nodded and watched while Rags led Savannah to the crawl hole and tried to go inside.

"We know there are kitties in there, Rags," Savannah said. "Let's see if there are any hiding out here anywhere, shall we?"

Margaret and Luke chuckled when they watched Savannah try to lure the cat out of the crawlspace.

She finally had to duck inside and pick him up. She carried him away from the opening and placed him on the ground. "Find kitties out here," she instructed. Savannah walked along behind the cat as he sniffed and pulled, circled back a few times, and sniffed some more. He poked his head into nooks and crannies among the debris and pawed at a few things that interested him, including the green plastic thing they'd tossed aside. Finally, Rags stopped. He sniffed the air, took a few steps toward an old wheelbarrow filled with topsy-turvy crates, then sat down and stared. After a few moments, he moved forward and put his paws up on the edge of the wheelbarrow. What happened next startled everyone, most of all Rags, for a cat emerged from the crates and slapped him on the nose.

"Uh-oh," Savannah said. "Poor Rags." She leaned down and checked him over. "No blood. You're okay, boy." She then said, "Auntie, I think we have some kittens over here. Or maybe just a cantankerous cat."

Once Luke and Margaret, with Lily in the stroller, joined Savannah, Luke began carefully moving things and eventually revealed a brand new litter of kittens and one very protective momma cat.

"Is she on your inventory list?" Savannah asked.

Margaret shook her head. "I don't think so. What are there—five kittens? I think we would have noticed a belly full of that many, don't you?" She then said, "Here, Vannie, watch your baby; I'll get a carrier."

Once the kittens and their mother were safely inside the carrier, Luke went to work loading the traps, which were holding some very vocal cats, into his van.

Margaret stood by with her inventory sheet. "That's four more."

"Ten counting the new feline family," Savannah said.

Luke looked around. "Gosh, this is one of the biggest colonies I've seen. Ms. June had a lot of cats living in that ravine on her property, but I don't think there were this many."

"Yeah, a record number," Margaret agreed. She looked around. "And still there are a lot of them left—including some inside."

"There are cats inside there?" he asked. "Are they being cared for?"

"You know what," Margaret said, "they're all in good shape. I do believe someone is living in there or else visiting often and taking care of those cats. We've left food for them, but they aren't eating much of it." She faced Luke. "There are birds inside too."

He looked up at the belfry. "Well, they could fly in through those open windows." He shook his head. "Must be a mess in there—I mean, with rain water coming in and birds flying around..."

"Not that we've seen," Margaret said. She pointed toward the belfry. "But we haven't been up there, yet."

"Auntie, just where do you think people would be living in there? Why would you think that? I mean, we've been through that whole place and we haven't seen even a stick of furniture—no belongings, food, nothing."

Margaret took a deep breath and faced her niece. "Well, someone's taking care of those cats." She glanced around the property. "I just wish I knew who it was."

"But we haven't even seen evidence of that," Savannah said, "except for the fact that the cats are in good shape. I mean, did you see any food or water bowls for them in there? I sure didn't."

Luke gazed out toward the new tract and the tract under construction. "Maybe someone's coming from over there and feeding the cats."

"Then why wouldn't they be feeding the outside cats?" Margaret challenged. "And, like Vannie said, where are their bowls?"

He removed his baseball cap and slid it back onto his head. "Maybe they don't know about these cats out here. They do tend to keep hidden."

Margaret and Savannah thought about what Luke had suggested, then Savannah said, "That's hard to believe. We see cats every time we come out here. And why would someone come here to take care of the cats inside rather than take them home or to a shelter. It doesn't make sense to me."

"And if it don't make sense, it probably isn't true," Margaret recited.

Luke stared at the building. "So you're feeding them?" he asked.

Margaret nodded. "Trying to, but they aren't eating much."

"Which is another reason we think someone is taking care of them," Savannah said.

Luke looked at Savannah, then Margaret, and asked, "Can I go inside?"

"As long as you're not afraid of ghosts and ghouls," Margaret teased.

"It's haunted?" he asked. He smiled. "Yeah, I like things like that, actually. Come on, show me around."

"Okay," Margaret said reluctantly. She turned to Savannah. "Bring Rags."

"Sure, if you'll help me. Which one do you want, the baby or the cat?"

Without delay, Margaret said, "The princess, of course."

"So no lock, huh?" Luke noticed when Savannah pushed open the door under the bell tower. He looked up. "Hmmm, no access from here?"

"To where?" Savannah asked.

"That tower up there." Luke looked around. "How old is this place, anyway?"

"I think it was built before 1900, probably," Margaret surmised. "And it was abandoned around the 1970s or so."

"Interesting," he muttered while walking through the place with a flashlight Margaret had handed him.

"How are the kittens in the manger?" Savannah asked, moving toward where they'd seen the black kittens.

"Kitty!" Lily shouted. "See kitty, Auntie?"

Margaret smiled at Savannah. "Isn't that cute? She's stringing her words together quite nicely."

"Yes," Savannah agreed. "So where's the kitty she sees? Oh, wait, I think Rags sees it too." She pointed. "There it is just inside the kitchen. It's one of the babies. I guess they have the run of the place now." She looked around. "Where's the momma?"

"Is she black?" Luke asked. "Is that her?" he pointed.

"Probably," Margaret said. "All of the cats we've seen in here are black."

Luke stopped and looked at her. "You've seen only black cats in here?"

"Yes, why?" Savannah asked. "You look stunned."

"Well…" He hesitated before saying, "I know of a group that uses black cats."

Margaret frowned. "Uses them?"

"Well, not in any bad way," he said. "They're just sort of around to help—you know, attract the spirits."

Margaret cocked her head. "Luke, I had no idea you were into that kind of stuff."

"What kind of stuff?" he asked.

"Witchcraft, the occult—things like that."

"Oh, I don't think it's witchcraft or that they're a cult. It's just a spirit-driven group. I attended their gatherings a couple of times when I was—you know, homeless."

Savannah chuckled. "You had a home, Luke. You just didn't want to be there."

He grinned shyly. "I know."

"So you went to a séance or something?" Margaret quizzed.

He thought for a moment before answering, "Yeah, sorta, I guess. I wasn't too savvy about what was going on. I'm not sure anyone else was, either. But it was interesting." He widened his eyes. "The gal talked to my grandpa—you know, from the other side. He had a message for me. He said I should get a good education." He smiled. "And I'm doing that now."

Margaret looked skeptical. "That was kind of a generic message, Luke."

"Well, it sure sounded like something he'd say."

"What did the witch tell the others?"

He turned abruptly in Margaret's direction. "She wasn't a witch." He explained, "One gal was looking for a ruby pendant that got lost when they were going through things after her mother died. The leader told her it's no longer in her mother's house. She said someone has it and it's safe."

Savannah stared at Luke for a moment, then said, "Shine your light over here, will you, Luke? I want to take a closer look at this kitten. Oh, there's another one. You know, they look healthy. So does the mother cat."

"And the other adults we saw in here too," Margaret reminded her. "Yes, I do believe someone's living here or visiting regularly and they're taking care of these black cats."

"I still wonder why they're not feeding those outside." Savannah said.

"I don't know," Margaret said. "Maybe because there are so many." She faced Savannah. "Some people believe that cats can survive just dandy on their own."

101

She grimaced. "Don't they know that once the rodents are gone, they could starve to death?"

"Can we go upstairs?" Luke asked.

"Sure. Just be careful; part of the railing broke the other day."

Luke motioned to Savannah. "Why don't you go ahead? I'll shine the light for you." Once they'd reached the second story landing, he said, "Not much going on up here, is there?"

Margaret shook her head. Then, sounding a little mysterious, she said, "We found a secret room, didn't we, Vannie?"

"Sure did. Want to see it?"

"Yeah," Luke said.

Margaret held back. "Um, what if that person's in there?"

"Oh yeah, you mean that thing we saw this morning?"

Luke laughed nervously. "Are you trying to freak me out?"

"No," Margaret said wide-eyed. "We saw someone in the bell tower."

"Oh, what did they look like?"

"I don't know…um…basically all we saw was a piece of cloth like someone was wearing a big scarf or something and it blew in the breeze." As the trio reached the end of the hallway, Margaret said, "Here's where we found that secret room, right, Vannie?"

"Yes."

Luke looked around. "Where? I don't see any doors."

"Well, I sort of fell against the wall over there and we ended up in another room." Before she could approach the area where they'd found the secret door, Rags began pulling on his leash, and Savannah yelped, trying to keep up with him. "Hold on, Rags! Auntie, he's interested in something behind that wall too. Look at him."

The three of them watched as Rags approached the wall, sat down, and cocked his head as if he were listening. After a few moments, he touched the wall with one paw and looked back at Savannah.

"Vannie, I think he wants you to open it. He senses that something's in there."

"Do you really want to see what's in there?" Savannah asked.

"What do you mean? We've already been in that room once."

"But that was before we saw…" Savannah whispered.

"Saw what?" Luke asked.

"Whatever that was in the bell tower."

Luke looked from one to the other of the women before saying, "Well, let's go check it out."

Margaret smiled at him. "You really do like this sort of woo-woo stuff."

He grinned. "Kinda, yeah."

All of a sudden they heard a strange grinding sound and turned in time to see a portion of the wall give way and Rags disappear into the shadows.

"Rags," Savannah hissed, holding tightly to the end of his leash. When he pulled her off balance, she stumbled into the room after him and to her dismay, she heard the door close behind her. *Oh no,* she thought. *Now what? What's going on? It's dark.* "Rags," she called quietly. She pulled on the leash and moved slowly in his direction until she was able to put her hands on him. She grasped his harness and held onto him while she tried to figure out what to do next. Suddenly, she became aware of an aroma. *A candle. Someone was burning a candle in here within the last few minutes.* "Hello," she said hesitantly. "Is anyone here?"

At the same time she felt Rags pulling off to the right. "Rags, stop it," she hissed. "Settle down." Again she called out, "I know someone's here. Where are you? Speak up, will you?"

Just then she saw a light shining into the room and she heard a familiar voice. "Vannie, where are you?"

It was Margaret. They'd found a way into the secret room.

"Cats!" Savannah said. "I just saw some of those black cats in the light." She spoke more quietly. "But cats can't light candles." She glanced around, then approached her aunt. "Give Lily to me. We're out of here."

"Where are you going?" Margaret asked. "Come on, let's look around."

"I've seen enough," Savannah groused.

"What did you see?" Margaret hissed.

"Actually nothing. It was dark. But that's all I care to see. We'll wait for you two out here in the hall."

"Oh, okay," Margaret said, handing the toddler over to her. "We'll be right there. I want to see if we can find that spiral staircase."

Savannah had been waiting outside the secret room with her daughter and her cat for several minutes when she heard something. She looked up in time to see what she thought was a woman carrying a bird cage swiftly down the wide hallway toward the staircase. She blinked a couple of times and silently wondered, *Is my imagination playing tricks on me?* She squinted into the dimness again, only to see nothing. *It was like one of those figures you see at Disneyland,* she thought, *sort of filmy and fleeting. But it is fairly dark in here.* "Rags, quit pulling," she scolded in a whisper, trying her best to hold him back.

She then decided, *you know what, Rags wants to follow something. I think I'll let him.* "Come on, Rags. Let's go."

Savannah noticed that there was just enough light for her to see her way down the staircase. *I'm not sure I can make it with both Lily and Rags, though. I think I'll just let him go. Surely he'll wait for me at the bottom of the stairs.* "Rags, you be a good boy now. Stay close," she murmured. However, when she reached the lower level, he was nowhere in sight. "Rags," she called softly. "Rags." That's when she heard the sound of a door closing. *Rags!* she thought. *Darn. Did he go outside, but who closed the door? Maybe the wind blew it shut.* Savannah quickly made her way through the reception area and toward the front door, when she noticed something. *Oh my gosh, it's Rags's leash. It's stuck under the door.* She placed Lily on the floor, took her little hand, and sprinted with her toward the door, arriving in time to step on the leash just before it disappeared. She quickly grabbed it, then leading Lily by the hand she opened the door and stepped outside, where she found Rags sitting on the porch staring ahead with interest. She peered into the distance. "What are you looking at, Rags?" *Nothing. I don't see anything.*

As she stepped closer to the cat, though, she noticed something. *Tire marks, like from a bicycle.*

Just then, Savannah's attention was summoned from behind her. "Whatcha doing?"

When she turned, she saw her aunt and Luke standing in the doorway. "Oh, just following Rags around."

"Well, look at this," Margaret said. "A black feather. We found it in that room."

As if she hadn't heard her aunt, Savannah continued to stare into the distance. "I think I saw her or him," she said. "It looked kind of like one of those illusions you see in the haunted house at Disneyland. I think she rode off on a bicycle."

"What?" Margaret asked, scrunching up her face.

"Yeah," Luke said, chuckling, "a ghost on a bicycle? Are you sure you're not confusing her with the witch in *The Wizard of Oz*?"

"Sounds like it, huh?" Savannah said. "All I have to go on is the filmy figure I saw moving quickly down the hallway past me in the darkness carrying a bird cage. Then there are these bicycle tracks."

"What tracks?" Luke asked.

Savannah pointed.

"Yeah, they look fresh. Could have been a vagrant or someone from one of those tracts taking their dog for a walk."

"Could be," Savannah said. She then asked, "So did you two find the staircase?"

Margaret shook her head. "No luck with that. We tapped and rapped and pushed on every inch of the wall up there—nothing."

Luke looked up at the bell tower, then at the traps. "Let's get these guys to a better place, shall we? Where are they going?"

Margaret thought for a moment, then said, "I'll take the mother cat and kittens. Can you take the rest of them to June's?"

"Yup," Luke said. "Let's load 'em up and move 'em out."

***

Later that day while Lily was napping, Savannah checked her phone and found a message from Rochelle. She returned the call. "Hi, Rochelle. Sorry it took me a while to respond. I had my phone turned off. How are you? Are you still planning to come stay with us?"

"Sure am. When Peter heard about our plans, he decided to join me, if that's okay."

"Absolutely," Savannah said enthusiastically. "We'd love to see you both."

"Great. We'll arrive sometime next Friday. I'll need to leave early Saturday for the show. I have a lot of set-up to do, and since this is all new to me, it'll probably take me a little longer at first." She then asked, "Hey, want to go with me?"

"Oh, that sounds fun. Would I be able to help you?"

"I was hoping you would." She spoke more quietly. "Peter is a dear and he's a genius with his art exhibits, but he's a bumbler when it comes to displaying my jewelry. I'd love a woman's touch."

"Great! I'll let Michael know he and Peter are on Lily-duty Saturday and I'll be your assistant."

"That'll be fun. Hey, Savannah, the reason I'm calling is that I've learned something that may be of interest to you and Maggie."

"What's that?"

"Well, I've been doing some research among some of the psychic and medium circles I'm aware of and I discovered something very interesting. There's evidently a cult or sect that seems to have originated in Hammond. Get this, Savannah, they meet at what they call a *mystic haunt*. The way it's described, I thought it might be your seminary."

"Really?"

"Yes, I signed us up to go there next Friday night."

"You did what?" Savannah shrieked.

"Yeah, I gave a fake name for you and Maggie, in case whoever's in charge happens to know who you are." She paused. "You want to know what's going on out there, don't you?"

Savannah hesitated, then said more quietly, "Rochelle, someone died out there earlier this week."

"Died? How?"

"Actually, they think it was probably accidental, but still…"

Rochelle thought about her friend's comments, then said, "If you don't want to go, I certainly understand. But I thought it would be a good opportunity. You gals want some answers, don't you?"

"Yes." Savannah was silent for a moment, then said, "Actually, it sounds rather like an adventure and I feel sort of adventurous." She giggled. "Maybe it's because I'm carrying a boy."

Rochelle laughed along with her. "Could be." She then asked, "So we're on for next Friday night?"

"I guess so."

"Okay then, we meet behind the old refuse-disposal plant at nine. I'm sure you know where that is. We'll be shuttled to a secret place. They don't want anyone driving to the site on their own."

"Interesting," Savannah said. "Okay, count me in. I'll tell my aunt about it. Hey, what are our names?"

"What?"

"What are the fictitious names you gave them when you signed us up? And what are we to expect, anyway? What's the program, do you know? Or is that a secret too?"

"Well, we're supposed to come with money, of course. We pay up front in the parking lot, if you can imagine—fifty-dollars each. And we should have a question about or for someone who has crossed over. We write that on a piece of paper and hand it to them when they pick us up in the shuttle."

"Oh, I see, so whoever does this…um… program channels spirits?"

"That's what she professes. Oh, and your name is Beverly Lyon and Maggie's is LeeAnn Rogers."

Savannah chuckled. "Okay. I'll let Auntie know. See you next Friday, then."

"Looking forward to it."

Once Savannah had ended the call, she listened for Lily. Hearing nothing, she placed a call to her aunt. "Got the kitties all settled?" she asked. "Sorry I couldn't stay and help. Lily was past ready for a nap and…"

"I know, Vannie. You looked pretty tired yourself. Have you had a chance to rest?"

"A little. Listen, I just got off the phone with Rochelle. Guess what?"

"I don't know, what?"

"She thinks someone is doing some sort of séance-type things out at the seminary."

"Really?"

"Yes, and we're attending one next Friday night with Rochelle."

"What?" Margaret shouted. "A séance? Me? I don't think so. No, Vannie, count me out. I'm not going there at night to spend time with that weird ghost thing you saw—or didn't see. No way, José."

By then Savannah was laughing hysterically. When she caught her breath, she said, "Really? You don't want to see close up and personal what's going on out there—if, indeed, that's where this thing is happening?"

"Hellooo," Margaret said dramatically, "someone was killed out there just the other day."

"Unrelated," Savannah said.

"Maybe. But no. I don't do woo-woo stuff. Uh-uh. Get someone else for that duty. Maybe Iris. She likes that sort of thing."

Still laughing, Savannah said, "Oh, good idea. But Auntie, you seem so curious about what's going on out at the seminary. You're the one who wants to go up into the bell tower and all."

"Well, that's different."

"How?"

"It just is, that's all." Changing the subject quickly, Margaret said, "Hey, good luck with your writing class tonight."

"Thanks. I may need it."

When Savannah noticed that the house was still quiet once she'd ended the call with her aunt, she decided to make another call. "Hi, Iris. Where are you today?"

Iris laughed. "Hey, are you old enough to remember when you never had to ask that question? If you called someone's home phone number, you knew they were at home. If you called their work number, you knew they were at work. In fact, you usually knew right where they were sitting or standing as they answered the phone. Do you remember when we were tethered by a phone?"

"Well, yes. We still have a landline phone," Savannah said. "So where are you?"

"At the inn. Just finished interviewing a new housekeeper. We're getting so busy we need extra help. So what are you doing? Where are you?"

"I'm home. Lily's napping. Just wanted to offer you an opportunity."

"Uh-oh. What sort of opportunity?"

Savannah hesitated, then said, "You know what, I hear Lily. I'd better go rescue her. I'll talk to you later, okay?"

"Sure. Kiss the princess for me."

"Will do."

Chapter 4

By six thirty that evening the dinner dishes had been washed and Michael was stacking blocks with Lily when Savannah entered the room carrying her purse, a notebook, and a jacket.

"Are you excited about your first class?" Michael asked.

"A little nervous, actually. It's been a while since I was a student."

"Oh, you'll do fine." He chuckled. "I don't imagine there'll be anyone else in the class who's writing their cat's memoirs."

"No. Probably not. I'll be interested in what the others are writing about, though. Could be a fascinating group of people."

"Could be," Michael agreed.

Savannah glanced at her watch, then leaned over and kissed Michael and Lily before stepping out into the night to attend her first writing class.

***

"So how did it go last night?" Michael asked the following morning over breakfast.

"Fine, I guess. The teacher's kind of odd. She shared some of her writings, which all seem to focus on fantasy. Quite different from what I'll be writing." She placed a plate of scrambled eggs and toast in front of Michael and began cutting up some fruit to add to Lily's high-chair tray. She faced Michael. "She singled me out."

"You mean she liked your writing?"

"No. She hasn't seen my writing yet. No.

She singled me out after the class to ask me if I was interested in the spirit world. I didn't know how to respond."

"How did you respond?"

"Well, I said something like, 'Not really.' And she proceeded to tell me that she has psychic powers and she senses that I'm about to move into dangerous territory."

"Really? What did you say?"

"Nothing. I just wanted to get into my car and come home."

"Will you go back?"

"I'm not sure. She seems to have a knack for teaching and I have a lot to learn. I want to tap into some of her writing wisdom. But I must say I felt pretty uncomfortable when she forced her supposed psychic powers on me." She tilted her head. "You know, I rather enjoy talking about that sort of thing with Rochelle and even Iris, but I sure didn't like a stranger approaching me with an off-the-wall warning."

"I don't blame you. So what do you think she was referring to?"

Savannah shrugged. "I don't have the slightest idea."

***

The next afternoon around four, Savannah and Margaret headed out to check on the cat colony.

"So Michael's with Lily?" Margaret asked.

"Yeah, he's home from work early today."

Margaret nodded toward Rags, who was hanging out in the backseat. "Why didn't you leave the troublemaker at home?"

"I thought we could use him. Didn't you say Luke's meeting us out there and he's going into the crawl hole? I think Rags could help him."

"Or hinder him," Margaret said under her breath.

Ignoring her, Savannah asked, "Did you set the traps again yesterday?"

Margaret nodded.

"It's been a few days since we've fed; those cats that are left are probably pretty hungry by now."

"That's what we're counting on." As Margaret pulled onto the property and looked around, she noticed, "Luke's not here yet." The two women and the cat climbed out of the car and approached the traps. "Goodie," Margaret said, "it looks like we caught us a few kitties." Just then she heard her phone chime and she pulled it from her pocket. "It's Luke." After finishing the call, she reported, "He's running late. He'll be here in about twenty minutes." She looked impishly at her niece. "I've been thinking about that spiral staircase Iris told us about—you know, the one up to the bell tower. I have an idea about where it might be. Want to go check it out while we wait for Luke?"

Savannah hesitated.

"Come on. It could be kind of cool." She looked down at the cat. "Rags will like going on an adventure."

"Okay." She motioned toward the traps. "I see that a few of the traps are in the sun. Let's move them into the shade, shall we?"

"Yes. By all means. Looks like we have four more cats. There shouldn't be many left, do you think?"

"Shouldn't be." Savannah chuckled. "I wonder how many of the neighborhood pets we've captured."

Margaret cringed. "Michael is checking for chips."

"Good, I'm glad he's doing that. Has he found any?"

"One. We're trying to locate the family. Evidently they've moved. Let's hope they still want their sweet little tuxedo cat." She let out a sigh. "Well, let's go exploring. I have the light." A few minutes later she warned, "Be careful, Vannie," as the two of them made their way slowly up the old staircase to the second floor. "Now, that spiral staircase should be at the end of the hall to the left. Iris said the door had a lock on it. But since then, someone may have created a less obvious way to enter the bell tower. For whatever reason, they may have camouflaged the entrance. If I'm right, all we have to do is feel around on that back wall. There's probably a hidden mechanism that will open a door and give us access."

Once they'd approached the end of the hall, Margaret handed Savannah the flashlight and began running her hands over the wall—rubbing, pushing, rapping, when suddenly she said. "I think I found it. Vannie, shine that light over here." Once Margaret got a better look at the area, she added, "Someone took the hardware off and it's almost impossible to see in the dark since the walls are all painted black." She looked at her niece. "Do you suppose it was all black in here when it was a seminary? Seems like it would have been dismal. We'll have to ask Iris."

"So, now that you've found it, how are we going to open it?" Savannah asked, holding the light steady for her aunt.

"I'm not sure," Margaret said, pushing and tapping on the door. She then said, "Oh, there it is—I think it's held closed by a magnet—like a kitchen cabinet." She curled her fingers around the edge of the door and pulled it open, revealing a very old, very narrow spiral staircase. "Wow!" she murmured, taking the flashlight from Savannah. "Let's go up and see what we find."

"Okay, I guess," Savannah said. She laughed nervously. "It's ironic, Auntie; you're afraid of séances and things like that, but you're all gung ho to climb those stairs into the unknown—the spooky unknown."

"And you're willing to attend meetings where dead spirits might be returning, but you're hesitant to go exploring." Margaret nodded toward the cat. "Rags isn't afraid. Look at him. He's sure eager to get to the top." The women and the cat had climbed about a third of the way up when Margaret noticed that Rags was tugging against his leash. Before taking another step, she asked, "Hey, want me to take him?"

Savannah hesitated, then nodded. "Yes. Maybe you should. I'm a little off balance already with this baby bulge and Rags isn't helping."

"Okay. Here, you hold the light; hand me the leash." But as the women attempted to make the exchange, somehow they lost their grip on the flashlight and it tumbled down the spiral staircase with a clang and a clatter. "Damn!"

"Oh no."

"I thought you had it," Margaret complained. Savannah let out a sigh. "Now what?"

"I guess I'd better go back down and get it. Or," she hesitated before saying, "we could scrap this witch hunt."

"So it's become a witch hunt, has it?" Savannah snarked.

"What would you call it?"

More quietly, Savannah said, "I guess that's what we were going to find out today. Yeah, it's getting late. Let's go back down and regroup."

"Okay," Margaret agreed. "Hold onto that railing and step carefully. It's pretty dark up here."

"I will. You hold onto Rags."

"Huh?"

Savannah stopped in mid-step. "Rags," she hissed. "Auntie, you have him, don't you?"

"No. You didn't hand him over."

"Yes, I did," Savannah insisted. "You took the leash before you dropped the flashlight."

"No, I didn't. And I didn't drop the flashlight, either. I handed it to you. You dropped it."

"Are you delusional?" Savannah spat.

Margaret tried to focus on Savannah in the near-darkness. "Are you saying you don't have hold of the leash?"

"No, I don't!"

"Good God," Margaret murmured. "What just happened?"

Savannah suddenly felt a familiar knot in the pit of her stomach. "Rags!" she called. "Here kitty-kitty. Where are you, Rags? Come on boy."

Margaret tried her hand at enticing the cat. "Here kitty-kitty-kitty," she trilled. "Rags! Here kitty, kitty, kitty."

Still holding tightly to the railing, Savannah leaned over and felt around for the cat on the steps. "Where is he, Auntie? Which way do you suppose he went?"

"I don't know. I'd better go get that light and see if we can figure it out. Maybe he went back down the stairs. At least, let's hope he did. Otherwise…"

"Otherwise what?" Savannah asked, not wanting to hear the response.

"Otherwise he went up and we don't know what in the heck is up there."

"Rags!" Savannah called more loudly. "Rags! Kitty-kitty-kitty."

Margaret sighed. "Come on, let's go back down. Now step carefully, Vannie. In fact, let me go first in case you stumble."

Before they could make any headway, they heard an ear-piercing screech. Margaret grabbed for Savannah. "What in the hell was that?"

Too shaky to stand, Savannah lowered herself and perched on one of the narrow steps, muttering, "Oh, my gosh. Oh, my gosh. Rags…"

"Didn't sound like a cat to me," Margaret said. "Where'd that weird noise come from, anyway?"

Savannah pointed toward the bell tower. "Up there, I think." She pulled herself to her feet using the railing. "Let's go." More quietly, she said, "Please be downstairs, Rags. Please, please, please."

Just then Margaret screamed. She slapped frantically around her head.

"What's wrong?" Savannah shouted.

"Something just attacked me—a damn bird or a bat, maybe."

118

"Are you okay?" Savannah shrieked.

"Yes. Let's just get out of here." As Margaret began taking the stairs more quickly, she turned and instructed, "Now, you take it slow." When she reached the bottom of the staircase, she picked up the flashlight and directed it at the few steps Savannah had left to descend.

"Do you see Rags?" Savannah asked.

Once her niece was on solid flooring, Margaret shined the light around the spiral staircase, then into the hallway. "Oh, my God!"

"What?" Savannah could feel her heart pounding hard in her chest.

"Your cat! The black bird's got him!" She shuddered. "It looks like he attacked Rags." Savannah gasped. "A bird? Is Rags okay?" she asked, her view obstructed by her aunt, who was running toward where the cat lay.

"Shoo!" Margaret shouted. "Get off him! Get off him!"

Meanwhile the large black bird unfolded its wings and flew over her head up toward the bell tower, emitting a piercing call as it disappeared into the darkness.

"Rags," Savannah said, kneeling next to him. She ran her hand over his body. When he didn't move, she quickly checked his vitals. "He's breathing. His heart rate seems slow." She shook him and called his name. "Rags. Rags."

Just then the cat opened his eyes and lifted his head. When he saw Savannah and Margaret, he stood, stretched, and yawned.

"Oh, Rags, you're okay," Savannah said, hugging him to her.

Margaret looked around cautiously. "That bird must have knocked him out or something."

Savannah ran her hands over the cat to check for injuries. She gazed toward the spiral staircase and said, as if thinking out loud, "Or he was hypnotized or drugged, maybe." She enveloped him in her hands and kissed him on top of his head. Then lifting him into her arms, she said, "Auntie, I'd like to take him outside."

"Yes," Margaret whispered. "Let's get the heck out of here."

As the two women and the cat slowly descended the wide staircase, they heard a voice echo up into the second-story hallway. "Ms. Savannah. Ms. Maggie. Hey, are you up there?"

"It's Luke," Margaret said. She grabbed Savannah's arm. "Come on, let's go down and get to work, shall we?" She then called out, " Here we are!"

"What were you doing up there?" Luke asked. "Did you find the stairway to the tower?"

Margaret nodded. "We sure did." As they made their way down the main staircase and out through the small door, she told him what had happened. "But we didn't make it to the top. Um…a dang bird about broke our eardrums with his screeching, then he attacked Rags and knocked him out or something."

"Attacked the cat?" he asked. "What was it, an eagle?"

"A raven, we think," Savannah said.

Luke stopped and stared at the women, then at Rags. He adjusted his baseball cap. "Well, let me take the cat and we'll see what we can find under the building, okay?"

"Keep hold on the leash," Savannah instructed. "I don't want to lose him under there or in the walls of that place."

"Yeah, I will," Luke agreed. He looked at Rags. "You'll stay with me, won't you, guy? We have work to do under there and you're gonna help me, right, fella?"

After Luke and Rags disappeared under the building, Savannah and Margaret entertained themselves by dropping treats into the traps for the cats. "Poor babies," Savannah said, "they're hungry."

"They shouldn't be," Margaret complained. "I left a whole can of tuna in each of those traps."

"Well, they act hungry," Savannah said. She faced her aunt. "Hey, let's take those black kittens, shall we? Do we have room?"

Margaret faced her niece. "Thanks for reminding me. Yes, I want to grab them before they start wandering off." She winced. "I hope we can get the momma cat too. Did you see her this afternoon?"

"No. Do you have a carrier?"

"Yes, I think so. I'll get it. Put on your gloves."

They'd just placed two of the black kittens in a carrier and set it in the shade near the car when they saw Luke crawl out from under the building. He stood up and brushed off his knees, then removed his jumpsuit and shook it.

"Well?" Margaret said, eager to hear what he had found.

"Yeah, there are still some cats under there, but not many—at least I don't think so. It appears that you have maybe five or six left."

"That's all?" Margaret asked. "What kind of shape are they in?"

He raised his eyebrows. "Pretty good, actually. No kittens and no pregnant females. Those I saw were either older cats or young ones—you know, teenagers."

Suddenly Savannah lurched forward. "Rags! Luke, where's Rags?"

He grimaced. "Yeah, about your cat—I think he crawled up into the building."

"Did you see any black cats down there?" Margaret asked.

"No black ones."

Savannah heaved a sigh. "So you think he went inside from down there? We'd better go find him. Luke, I thought you were going to hold onto him."

He noticed an edge to her voice. "I did, actually," he said in his defense. "…that is, until…"

"Until what?" she groused, as she trotted toward the door to the building.

He followed her. "Well, I had the leash in my hand and when I noticed he had jumped up onto the wood framing under there, I tried to get him to come back down. But by then he'd disappeared and I figured the best way to get him was to go inside and nab him."

Savannah stepped in through the door with a flashlight and walked into the former reception area. She shined the light around the room. "Where do you think he went in, Luke?"

He thought for a moment, then pointed. "Probably like eight feet in that direction."

"Under the staircase?" Savannah asked, her voice shrill.

She and Margaret both shined their flashlights around the sides of the staircase.

"Sometimes there's a door under a set of stairs for storage," Margaret said. "Do you see one?"

"No, but they could have wallpapered over it. Luke, do you have a knife or something we can use to cut into that wallpaper?"

He pulled out a pocket knife. Before handing it to Savannah, he said, "Let's feel around and see if we can find a door before we go to cutting, shall we?"

"Rags!" Savannah shouted. "Rags!" She turned to her aunt. "Did you hear that? I think he's in there. Yes, let's feel around and see if we can find an opening. If not, I'll have Michael come over here with his saw and sledgehammer." She put her ear up to the wall around the space under the stairs and called, "Rags?"

"Do you hear him?" Luke asked.

"Not anymore." She put one hand out. "Wait." She shushed the others. "Listen. I hear something." She jumped away from the wall for a second, then went back to listening. "What in the heck is going on in there?"

"What?" Margaret asked, joining her with her ear against the wall. "I don't hear anything."

"I don't feel anything that appears to be a door of any sort," Luke admitted.

"There, I hear a cat," Savannah said excitedly.

"Vannie," Margaret said sternly, "look."

When Savannah turned in the direction Margaret indicated, she saw the third black kitten sitting on a stair step, looking down at them and mewing. "Oh, hello there," she said. "You want to go home with us, huh?" She thought for a moment, then said, "I'm going back to the crawl hole and see if I can talk him out that way."

But all of their efforts were unsuccessful. Rags seemed to be trapped inside an unknown void in the construction of the building, or else he was adventuring and didn't want to be discovered.

Feeling defeated and frustrated, Savannah finally said, "I'm going to call Michael and have him bring some tools."

"Look, Vannie," Margaret said, "it'll be dark soon. Why don't we board up the crawl hole and come back in the daylight with Michael and his tools?"

"No!" Savannah insisted. "I'm not leaving him here in this creepy place overnight. Those other cats might attack him. He is an intruder, after all."

Margaret started to protest, but when she saw that her niece was near tears, she let out a long sigh. "Okay, give your husband a call and see what he thinks."

Savannah dabbed at her eyes, then edged her phone out of her pocket and made the call. "Michael, Rags is lost inside the walls of the seminary building and we can't get to him. I'm afraid for him, Michael. Would you bring your saw over here and see if we can get him out?"

"He what?" Michael asked. "He's lost in the walls? That's a big place, Savannah, how are we going to find him?"

"We think we know where he is. We just can't find a way to reach him. Please, Michael," she pleaded.

Upon hearing the emotion in her voice, he agreed. "Okay, hon, I'll be right over." He paused

124

before saying, "I'll see if I can drop Lily at Iris's and Craig's. I hate to drag her out to that place."

"Good idea. I'll call Iris while you're getting her ready."

When Michael arrived at the seminary, he found Savannah and Margaret struggling to block the crawl space with a piece of plywood they'd found among the debris. "Here, let me help you with that," he offered. "Why are you doing this, anyway?"

"We don't want Rags to escape through here," Savannah explained. Then she noticed that Michael wasn't alone. She smiled at the man who accompanied him. "Well, hi Craig. What are you doing out here?"

Michael chuckled. "He wants to see how I use some of the new techniques I've been learning at the home-repair class."

"Darn right," Craig confirmed. His voice softened. "And I want to make sure my buddy gets out okay." He frowned. "How did Rags get into this mess, anyway?"

"Oh, Craig," Margaret carped, "you know how it is with that cat."

Ignoring her aunt's comment, Savannah explained, "Luke took him under the building to help find any cats that might be hiding under there and Rags pulled one of his shenanigans…"

Margaret interrupted. "Yeah, his Houdini act."

"Somehow he found his way up into the interior of the building and we think he may be stuck inside there." Savannah motioned. "Come on, we'll show you where we think he is."

Michael looked around. "Where's Luke?"

"Oh, we sent him on his way with the cats we'd trapped," Margaret explained. "He still had work to do with them before he could call it a day and there's not much daylight left."

Savannah smiled. "He was reluctant to leave us, but we told him you were on your way."

Michael gazed at the building. "Okay, show us where you think your delinquent cat is." After surveying the situation inside the building, he asked, "So you think that where he went in from down there is right under these stairs, do you?" He walked around the staircase a few times with a flashlight and ran his hand through his hair. "You know, often this space is used for storage; there's probably a door somewhere. Did you check for a door?"

Margaret nodded. "As you can see, we tore into the wallpaper looking for one."

"That's odd. Don't you think so, Craig?" Michael asked.

Craig shrugged.

"I mean, it would be unusual to let so much space go to waste." He began tapping on the enclosure under the staircase. "I tend to agree that there probably was a door at some point. I wonder what happened to it. Why would they hide it?" He continued to tap and knock on the wall on both sides of the enclosure, finally saying, "Did you hear that?"

"What?" the others asked.

"Well, listen," he instructed. He tapped the wall, then moved over a few feet and tapped it again. "Hear the difference? I think this is your opening, right here." He pulled out his knife and cut away at some of the wallpaper. "They did a pretty good job of concealing this door."

Once Craig got a look at what was underneath the wallpaper, he ran his hand over the putty and tape. "Boy, I'll say. Smooth as a baby's bottom."

At that, Michael picked up his battery-operated power saw and began cutting into the door. Once he'd removed it, Craig shined his flashlight inside the space. "Yup, storage," he said.

Margaret pushed closer. "I want to see, I want to see."

Savannah stood back and asked quietly, "Is Rags in there?"

"No, I don't see the cat," Craig said.

Savannah grimaced and glanced around the room. "Where could he be?"

"So what is all this stuff?" Margaret asked, stepping into the space with her flashlight.

"I don't know," Craig said. "Looks like boxes of books and papers. Probably old records from when this was a school."

"Yeah, administration forms, curriculum materials, and such, I would imagine," Michael agreed. "It doesn't seem as though they'd leave all this stuff behind, though."

After peering into the alcove for a few moments, Margaret said, "They didn't leave very much. I mean, that school operated for a long time. I wonder where the rest of the records are."

"And I wonder where Rags is," Savannah said, stepping inside the small room and looking around using the glow from Michael's and Margaret's flashlights. "Do you see any way in or out of here from under the building?"

"Sure don't," Michael said. "If he crawled up into the structure, he wouldn't be able to make his way into this area."

Savannah covered her face with her hands. "Oh no. Where is he?"

Michael winced. "I sure don't know. I guess we'll have to go under there to find out. Craig, you stay up here. I'll see if I can find where he went in and I'll tap in the area. You mark it on this end."

"Now, Luke said Rags sort of disappeared up into the framework under there," Savannah said. "Michael, he still has his harness and leash on. Luke tried to hold onto the leash and back him out of there, but he said there was no way. By then, the leash was wrapped around something or Rags had turned a corner, maybe. Gads, I hope he's not tangled up somewhere inside this building. That could be it. He could be caught and he's stuck in there."

"If that were the case," Michael said, "I think he'd be yowling his head off." He turned to Savannah. "Give me Luke's number. I'll call him and see what information I can get from him. Then we'll go take a look."

"Hey!" Margaret shouted. "Check this out, you guys. Wow, this is scandalous!"

"What?" Craig asked, moving to where she stood holding a handful of documents.

"Well, it appears that some of the people hired to teach here and maybe even some of the administrators were into something outside of the divinity of the seminary doctrines, if you know what I

128

mean." When she noticed the others were waiting for an explanation, she said more quietly, "I think there were some undercover witches working here. These boxes seem to be full of reports of evil witchcraft and unauthorized spells and other mysticism being perpetrated on students and staff—counter, of course, to the theology this seminary was accredited to teach." She looked at the others. "At least, that's what I'm getting from some of these documents."

"Well, that *is* scandalous," Craig said.

"So someone didn't want this stuff leaked, it seems." Savannah stared at the items her aunt clutched. "I wonder if this has any bearing on why the seminary closed."

"Yeah," Margaret said. "And I wonder who hid all this stuff in here and why?"

"Look at this!" Savannah shouted.

When everyone looked in her direction, she picked up a statue that she'd uncovered.

"A black cat," Margaret said under her breath. "Vannie, do you think those black cats we keep seeing inside this place are somehow related to what used to go on out here—I mean the mystical, woo-woo stuff?"

"Yeah, and that could still be going…" Savannah said, her voice trailing off. She took a deliberate breath. "Hey, let's go find my cat before it gets as dark outside as it is in here."

"Yes, I'd like to get back to my newspaper…and dinner," Michael said, having finished his conversation with Luke. "Okay, so listen for my knocking," he instructed as he left the room and headed for the crawl hole outside the building.

"Wait," Margaret said before Craig and Savannah left the small room. "Here are some old photographs."

"Not now, Auntie. One thing at a time. Let's get Rags back and get home out of the cold. We can look at pictures tomorrow."

Margaret stared at her niece for a moment, then grabbed a handful of the photos and stuffed them into her jacket pocket before following the others out of the storage area.

"Over there!" Craig pointed when he heard Michael's tapping. He rushed to a spot six feet from the storage area and close to a stone fireplace. "Listen now," he instructed. "Where, exactly, is he?"

"I think it's under the fireplace," Savannah said.

Craig frowned. "Could be." He walked closer and examined a small compartment built into the side of it. "For wood storage," he said, opening it. He picked up a piece of wood and tapped against the far wall of the small space and promptly heard a tap in response.

"Michael, did you find where he went in?" Savannah called.

"Yeah. I think so. I'm coming up."

"Wait," she said. "Michael, call him. See if you can get him to come out of there."

"Okay."

The others stood quietly while Michael called out to Rags. Then they listened for the cat's response.

Michael yelled from down below, "Did you guys hear anything?"

"Not a sound!" Craig shouted.

"Where could he be?" Savannah whined.

Once Michael had joined the others inside the building, he studied the fireplace and the area all around it. Finally, taking a deep breath, he said, "I don't even know where to start. He could have found a maze that takes him all throughout the ground floor—a tunnel just his size." He turned to Savannah. "Oh, I did find what looks like his fur around that opening down there where Luke saw him disappear. Of course, it could be some other cat's fur."

"So what are we going to do, Michael?"

"Start cutting into the floor, I guess." He shook his head. "Sure hope we don't have to cut into that old stone fireplace."

"Did you bring the right tools?" Savannah asked.

He looked at her. "Hon, why don't we block off the crawl hole and go on home. I'll think some more about how to approach this. We can come back tomorrow when we have more daylight and a fresh perspective. In fact, maybe he'll come out of the crawl hole in the morning after spending the night here."

"Michael…" Savannah complained.

"He'll be okay, hon. Come on, now. Let's go get our child and have some dinner."

"Michael," Craig said, "you might pull some of those boards off the windows to let more light in here for you to work in tomorrow."

"Yeah, I think I will. And I'll bring my shop lantern. Maybe Damon will come out and help me with this in the morning." He looked at Savannah and Margaret. "Were you gals planning to do more trapping tomorrow?"

Margaret nodded. She glanced at the stairwell and patted the photos in her pocket. "Yeah, and I'd like to snoop around in here some more."

Chapter 5

At round nine the following morning when Margaret picked Savannah up, she asked, "Where's the princess?"

"Michael took her to Colbi's when he picked up Damon."

Margaret glanced at her niece as she drove. "How are you feeling today, Vannie?"

"Okay. Just a little tired. I sure hope we can find Rags and release him from that monster of a building."

Margaret chuckled. "The building is a monster?"

Savannah pouted. "Yes. It has captured my cat, hasn't it?"

"Pshaw, he's probably on one of his adventures. Hopefully, he's hungry and ready to surrender by now." She changed the subject. "Hey, I guess Luke went out after we left last night and set the traps again."

"Well that won't do much good. We blocked off the crawl hole." After thinking about it, Savannah said, "Unless there are cats hanging around in the debris piles."

Margaret cringed. "He removed the board Michael put over the crawl hole."

"What? Why did he do that?"

"Well, he didn't know Rags was still stuck in there. He wanted to make sure the cats could get to the traps—you know, in case they were hungry."

Savannah started to respond when her phone chimed. "It's Michael. He and Damon are probably already out at the place." She put the phone up to her ear. "Hi, Michael."

"Hi. Well, you're not going to believe this."

"What? What happened?"

"We caught Rags."

She relaxed against the seat. "Oh, good. How is he?"

"A bit indignant, actually."

"Why?"

"Well," he hesitated. "…when will you be here?"

"Um…we're almost there. Why?"

"I think I'll just wait so you can see for yourself."

Savannah let the phone drop to her lap. "Well, that's odd."

"What?" Margaret asked.

"Michael said they found Rags and he's indignant." She frowned. "I wonder what he means."

"Well, here we are. Let's go find out."

"What's going on, Michael?" Savannah asked as she stepped out of the car. She glanced at Damon. "Why are you guys staring at that trap?"

Michael pointed. "Look."

Margaret couldn't help herself. She burst out laughing. "Oh, my gosh. Will you look at that? He got himself trapped, did he? And I thought he was supposed to be a smart cat." She did a double take and squinted at the cat. "What's that he's got on him?"

Savannah simply stared for a few seconds before kneeling next to the trap. "Rags, I'm so glad to see you." She frowned. "But what has happened to you?" She opened the trap to let him out and continued checking him over.

Margaret chortled. "What is he, a butterfly? Vannie, he's wearing wings."

"Yes, I see that. Crumpled angel wings."

"And bloomers," Margaret said. "Ewww. Dirty bloomers, I might add."

Savannah shook her head. "How disgusting. Why would someone put panties on a cat?" She looked up at the bell tower and shuddered. "I guess there's no denying that someone other than us has access to this place." She started to pick up Rags when Michael stopped her.

"Let me take care of those soiled britches," he said, reaching down and removing the clothing.

"What's that?" Savannah asked, leaning over to peer more closely at Rags. She looked up at the others. "Someone has shaved him. Look, he has a strange emblem on his shoulder. What is that? Who would do that?"

Margaret gasped and put her hand up against her mouth.

"What?" Savannah asked. "What do you know about this?"

"Well, when I spoke to Luke this morning, he told me something odd."

"What?" Savannah insisted, holding her breath.

"After he set the traps, he went inside because he thought he heard a cat carrying on in there."

"It was probably Rags trying to get his attention," Michael said.

She nodded and continued. "He said all the black cats inside seemed to be okay, only he discovered something kind of weird." She tilted her head inquisitively. "Vannie, did you notice that the black cats have been marked?"

"Marked?"

"Yes, he saw two of the adult cats with shaved patterns on their shoulders. You didn't notice that? I must say I sure didn't, but it's so dark in there and they are black."

"And they haven't let us get that close to them," Savannah said. She looked at her aunt. "What sort of pattern?"

"Some kind of crude pentagram. Luke thinks it's an occult symbol, but it's not one he's familiar with."

"Gosh, do you suppose it's the same as this one on Rags?" Savannah shivered. "Ohhh, it creeps me out to think that someone who may worship demons had their hands on my cat."

Margaret looked up at the bell tower. "It sure confirms that there's something mysterious going on out here."

"Well," Michael said, "we found your cat. Think we should take him home?"

Savannah nodded. "I'd sure like to get his harness and leash back."

"Do you want to go up those skinny stairs and see if you can find them?" Margaret teased.

Savannah glanced at the bell tower and cringed. "Maybe. But not right now. I just want to take Rags home and relax with him and my little girl today." She turned to her aunt. "If you don't mind."

Margaret shook her head. "No. I wasn't planning to stay long this morning anyway, and Luke should be here soon in case I need any help."

"Okay then," Michael said. "I'll put him in the car and gather up my tools."

Before walking away, Margaret asked, "Hey, Vannie, is Iris excited about going to that psychic thing next week?"

Savannah stared at her aunt for a moment. "I still don't get why you're not coming with us."

"Too creepy and weird," she said.

"But you seem so curious about what's up in the bell tower. You have no fear when it comes to climbing that scary staircase to…to who knows where."

"That's different," Margaret insisted.

"How?" Savannah challenged.

"Um…I don't know. I guess because I feel sort of in control when I choose to explore around here. You guys don't have a clue as to what you'll encounter Friday night."

Savannah lowered her brow. "Hmmm. I don't get it. I sure haven't felt in control of anything going on out here these last few days—Rags…" she laughed. "…the flashlight, that nasty attack bird, or anything else, have you?"

"Yeah, I suppose not. But I'm just freaked out about attending an organized black magic encounter, not knowing what in the heck might happen."

Savannah grinned at her aunt. "Not even for the sake of research, huh?"

Margaret shook her head. "Not even…" She asked, "So is Iris going with you and Rochelle?"

"I don't know. I haven't told her about it. I thought I'd spring it on her Sunday. We're meeting at Bud's, aren't we? I think Bud's parents and grandmother are joining us."

"That will be something different. Bud doesn't cook, does he?"

"No, but his mother's a good cook and I guess Brianna's going to help her prepare something. Brianna mentioned beef pot pies and a garden salad." She smiled. "They have a lot of greens in their garden right now."

* * *

The Iveys arrived at the Bogart ranch shortly after church on Sunday. "Come in," Edith Bogart invited. "Good to see you."

Savannah smiled. "So nice of you to have all of us."

"Oh, we love to entertain. We don't do it often, but we've been looking forward to this gathering." She turned to her husband. "Gunther, of course you know Dr. Mike. I'm sure you remember his wife, Savannah, and this is their daughter, Lily, isn't it?"

"Yes."

Edith smiled at the child. "Brianna speaks of her often."

"Hello Gunther," Michael said, shaking hands with him.

Savannah greeted him, as well.

Gunther then took Lily's hand. "She's a mighty fine filly."

"How old is she now?" Edith asked.

"Two," Lily said, holding up two fingers.

Edith chuckled. "Cute. And smart too."

Savannah smiled, then she handed Edith a vase of spring flowers. "This is for you."

"Thank you!" she gushed. "They're beautiful, and perfect for our table this afternoon."

Just then another woman stepped into the room and admired the flowers. "Aren't they lovely?"

"Savannah, Dr. Mike, have you met my mother, Serena?"

"No. Nice to meet you," Savannah said.

"Oma," the woman said. "Everyone calls me Oma."

"Okay, Oma it is," Savannah agreed. "I recall my sister speaking of you."

"Oh that girl—we sure do love her. She's a jewel, that one."

Just then Brianna stepped into the room and reached for Lily. "Want to see the piggies and horsies and duckies?"

Lily nodded brightly.

"Hi, Sis," Brianna said, giving Savannah a one-armed hug. Brianna hugged Michael briefly, then bounced Lily in her arms and said, "Let's go visit the zoo—the farm zoo." Before leaving the room, she asked Savannah, "Want to come with us?"

"Sure." Savannah glanced around. "Are we the first ones here?"

Overhearing this as he walked in, Bud said, "Yes. Isn't that some sort of record? Aren't you usually always late?"

"Since we've had Lily, yes, it seems so," Savannah confessed.

Michael nodded. "So true. But today she was cooperative."

"Well good; it'll give us a chance to get acquainted," Edith said. She turned to her mother. "Mom, would you make sure the salad's tossed? I'm going to accompany these ladies out to the…" she paused and laughed, "…the farm zoo."

"Yes." Oma gestured dramatically. "Go. Take the little one to see the animals."

Savannah gazed around the property. "You have a nice-sized place here."

"It gets bigger all the time," Edith said. When Savannah looked confused, she explained, "It's so much work. But when we speak of—what do you call it?—sizing down, we decide we aren't ready. With Bud's help, we can still manage. But there will be a time when we'll have to slow down." She put her hand on Brianna's arm. "Hopefully, by then, Bud will be ready to take a bride and they can run this place."

Savannah glanced at her sister in time to see Brianna's expresssion. *Hmmm. I wonder what's going on. I'll have to get her aside and find out. Looks like maybe she's feeling some pressure. I learned a long time ago not to back Brianna into a corner. She always comes out fighting or she runs away.* Savannah studied her sister for a moment. *I wonder which one she's about to do this time.*

"See the baby piggies?" Brianna chirped.

"Piggies," Lily squealed. "Piggies, Mommy."

"I see them," Savannah said, smiling.

Lily gazed up at Brianna, a more serious look on her face and said, "Piglet."

"Piglet?" Brianna repeated, giving her sister a sideways glance.

Just then, Lily pointed and shouted excitedly, "Horsie! See horsie, Auntie Bri?" She ran toward the corral. The others rushed to keep up with the toddler.

"You have a horsie, don't you?" Brianna asked the toddler.

Lily opened her blue eyes wide, turned her palms up, and said, "Horsie all gone."

Brianna looked to Savannah for an explanation.

"Oh, we're boarding Peaches with Bonnie until after I have the baby. She's making sure she gets her exercise and all. We were just out there visiting her a couple of days ago."

"Peaches apple," Lily chirped.

"You gave Peaches an apple?" Brianna repeated. Lily nodded.

"Sounds like a fruit salad to me," Bud said as he approached. "Hey Lily, want to see the baby cow?" Bud asked.

"Baby cow?" Gunther repeated sarcastically as he joined them.

"Well, she doesn't know calf, yet, does she?" Bud asked.

Just then Lily pointed through the slats of a corral fence. "Calf," she called out. "Baby calf."

Bud and Gunther looked at each other and burst out laughing.

"She is a veterinarian's daughter, after all," Brianna said proudly. She then corrected herself. "Two veterinarians' daughter."

Bud put his arm around Brianna's waist and pulled her to him. "Does that mean our children will use medical terms to describe their body parts?"

Brianna didn't respond. Instead, she wriggled free of his grip, took Lily's hand, and asked, "Want to see the baby duckies? Bud has baby duckies."

"Duckling," Lily said as they walked together across the yard.

"Yes, she's a smart cookie," Edith remarked.

When Lily heard this, she looked up at the woman and asked, "Cookie?"

Savannah chuckled. "Later, sweetie. We'll have cookies later."

Lily stopped and looked at her aunt. She pointed to something dangling from her jeans pocket and said, "Keys. Auntie Bri's keys."

"Keys?" Brianna repeated. "Oh yes, those are my keys."

Lily looked up at her aunt, a hint of a pout on her sweet face. "My keys all gone."

"You lost your keys?" Brianna asked.

She shook her head. "All gone," she said.

Savannah chuckled. "Yeah, they went missing under rather strange circumstances. She brought them out with us yesterday while we were playing on the porch. She likes to pretend she's unlocking the door, and she also uses them with her little princess car. She's quite attached to those keys."

"All gone," Lily repeated, staring down at her shoes.

"Yeah, after we went inside," Savannah continued, "she remembered she'd forgotten her keys and when we went out to get them, they were gone. Vanished, just like my bracelet and Michael's tools."

"You don't have another…what was his name… Luke in your neighborhood, do you?" Brianna asked. "Wasn't that the name of the kid who was helping himself to your trash and tools and things?"

Savannah nodded. "Yeah, it's not Luke. He has reformed. I just can't imagine what's happening. I sometimes feel as though I'm going crazy."

"Maybe it's a raccoon," Edith suggested. "We've had raccoons mess with things around here."

Just then Margaret called out to them. "Hey, what's going on out here, a treasure hunt?"

"Hi, Aunt Marg," Brianna said. "We're visiting the animals. Come join us."

"I'm Edith Bogart," the hostess said, offering her hand. "You must be these lovely ladies' aunt."

Margaret shook Edith's hand. "Yes, I'm Maggie. Thank you for inviting us." She glanced around the property. "You have a lovely place here."

"Thank you." When the conversation seemed to lag, Edith said, "Savannah was just telling us about missing things around her place."

"Pshaw," Margaret said, "did she tell you about her kleptomaniac cat?"

Edith's eyes grew wide. "No. So is it the cat that took the bracelet, Lily's keys, and the tools?"

Savannah shook her head. "I don't think so. He's never outside unsupervised. But on the off chance that he has been sneaking out, I did look through his stash."

"His stash?" Edith asked.

"Yes, he hides things in a closet upstairs. Yesterday I found just the usual: used tea bags, a pot holder, some of Lily's socks, her doll's bonnet, and a few bills."

"Bills that need to be paid," Margaret asked, "or dollar bills?"

"Both," Savannah said, laughing.

"So you've had something else go missing?" Margaret asked.

Savannah nodded. "Lily's set of keys—you know how she used to like our keys. I put together a set for her with old keys that don't go to anything. Now they're gone." She turned to her aunt. "So keep an eye out at your place."

"Why?" Brianna asked. "Do you think Max took them?"

"No," Savannah said definitively. "Auntie found my bracelet at her house a few days after it went missing. Remember, we talked about it last Sunday at the inn." She poked her sister in the arm. "You thought one of us was into levitation."

Edith glanced at Brianna, then said to Savannah, "Well that sounds like a real mystery, for sure." She leaned toward the women. "You know, my mother is a bit of a seer. Maybe she can shed some light on what's happening to your belongings."

Savannah's face lit up. "Oh, I'll have to ask her. Hey, here she comes."

"So how does the little one like the animals?" Oma asked. She stooped to Lily's level. "Did you see the duckies, and the baby cow?"

"Duckling," Lily said. She pointed toward the corral. "Calf. Brown calf."

"Oh my, she is a smart one." She looked at Savannah. "And she's only two?"

Savannah nodded.

"Hey, Mom," Edith said, "the Iveys are missing some things from their home. I told Savannah you might be able to give her a clue as to what has happened to them."

Oma stood straight and looked at Savannah. After staring at her for a moment, she said, "Your cat takes things, doesn't he?"

"Oh my gosh," Margaret said, "you picked up on that?"

Oma laughed. "Well, Brianna mentioned something about it once."

"Oh."

"Do you have a bird?" Oma asked.

Savannah shook her head. "No, that's about the only thing we don't have. We have a horse, cats, a dog..."

"I see feathers. I can't be sure if the image relates to Indians or birds—maybe a costume of feathers." She let out a sigh. "I'm out of practice and looking forward to what comes of this festive gathering today. Let's not dwell on what's lost to us, shall we?"

Before Savannah could respond, Bud announced, "The Sledges and the Jacksons are here."

"Oh, goodness," Edith said, heading toward the house, "we'd better put the finishing touches on the meal and start serving."

Once everyone had visited over mimosas and sparkling water, Edith invited their guests to be seated around two tables set up in their farm-style kitchen. Savannah, Michael, and Lily sat at the larger table with Craig, Iris, Edith, Oma, and Gunther. Margaret and Max sat nearby with Brianna, Bud, Colbi, and Damon.

"This is lovely," Savannah said as she gazed at the feast arranged on the table.

"It sure is," Iris agreed. She swooned. "I love a fresh garden salad."

"You serve fresh greens at the inn, don't you?" Savannah asked.

"As often as possible. But Edith, you have things in here I haven't seen. I'd love to know what some of this is so we can plant it at the inn."

"Mom's in charge of the garden," Edith said. "She can tell you."

"Well, the gardener and I," Oma corrected. She then said, "I saved the seed packets. I'll get them after our meal and you can write them down." She swallowed a sip of tea and added, "Or you can take the packets to get you started."

"Perfect," Iris said. "Thank you."

"The meat…" Craig started, "is it from one of your…"

"It sure is," Gunther said proudly. "We grow real good beef around here. Pork, too."

Bud heard his father's brag from the other table and grinned in his direction.

Once Gunther, Craig, and Michael were in deep conversation about growing beef and other ranching issues, and Edith and Oma were discussing something, Savannah turned to Iris. "Hey, what are you doing next Friday night?"

"Um…nothing that I know of, why?"

With a sparkle in her eyes, she asked, "Would you like to go on a witch hunt?"

"Huh?" Iris said, almost choking on her food.

"Yeah, out at the seminary. We think there may be some sort of odd other-worldly or wannabe other-worldly activity going on out there."

Iris dropped her fork, sat up straight, and said, a little too loudly, "I told you so." When she noticed that

Edith, Oma, and a few from the other table were staring at her, she slunk down in her chair a bit. When some of them went back to eating and chatting with their close tablemates, Iris asked quietly, "What's going on?"

Savannah glanced around, then said, "Well, we think someone...or something has taken up residence in the old place and Rochelle is coming to help us ferret out whatever or whoever it is."

Iris narrowed her eyes. "And you want me to...a...do what?" she asked suspiciously.

"Well," Savannah started, trying to be inconspicuous, "she has signed us up for an evening of woo-woo adventure—maybe a séance or something that we believe will occur at the seminary."

"Oh?" Iris said.

When Margaret overheard this from the other table, she said, "Yeah, you meet in a parking lot, hand over money, then you're taken somewhere in the dark."

"What?" Iris shrieked.

Edith shivered. "That sounds frightening."

"What's frightening about it?" Oma asked. "Sounds like the way Charmaine operates." When she saw that the four women were staring at her, she said, "But she's a scammer if I've ever seen one."

Edith smiled. "Mother spends a lot of her time exposing fakes—you know, through her blog."

Savannah made brief eye contact with Margaret, then focused on Oma. "Oh, really? Fake psychics...that sort of thing?"

"Yeah, I believe in the supernatural, but I'm not holding to the hocus-pocus some of those phonies try to sell. No way." Oma gestured toward Brianna and said, "That one believes."

"Brianna?" Edith asked.

At that, Brianna turned away and asked for someone to pass the rolls.

In the meantime, Oma smiled a self-satisfied smile.

Savannah noticed this and thought, *I must remember to ask Brianna what she's been up to lately.* She looked at Oma. *And I definitely want to speak to Oma about this.*

"So, Savannah, you want me to...what?" Iris asked.

After seeing that Edith was discussing with Michael something that had happened at the last steer auction, Savannah spoke quietly to Iris. "Well, Rochelle signed us up for an evening of...um...I don't know quite what. But we think it will lead to the seminary. We're trying to find out what's going on there and we think this person who's overseeing the evening..." she glanced at Oma, "...maybe it's Charmaine—will help us to find out. Are you in?"

Iris looked around, then said, "Sure. Sounds... um...well, interesting. Yeah, I'll be there."

***

Savannah got her chance to speak to Bud's grandmother after dinner when Oma stepped outside with a small bucket of vegetable scraps. "Can I go with you?" she asked.

Oma turned. "Yes, I'm going to feed my rabbits. Bring the little one. She'll want to pet the bunnies."

Savannah found Lily sitting next to Iris and baby Rosemary in the living room and asked, "Hey sweet pea, want to go feed the bunnies some supper?"

Lily scooted off the sofa and took her mother's hand. "Bunnies?" she said excitedly.

Once outside, as Lily handfed lettuce and carrot tops to the rabbits, Savannah said, "I'd really like to hear more about your experience with Charmaine."

Oma looked around, then said, "My daughter does not share my fascination for the supernatural." She put her hand on Savannah's arm. "But your sister does."

"Yes, I remember when you helped her with something I was struggling with before I got pregnant with Lily. It had to do with believing."

"Yes. But you did not need an intuitive for that." She shook her head. "Actually, we all have in us whatever it is we need in order to make our way in this world. Do you believe that, Savannah? We know all that we need to know—it's just a matter of believing and knowing how to reach the information." She paused and smiled at Lily as the child delighted in feeding the rabbits. She then leaned toward Savannah and said quietly, "Charmaine is a fake. Now that's my opinion only, but I'm pretty keen on these things. I sense that your reason for seeing her and playing her little game— it is a game, you know—is for a greater purpose and not in order to feed into her scam."

Savannah nodded. "You got that right."

"Then go without fear. Nothing will harm you, although she will want you to believe that it could. Fear is her control mechanism." Oma shook her head. "She's an odd one and her scheme is kind of entertaining." She looked around to make sure no one was listening. "Actually, I've taken her little trip a couple of times for the entertainment value and," she stood straighter, "to get material for my blog." She peered into Savannah's eyes. "Do you read my blog?"

"No, I wasn't aware…" Savannah started.

She put her hand on Savannah's arm. "I'll get you the link. You visit and you'll learn something about Miss Charmaine before you go on this adventure. For someone like you, who, I assume isn't a follower of the paranormal, it will be an adventure. Just know there is nothing to fear."

"Thank you," Savannah said. "I appreciate that."

Oma stared at Savannah for a moment, then said, "Believe me, there are bona fide mystics and psychics and seers. Me, for example. I have some gifts, but I don't use them for gain. Some do. And then there are some who do not have it, but fake it."

"Wannabes?" Savannah said.

"Exactly." Oma looked down at Lily and smiled. "I know things—like I know you are carrying a boy." She smiled. "And he will be robust and healthy. He will adore his sister and grow into a loving being with a big heart for animals, like his sister." She squinted up at Savannah, then pointed. "You will do some writing. Do I see you struggling with it? Do not. Your writing is good enough. Just come to terms with the content and its arrangement and the writing will not be troublesome for you." When she saw Savannah's puzzled look, she said, "I hope I have not overstepped. Sometimes it just comes out—what I see or sense."

"No, that's fine," Savannah said. "Actually, you're right on—I mean about my writing. And I hope about our son."

"I'm right," Oma assured her with a smile. When they heard Lily giggle, Oma asked her, "Want to hold a baby bunny?"

Lily looked up at her with big eyes and nodded.

Oma laughed. "She is a wonderful child." She opened the pen, lifted out a small bunny, and helped Lily hold it in her arms. "Don't squeeze. No squeezing, now." She chuckled. "We don't want to give baby bunny too much love."

"Baby bunny," Lily said. "Look, Mommy, baby bunny."

"I see, honey." Savannah leaned over and stroked the tiny creature. "So cute. Look at him wiggle his little nose."

Lily laughed.

Oma held the bunny up against Lily's cheek and she giggled. "Bunny tickle me!" she exclaimed.

Meanwhile, Oma nodded off to the right. "Your sister is struggling."

Savannah looked up and saw Brianna showing Colbi and Iris around the garden area. "Struggling?"

"Yes, but she doesn't want anyone to know it." Oma laughed. "She sometimes forgets that I can read her. She's an easy one to read. She loves my Bud, but she's torn. I don't think she embraces his lifestyle." She shook her head. "He'll never be a city boy. For him and his father, it's like wearing a straightjacket. And I don't know how long it will take Brianna to realize she can fit in here. She hasn't found her place yet. She thinks she knows what she wants, but Oma knows better." She continued speaking as if Savannah weren't there. "Oh, she may go away and search for what she thinks she wants, but she will come back. I just hope…"

"What?" Savannah asked.

"I hope Bud can wait it out." She chuckled. "He has a live one there and he'll have to step it up in order to keep her. I think he's learning that, little by little." She faced Savannah. "Your Dr. Mike is a good influence. He shows Bud that a man who wants an exciting woman cannot be one-dimensional."

Savannah's eyes widened. "Interesting."

Oma took Savannah's arm. "Well, isn't that true?"

After thinking about it, she said, "I guess so. Yes."

Oma leaned toward Savannah. "Maybe you could have a little talk with your sister. I sense that she will talk to you." She rolled her eyes dramatically. "But will she listen—that's another matter, isn't it?"

As the women returned to the house with Lily, Oma put her hand on Savannah's arm and stopped her. "Oh, you will find your lost belongings, but not where you expect. As I said, I see feathers." She looked off into space for a moment before saying slowly, "Is it a creature or someone dressed as a creature?" She shook her head. "I cannot be sure."

***

"You're quiet," Michael said as he drove his family home later that day. "Something bothering you?"

Savannah shook her head. "Not really. It was quite a…um…stimulating day."

"I saw you deep in conversation with Bud's grandmother."

"Yes. She's an interesting woman. She gave me a lot to think about."

"Oh?"

When Savannah realized that Michael was fishing for information, she said, "Yeah, just concepts and beliefs and...oh, I don't know...stuff."

"I'm sure I'll be hearing about it once you sort it all out in your mind, right?"

She grinned. "Probably." She faced him. "Oh, she said our baby will be robust, healthy, and he will love his big sister."

"Of course," he said. "I could have told you that."

She smirked playfully at him.

"What's his name?" Michael asked.

"Who?"

"Our son."

"Oh, well, our discussions on that subject haven't been very successful. You like the strong Nordic names and I'm more fond of Biblical names. But we do agree that a family name would be nice. What was your grandfather's name—the one you liked so much?"

"Harry."

"Oh," she said sounding disappointed. "Was that his given name?"

"No. That's what he was called. His real name was Horatio."

"Ugh. Was there a middle name? Or what about his maternal grandparents' last name?"

He thinned his lips. "Oh, let's see. His middle name started with a V, as I recall. Horatio V. Tilford." I know that somewhere in the line there was a Calvin. I recall a Simon Lee Calvin."

"Gosh, Michael, what a lame bunch of names. I guess we'll have to look elsewhere for ideas." After thinking for a moment, however, she said, "Simon. That's not bad. I kind of like that."

"Naw," he said, shaking his head.

"I hope we can come up with a name before he gets here." She stiffened in her seat. "Michael, what if we can't agree and we bring him home from the hospital without a name?"

He patted her knee. "Oh hon, that's not going to happen. We have several weeks now. We'll agree on a name. Don't you worry about that." When he could see that she was brooding, he changed the subject. "Are you ready for your next class? Did you do your writing assignment?"

"I've been working on the beginning of Rags's book. It seems a little hokey, but then how many ways are there to start a story?" She sighed. "I'll have a little more time to work on it before the class Wednesday night." She turned to Michael. "How are you doing in the home-repair class?"

He frowned. "Well, it's pretty simplistic. It's for the beginner, you know. Damon and Max are getting a lot out of it, so I'll stick it out for them. But I'm pretty well-versed on most of what they've presented so far. Oh, I've learned a few shortcuts I hadn't thought of. And there are some techniques coming up that I'm interested in. It's not a complete wash."

"Well, good. I doubt that Damon and Max would go without you."

"Probably not." He chuckled. "I'm sticking with it partly for selfish reasons."

"What?" she asked.

"Once they know how to handle simple tasks around their houses, they won't be calling on me so much."

"Yeah, that's selfish. That would be like me planting fruit trees at Auntie's, Iris's, and Colbi's so we don't have to share fruit with them."

He laughed.

"Where are you going?" she asked when she noticed he'd turned right instead of left.

He grinned. "I thought we'd go out to the seminary and see if you've caught anything."

"Oh."

"Do you have any traps set this weekend?"

"I'm not sure. Auntie and Luke are pretty much taking care of that. We have only a handful of cats left to deal with. We've sure trapped and caught a lot of them."

"I know. I've had a lot of patients from out there."

"I'll open the gate," she said when they got close enough.

He put the car in park. "Naw, you stay here. I'll get it." Once he'd driven inside, he turned to speak to Lily and saw that she was sound asleep. "Someone had a big day."

"I guess she did, sweet sleepy baby."

He stepped out of the car and stared at the building, then walked around to where he could see the bell tower. "It's a big place. Looks like it was a nice place in its heyday."

"Michael, you've been out here before," Savannah said, catching up to him. "You were just here yesterday."

"Yeah, I know. But I didn't have time to check it out." He grinned at her. "I was called out on an emergency for your cat, remember?" He then asked, "Have you been up in that tower?"

"No. We tried to go up there one day. I think I told you that we lost the flashlight, Rags got loose, and a bird attacked us."

He abruptly faced her. "Huh?"

"Didn't I tell you that?"

"No. A bird?"

"Yes, it attacked Rags, too." She chuckled. "Or he fainted when he saw the bird. I don't know exactly what happened that day."

Michael looked at her, then glanced at the building. Suddenly something caught his eye. "Did you know there are cats inside there?"

"Yes. Didn't you see them when you were in there Friday night?"

"No." He ran his hand through his hair. "I guess I heard Luke say something about them, though. How do they get in? I mean, we sure didn't find any openings in the floor."

"There seems to be a colony of all-black cats that live inside there. We've never seen them outside at all."

"Can't you catch them?" he asked.

"Yeah, we might be able to." She leaned toward him and spoke more quietly. "We're pretty sure someone's taking care of them. They seem to be in really good shape."

156

He frowned. "Well, that's odd. So you think someone comes out here and feeds them?"

She nodded. "Either that or someone's living in there." She grasped his arm. "But Michael, we've been all through that place and we haven't seen evidence of anyone having set up housekeeping. We can't even find a feeding station for the black cats. So we're feeding them, just in case."

Michael contemplated Savannah's comments for a moment, then looked back at the car to check on Lily before gravitating toward one of the debris piles. "Boy, there's a lot of good junk out here."

"Good junk?"

"Yeah, that's a nice wheelbarrow."

"Michael, we don't need another wheelbarrow."

"No, but someone we know might." He tossed a few things aside to see what was underneath. "Damon might want to look through this stuff. Hey, there's a good metal rake." He glanced in Lily's direction again, then said, "What's this?"

"What?" she asked, pulling her jacket more tightly around herself.

He moved a few more things around, then quickly stepped back. "Good Lord!"

When Savannah started to move closer, he turned her away. "I don't think you want to see this." He put one arm around her and walked with her toward the car.

"What is it?" she asked, trying to look over her shoulder.

He pulled his phone out of his pocket, took another look behind him, then made a call. He let out a deep sigh before saying into the phone, "Nine-one-one, this is Michael Ivey. I'm at the old seminary at..." he glanced around, "...on west Carter." He looked briefly at Savannah and said more quietly, "I've found a body." He paused. "Yes, I'll wait here."

"A body?" Savannah screeched.

She tried to turn and look behind her, but Michael discouraged it. "Hon, it's not something you'll want to see. Now, why don't you go move the car so the emergency vehicles can get in. Stay with Lily, will you?"

***

"Do they know who it is, Michael?" Savannah asked when he joined her several minutes later.

"Not yet," he said. "The investigator wants to talk to you. I'll stay with Lily." When she looked unsure, he said, "He's on the other side of the coroner's car, waiting for you."

She walked slowly between a couple of emergency vehicles and spotted a man with a notepad. He motioned to her. When he saw that she was pregnant, he pulled two folding chairs from the back of a large van and placed them on the outskirts of the activity. "Please sit down, won't you?" he invited. "Would you state your name?"

She chuckled nervously. "Like in a courtroom?" When he just stared at her, she said, "Savannah Ivey."

"And what were you and your husband doing out here, Mrs. Ivey?"

"Um...I'm helping to trap a colony of cats that have been living out here for a long time."

"Colony?" he questioned.

"Yes, that's what they call it when a group of feral...um...wild cats band together. The owner's going to demolish the building in August and he's asked us to relocate the cats."

He looked at her over the rim of his reading glasses. "Relocate?"

"Yes, we trap them in humane traps and move them to a safe place where we can try to socialize them and place them in homes—you know, as pets."

"Got it," he said.

"And you were trapping this afternoon?"

"Actually, no. My husband and I just stopped by to check on the cats."

"And how was the deceased discovered?" he asked.

"Didn't Michael—my husband—didn't he tell you? He was looking through some of the trash and I guess he saw it. I didn't see it."

"Have you seen anyone around here at all since you've been…um…trapping cats?"

"No. Not really."

"What do you mean by *not really*?"

"Well, a couple from that tract over there came by one day. They wanted to know what we were doing out here. Their name is Ward." She hesitated before saying, "And we saw someone else. At least we think we saw someone…"

"Where?"

She glanced at the structure. "Once up in the bell tower and once…" She winced, "…I thought I saw someone in the second-floor hallway inside there."

He looked at her for a moment, then asked, "Do you think that was Mr. or Mrs. Ward?"

She shook her head.

"Do you know who it was—I mean, in the bell tower and in the hallway?"

"No."

"Can you describe these people you think you saw?" he asked.

She gazed at the bell tower. "Well, once we saw a piece of fabric blowing in the breeze up there. We thought it might be a scarf, maybe. Another time, I saw what looked like a woman carrying a bird cage, running—no, sort of gliding along the second-floor hallway toward the staircase."

The investigator stared at Savannah. "Gliding? With a bird?"

"Yeah, sort of. I don't know if she was real or one of those ghost figures like you see at Disneyland."

He made some notes, then asked, "Who's *we*?"

"Huh?"

"You said, 'we saw someone…'"

"Oh, my aunt is working with me to trap the cats. We both saw something in the bell tower."

"So, as far as you know there's no one living in this place. Is that right?"

"Not that we can tell, only…"

"Only what?"

"There are several all-black cats that seem to stay inside and appear to be well cared for. We're sure that someone has been taking care of them. But there's no sign of anyone living here—no furniture, clothes, food or anything."

He looked up from his notepad. "Just well-fed cats, huh?"

Savannah nodded.

He looked at the structure, then at Savannah. "So you've been inside there?"

"Yes. There's an open door below the bell tower."

He peered at her for a moment, then made more notes. "Ma'am, we've checked every door to this place and we didn't find any that are open and the windows are all boarded up solid. There's a broken window here and there, but there's no way inside that place unless you happen to have a key or maybe a crowbar."

She looked puzzled. "No, we don't have a key..." she chuckled, "...or a crowbar."

He stared at her for a moment before saying, "That small door you mentioned under the bell tower... well, that door seems to be locked from the inside."

Savannah frowned. "I don't know what to say."

He tightened his lips. "I'd say there's someone inside or someone with a key. Do you know which it is?"

Just then Savannah heard a familiar voice. "Well, I should have known the Iveys would be involved."

"Craig," she said, feeling a sudden sense of relief.

"You know the detective?" the investigator asked flatly.

She nodded.

Craig approached and put his arm across Savannah's shoulders. "The Iveys are some of my best friends. Now, Leonard, why are you interrogating her?"

"Well...um...her husband found the deceased. She's been hanging around out here doing something with cats and she says she's seen people out here, but

161

that no one lives in the building." He squinted toward Craig. "Detective, the building is locked up. The door Mrs. Ivey says they found open in the past is locked from the inside. We believe someone's in there."

"Or," Savannah reminded him, "as you said, someone may have a key."

"Exactly." The investigator looked her in the eyes. "Maybe we should talk to your aunt."

Craig chuckled. "Oh yes, your aunt's mixed up in this too, isn't she?"

Savannah frowned. "Mixed up in what?"

Just then Michael approached with Lily in his arms.

"Hi, princess," Craig said, addressing the toddler. "Sleepy, huh? Me too, after that big farm-style meal."

"What's going on?" Michael asked. "Can I take my wife and daughter home now?"

"Yes," Craig said. "If we have any further questions, we'll be in touch. Come on, I'll walk you to your car."

Savannah stood up and Michael squeezed her around the waist. "Are you okay?"

"I guess so. For a while there I felt as if I'm some sort of suspect."

"Why?" he asked, looking from Savannah to Craig.

"I guess because I've been spending time out here."

"Oh, don't take Investigator Leonard too seriously. He's just trying to do his job. He's after more feathers in his cap, you know. And he's pretty good at what he does. What he doesn't have yet is street sense—instinct. But he'll get there."

Savannah looked back at the building. "Craig, you heard him; he said the place is all locked up, but anytime Auntie and I have been here we've found that small door under the bell tower open."

He rubbed his chin. "Now that is odd. So have you seen anyone else out here?"

Savannah thought about the question before answering. "We think someone's feeding the black cats."

"Huh?"

"There are maybe three black cats still inside and they seem to be well fed. Luke says they're marked with some sort of odd spiritual symbol."

"Oh, voodoo stuff, huh?" Craig complained. "Someone wants us to believe there are ghosts walking the halls? I hate those cases."

"Do you get many of those, Craig?" Michael asked.

"No, thank heavens. They're a pain in the butt. You don't know what's real and what's illusion and who's fantasizing and who's rational." He thought for a moment and said, "But when there's a body involved, you know you're dealing with a living being, not mirrors and smoke. And we do have a body."

Savannah looked at him. "Who is it, Craig? Do you know?"

He shook his head. "A woman about five foot three, plump, in her early sixties, I'd guess. She's wearing a lot of material and jewelry."

"Material?" Savannah asked.

"Yeah, you know—layers of filmy fabric like some women wear." Craig turned to the couple. "Did you happen to see a bird?"

"A bird?" Savannah asked, perking up. "A black bird?"

"Yeah, someone said it's a raven."

"No. I didn't see it today. Did you?"

He shook his head. "But I guess someone did. As I walked up, they told me it watched from the bell tower for a while, then flew down and skimmed their heads while they were working with the corpse."

"I saw that," Michael said. "He darn near knocked that one gal's glasses off her nose."

Craig looked into the sky. "Now that's odd. So Savannah, you've seen the bird before?"

"Yes, a couple of times. We think it attacked Rags inside the place one day."

Craig just stared at her, then said, "Well, I'll let you go. I'd better get to work here. Tell your aunt we may come a-knockin' at her door with some questions."

"Will do. Thanks, Craig."

Chapter 6

"Her name was Charmaine Lorraine," Margaret told Savannah the following morning over the phone.

"What about her?" Savannah asked.

"She's the dead gal you found at the seminary yesterday."

Savannah gasped. "Oh my gosh! That's just too weird."

"Why? Did you know her?" When Savannah didn't respond, Margaret said, "Vannie?"

"Yeah, I did know her. I think she may have been my writing teacher. Her name was Char Lorraine."

"Yowza! Now that *is* weird."

"Not only that," Savannah said, "Charmaine is the name of the witch or psychic or whatever that we were supposed to meet on Friday. What do you suppose happened?"

"Holy cow. That's creepy."

"Yes," Savannah said, her voice an octave higher than normal. She shivered. "I've got goose bumps." She paused. "Oh, wait, the house phone's ringing. I'll call you back."

"You still answer that thing, huh? It's probably a telemarketer."

"Probably. I'll call you. Hello," she said into the landline phone.

After a period of silence the caller spoke. "Is this Savannah Ivey?"

"Yes."

"I guess you heard what happened to your teacher. She's no longer among the living."

Savannah felt her stomach tighten. *So that was her.* She paused, then asked, "Who's this?"

"Oh…um…my name's Rita Johanson. I just wanted to let you know that I'm taking over the class that Charmaine was teaching, only it's been moved to a new location. Here's the address: 1124 Samson Way."

"That's a residential street, isn't it?"

"Um…yes…yes, I want to provide a more intimate setting where students will feel more comfortable."

"Oh, okay," Savannah said. "Do you want me to bring the assignment Ms…um…Ms. Lorraine gave us?"

"Oh…yeah…sure. Bring it. That would be just fine. I'll see you at eight fifteen Wednesday night."

"Eight fifteen?" Savannah questioned.

"Yes, I can't start the class until eight fifteen. So tell your loved ones that you'll be home later than usual Wednesday night."

"Oh, okay," Savannah said, feeling a little unsure about the situation.

Before hanging up, Rita added, "Oh, and bring your cat. I understand that you're writing about your cat."

"Huh?"

"Yes, students are to bring something representing the topic they're writing about. So bring your cat. You can do that, can't you?"

"Yes, I suppose."

"So, who was it?" Margaret asked when Savannah called her back a few minutes later.

"My new weird writing teacher. Auntie, I thought Char Lorraine was strange, but her replacement sounds just as peculiar. Maybe it's the way teachers are these days." She chuckled. "Actually, I wasn't all that thrilled with Char—may she rest in peace. I can only hope this teacher has more to offer me." She let out a sigh. "I guess I'll find out Wednesday night, won't I?"

***

"Got your binder and pencils—and an apple for the teacher?" Michael teased as Savannah prepared for her writing class a few nights later.

"Yeah. I'm all ready, just waiting for my aunt. She's driving tonight."

"Now, why is your aunt going with you?"

Savannah smiled. "She's thinking about writing a book focused on managing cat colonies and she thought the class might help her get organized. She's not sure if she wants to make it a how-to or a have-done."

"Huh?"

"Oh, you know, whether she should teach others how to do it or write about her experiences with cat colonies."

"I can't imagine your aunt a writer."

"I don't know why not." When she saw the approaching headlights through the window she said, "Oh, here she is." She kissed Michael and Lily, then picked up Rags's leash and led him out into the night, calling over her shoulder, "See you later."

"Hi," Margaret said as Savannah opened the door and urged Rags to jump up onto the seat. "What's he doing here? Has Michael refused to take care of him?"

Savannah ignored her aunt's remark. "Michael wonders why you're coming with me tonight. He can't see you as a writer."

"Oh?" she said, obviously offended. "I don't know why not." She grinned. "Maybe he means I'm not weird enough. Yeah, that's probably it."

"Probably," Savannah said, grinning.

"So why do you have your cat?"

Savannah looked at Margaret. "Well, you could have brought cats too. We're supposed to bring something that represents what we're writing about."

"You didn't tell me that. Yeah, I could have brought Layla."

"She's not a colony cat."

"No, but she's a pleasure to have around." Margaret glanced at Rags. "Unlike someone else we know."

Ignoring her aunt, Savannah asked, "Do you know where Samson Street is?"

"Yes, I think so." Once they had turned onto the street, Margaret said, "Holy cow, how many people are in your class, anyway?"

"What do you mean?"

"Well, I don't see any place to park. The whole block and...well, another half block are loaded with cars."

Savannah pointed. "There it is, 1124." She glanced around. "Gosh, there is no place to park, is there?"

Margaret continued to drive around the corner and almost to the end of that block, then she looked at her niece. "Okay if I park here? It looks like quite a walk."

"Yeah, that's okay. I need my exercise."

Before getting out of the car, Margaret reached into the console. "Glad I carry this flashlight in my car…with extra batteries."

"You still do that, huh? I mean, I know you started doing that after the fiasco in the swamps of San Francisco."

"And I've never wavered. I always have a working flashlight with me."

"You are disciplined; I'm proud of you. Come on, Auntie, light the way." The two women walked the block and a half or so struggling a bit with Rags as he wove himself in and out and between their ankles and tried to explore some of the neighborhood yards. Finally, Savannah picked him up and carried him the rest of the way. When they drew closer to the house, she slowed. "That's odd. It looks dark in there." She looked at the house number again. "Yup, 1124."

"Maybe they've already started and someone's reading a spooky story, so they dimmed the lights." Before Savannah could respond, Margaret said, "Oh, wait, I meant to bring a trap. I figured I could share a trap—and maybe educate people while doing my show-and-tell."

"Oh, you have one in your car?"

Margaret nodded. "I'll be right back. Want me to leave the light?"

Savannah shook her head. "No, you'll need it more than I will. Besides," she said, placing Rags on the ground and digging in her purse, "Michael gave me this little flashlight and made me promise to always carry it." She turned it on. "See, it's pretty bright for being so small. Go on, I'll see you in a few."

"Okay," Margaret said, heading back toward her car.

Meanwhile, Savannah walked up to the house, leading Rags. *Hmmm. It is weird that it's so dark in there.* She checked the number again. *Oh wait, there's a note on the door. Maybe class was cancelled.* She read the note. "Door's open. Come in." *Maybe Auntie was right—the class is in session and they've darkened the room to create a mood.* She dropped the flashlight into her pocket, pushed the door open, and stepped one foot inside the room. When she didn't hear anything, she called out into the stillness, "Hello." Then she heard a woman's voice.

"Come in."

Savannah took a step inside, then hesitated. "Where are you?" she called quietly. But before anyone could reply, Rags emitted a low growl. *Uh-oh,* she thought. *Danger.* She started to back out through the door, but promptly ran into something solid behind her.

She felt a hand on her arm and a man said into her ear, "You're not going anywhere."

Once he'd rather forcibly ushered her into the room far enough that he could close the door, Savannah heard the woman speak again. "Get the cat." She also heard the door lock engage.

Oh my gosh. What's going on? I must be at the wrong house. Who is that? What do they want? Savannah held tightly to Rags's leash. She felt as if her heart would pound right out of her chest. "No!" she asserted when someone—*probably the man,* she thought—roughly pulled on the leash. Despite her attempt to hold on, he pried Savannah's fingers from the leash, picked up Rags, and walked away with him.

"What's going on?" Savannah demanded. She looked hard in the direction the man had taken Rags and could just see the outline of two figures standing in the shadows. The one carrying Rags wore a cloak-like garment with a large hood. *He looks like the damned grim reaper,* she thought. *The other one is a woman—the teacher, Rita? What is this, some sort of initiation? A game we're playing in class tonight? Well, I don't think it's funny.* "What do you want?" she asked, her voice quivering.

"What do I want?" the woman repeated from across the room. "I want my sanctuary. You've disturbed my sanctuary—you and that other female, the young man you brought there and, of course," she cackled and scowled at Rags, "this cat."

"What are you talking about?" Savannah asked. "What sanctuary?"

"Oh, people have been coming around now and then, but you," she said with venom, "you won't leave. You keep coming back and bringing others. You must be punished just like Charmaine was." The woman's voice accelerated. "I have work to do there and I can't let you interrupt it." She spoke more sternly. "If you hadn't brought that man and that little child out there Sunday, they'd never have found her. But oh no, the man—your husband, I presume—had to snoop around and then the place was swarming with people, all wanting to destroy what I've built." She slammed something down hard on the desk and shouted, "I won't have it!"

Savannah gasped. She didn't mean to say it, but the words just tumbled out. "Oh my gosh, you killed Charmaine Lorraine!"

"Yes. She was trying to destroy my life's work. I don't know who she thought she was. She pretended to be a friend, then stabbed me in the back when she brought all those black cats in there and began taking over." She snarled, "Well, those cats aren't long for this world, I can tell you that. She won't be needing them any longer, anyway."

"Oh my gosh. You mean the seminary. No, don't harm the cats. We'll take care of them. We'll take them off the property. I promise." She paused, her head spinning, her mind trying to process what was happening. *The woman's crazed. Maybe I can talk my way out of this.* "We'll leave. We'll take all the cats and leave. Don't worry," Savannah said, backing toward the door, "we won't bother you again."

"You're not going anywhere," the woman said, her tone reeking of evil. "Nelson will see to that."

Savannah became aware that the man was now standing behind her blocking the door. She felt the most awful pang in the pit of her stomach. Her heart raced. She looked around the room. *God, they've covered the windows with black paper. And he's guarding the door. How will I ever get out of this?*

"You won't get out of here alive," the woman said. She laughed. "You probably wonder how I knew what you were thinking. I'm psychic. I hear what's in people's minds. And I think you should know that this is your last day on earth—in fact, the moments are clicking away. Is there anything you'd like to say before you die?" The woman laughed again. "Never mind. You won't be given the chance. You're going to drink this potion, then Nelson will take you where no one will find your remains and you won't ever be able to disturb my peace again. Grab her, Nelson!" she demanded.

"No!" Savannah shouted when she saw the man move around in front of her. Before he could put his hands on her, she lurched past him and somehow tripped him and he fell to the floor.

"Get her!" the woman shouted.

He rose to his feet and this time he caught up to Savannah, grabbed one arm, and held her until the woman joined him. They moved with her into another dimly lit room and pushed her down onto a sofa.

"Hold her," the woman said as she walked away.

"Who are you?" Savannah asked, unable to make out her features in the low light.

"Rita, your new teacher," the woman said with feigned innocence.

There's that danged evil laugh again, Savannah thought. She strained to see the woman. "Where's my cat?" she demanded.

"You won't be needing a cat," Rita said from across the room. "…not where you're going." She cackled again, then said dramatically, "Although you may actually see him there. Yes, Nelson, don't you think we should let the cat follow her? Yes, yes," she said excitedly, "that's a good idea. Where is he, anyway? Nelson," she asked, rather impatiently, "what did you do with the cat?"

The hooded man motioned with his head. "Down the hall."

"No!" Savannah shouted, "just let him go. Let both of us go. We won't bother you again. You have my promise." She began to cry.

"Awww, don't cry now," Rita said. "It'll all be over soon. My work, you see, is much more important than you, that cat, and your little family. You're insignificant in the big picture and the big picture is all I'm concerned with at the moment."

Savannah could see the outline of the woman as she walked into the hallway. She heard a door open and Rita said, "Come out, kitty-cat. Come out and share your fate with your busybody owner." But before the woman could return to the living room with Rags on the end of his leash, he ran in the opposite direction, pulling her off balance. She fell against the wall and let go of the leash. "Damn cat!" she shouted. "Oh never mind. I'll deal with you later. First your owner—Ms. Savannah." She picked up something from a table.

It appears to be a small bottle, Savannah noticed. She began struggling to free herself from the man's grip, but to no avail. He had her pinned against the sofa. There was nothing she could do but watch as the woman approached with the bottle in her hand. *Rags,* she thought. *Maybe Rags will sense the danger and do something.*

"If they ever find you," the woman said, "they'll think you decided to commit suicide. You'd been told the class was cancelled. Your dear teacher is dead, after all. And you knew the classroom would be empty—a good place to end your miserable life." She stopped and seemed to be pondering her idea. "Yes, Nelson, we could leave her remains at the classroom. Good idea!"

"No!" Savannah shouted again. "No! You can't do this!" She tried to look into the woman's face, but noticed she wore a mask made of some sort of gauzy material. She couldn't even make out her hair color.

Once she was close enough, the woman grabbed Savannah's ponytail and pulled her head back, then leaned forward with the small bottle, bringing it closer and closer to Savannah's lips.

Suddenly there was an ear-shattering crash and the room lit up like a busy night on Broadway. Everyone froze upon seeing a uniformed officer scramble to his feet after jumping in through the window. Before anyone could react, a second officer leaped through the broken window and rushed the woman, knocking her off her feet. Within seconds, the first officer pulled the man off of Savannah and quickly unlatched the front door, letting in two more officers—one of whom ushered Savannah outside and into Craig's arms.

"Oh my gosh, oh my gosh," Savannah said sobbing against Craig's chest.

"Are you all right, honey?" Craig asked.

"Yes, just scared...oh, Craig, she was going to..."

He held her close and patted her. "It's okay, honey. Just let it out."

In the meantime, Margaret put her hand on Savannah's back and rubbed it. "Here, let me help her to sit down," Margaret said. She led Savannah to a small retaining wall that surrounded the grass in the front yard and sat down with her. "What happened, Vannie?"

"I don't know," she said between sobs. "There's a weirdo man and even weirder woman in there and they decided we need to be punished." Savannah took a few shallow breaths.

"We?" Margaret questioned.

"Yes, you and me." She sniffled. "We disturbed her peace."

"What are you talking about?" Margaret insisted.

Savannah shook her head and groaned. "Oh, I don't know, it's all so unreal—surreal." She suddenly stood up and nearly shouted, "Rags! Rags is in there with those creeps."

Margaret gently pulled her back down onto the wall. "Just stay here, they'll take care of Rags. Craig knows he's in there." Just then, Margaret did a double-take. "What was that?"

"What?" Savannah asked, her eyes still overflowing with tears.

"Someone just ran out of there."

"Where?"

Margaret pointed. "They went between those two houses. Whoever it was wore a sort of filmy dark blue or black cape or dress."

"Oh my gosh," Savannah said. "That sounds like the woman who was trying to kill me. She got away?" she screeched. When she saw three officers step out of the house, she pointed and shouted, "She went that way! My aunt saw her go between those two houses!" The women watched as the officers ran in the direction she indicated.

Just then Craig appeared with Rags in his arms. "Here's your cat." He chuckled. "He sure nailed that guy in there. Evidently while the officer was trying to get the bottle of whatever that was from the woman, the man pulled a knife. Rags jumped him and he lost his balance and fell. He hit his head on something."

"He's dead?" Savannah asked, her voice shrill.

Craig nodded. "And she got away."

"So that was her we saw just now?"

"Yes. Do you know who she is?" he asked.

"I don't have a clue," Savannah said. "Some loony tunes who has it in for me and Auntie." She swallowed hard. "She says we've disturbed her peace."

Margaret tilted her head. "Out at the seminary?"

"Probably." Savannah looked pleadingly at Craig. "Can I go home now? I just want to go home."

"Sure. But we're putting a guard on you." He stared into her eyes and took a serious stance. "Do not get out of his sight. Do you hear me? And do not let him go, no matter what happens. In fact, I think I'll put two people out there at your place. They'll be there when you arrive home."

"Okay, Craig," Savannah said, hugging Rags to her. She stood and walked with her aunt and two sheriffs officers toward her car.

***

"What's wrong, hon?" Michael asked when Savannah walked into the house with Margaret a few minutes later. "You look like you've seen a ghost."

"Worse," she said.

Michael approached Savannah and took Rags from her. "Here, sit down. Tell me what happened." He kneeled in front of her.

"A woman tried to kill her," Margaret explained.

"Who?" he demanded. "Your teacher?"

"Yeah, but I don't think she was really the teacher. I believe she got me there under false pretenses."

"What did she want, for cripe's sake?" he asked.

"She said Auntie and I were disturbing her peace."

Michael stood up, ran his hand through his hair, and paced across the living room, muttering, "Good Lord." He stopped and asked, "Where were you, Maggie?"

"I had to go to the car for something and when I came back, I heard strange voices. I noticed the door was locked and I listened. What I heard didn't seem to be someone reading their story, so I decided I'd better call Craig. He sent the riot police out there and they broke in."

"Just in time, Michael," Savannah said. "That crazy person wanted me to drink a potion."

Michael removed Rags's harness, then sat down next to Savannah and held her tightly. "Oh hon, you must have been terrified."

"Yes." She rubbed her stomach. "For both of us."

"Well, I'm leaving," Margaret said. "Just wanted to make sure I delivered her home safely."

Michael stood and walked to the door with her. "Thank you, Maggie." He opened the door, looked out, and asked, "Who's that out there?"

"Your guards," Margaret said.

"Guards?" he asked, glancing back at Savannah.

She nodded. "Ordered by Detective Craig."

Michael ran his hand through his hair again. "So why the guards? Didn't they arrest that woman?"

Savannah shook her head. "Her accomplice is dead—Rags saw to that. But she's on the loose. She got away."

He looked at Rags. "Rags...um...he killed someone?"

"I guess he attacked the man when he saw a knife in his hand and the guy fell and hit his head."

"Good Lord."

***

The following morning Craig stopped in at the Iveys' for coffee and a sweet treat. Upon seeing Savannah, he asked, "How are you this morning, honey?"

"Still shaken, but okay." She gazed at her baby daughter. "We're all okay."

Craig smiled at Lily, then focused on Savannah. "So what do you think that was all about last night?"

Savannah took a deep breath. "I've been trying to make sense of it. But I guess when you're dealing with crazies, there's no sense to be made. I believe there's a connection between that woman's wrath and the old seminary." She looked expectantly at Craig. "Did you search that place?"

He shook his head. "We haven't caught a break. We can't get in without breaking in."

"I told you that one door's always open."

"No it isn't—not anymore. We're staking it out, and so far we haven't seen anyone come or go—well, except for Luke. He picked up some traps last night and set a couple more. I think we'll ask him to stop the trapping for now."

"But we'll still have to go out there, Craig, to feed. And what about the black cats?"

"Black cats?"

"Yes. They live inside and someone's been taking care of them, I'm sure of it. Oh wait—the woman last night, she said the black cats will be gone. Oh my gosh, they're beautiful cats. I think she plans to destroy them. We need to get them out of there."

"How?" he asked. "The place is locked up. I mean, we can sure pull boards off the windows and break in, and we will if we need to, to get to the murderer or to save those cats, I guess. But that's our last resort."

The two of them sat silently for a moment, then Craig said, "Iris tells me you girls are planning some sort of mystic thing out at that place Friday night."

"Oh, I'd forgotten about that," Savannah said. "I'd better call Rochelle and cancel that nonsense."

"What nonsense?" Craig asked, a crooked smile on his face.

She stared at him. "You want us to go ahead with that—after what has happened? What are you thinking, Craig?"

He leaned back in his chair. "Yes. I think you ought to go ahead with the plan. If it takes you out there, we might be able to work our way in without the perp knowing we're even there." He grinned. "… unless, of course, she's actually psychic."

Savannah remained silent for several moments. Finally she asked, "What did you find out about the guy who died?"

"Oh him? Not much. It's as if he landed on earth yesterday just before your encounter with him. We have absolutely nothing to go on other than you said she called him Nelson. He has no significant birthmarks, carried no ID, and he had no viable fingerprints."

"You couldn't identify him through his fingerprints? Why?"

"He'd evidently burned his hands fairly recently."

"On purpose, do you think?"

Craig nodded. "Could be, I guess, or someone did it to him."

"Wow, I'll bet you don't see that very often."

"No. However, there are other factors that can cause fingerprints to be compromised. I've actually seen a few of them: chemo used for cancer can destroy fingerprints on some patients. And there are people actually born without fingerprints. It's a rare genetic disorder and often affects more than one member of a family."

"Odd," Savannah said.

Craig grinned at her. "You're stalling."

"Huh?"

"I want to know if you'll go ahead with the Friday night thing."

She grinned. "Yeah, I guess I am stalling. Okay, we'll be protected if we go ahead with it?"

"Absolutely," he said. "I wouldn't let anything happen to you or to my wife, for heaven's sake."

"So what do you want us to do?"

"Just go along with the program. We'll be at the site where they pick you up. I understand that you'll be shuttled to the secret place, which you're assuming is the seminary."

"Right."

"We might be able to slip a plant in." He looked at her. "Hey, can you tell me how you made reservations for this gig?"

"Rochelle did it."

"Oh. Can you give me her phone number?"

"Sure," she said, writing it down for him. She looked up and asked, "Will it be a man or a woman?"

"Never mind. Just know this: we will protect you all. No innocent bystanders will be harmed. I can promise you that."

Savannah let out a sigh. "Okay, I'll see what courage I can muster by tomorrow."

Just then Savannah's phone rang. "It's my aunt." She hesitated, then said, "I suppose I'd better take it."

At that, Craig stood up and started to head for the door. He gave Savannah a casual salute. "Thanks for the coffee and pie."

Before he could leave, however, she called out, "Wait, Craig." She spoke into the phone, saying, "Craig's here now. So what happened?"

"I guess Luke was accosted this morning," Margaret said. "He went out to the seminary to check the traps and someone began throwing rocks at him. He said he was able to load one trap into the van. He sprang the door on the other one and left it, then he hot-footed it out of there."

Savannah addressed Craig. "Auntie says someone threw rocks at Luke when he was out at the seminary checking the traps."

"Crap. How long ago? Did he see who it was?"

Savannah asked, "Auntie, he wants to know how long ago and did he see the person at all?"

"I'd say about half-hour or forty-five minutes. He didn't say he saw anyone. And he left before he could feed the cats, so they still need to be fed."

Into the phone, Savannah said, "Maybe Michael and Max will go out there and take care of that this evening." She then told Craig, "He didn't see who it was. My aunt thinks this happened thirty or forty-five minutes ago."

"Where is he now?" Craig asked.

"I suppose back at June Balcomb's cat ranch."

"Okay, I'd better go talk to him. Thanks again." He started to leave, but when Savannah stood up to see him out, he noticed that she was kind of shaky. He put his arms around her and held her for a moment. "Everything's going to be okay, honey. That evil witch woman will never be able to hurt anyone again. We'll make sure of it."

"Thanks," she said, forcing a weak smile. She watched him walk toward the door, then said, "Craig, she killed Charmaine—she so much as told me so. Do you think she killed the man in the pond too?"

"Probably." He gave her an off-handed wave and left.

***

"Are we all set?" Rochelle asked as she descended the staircase in the Ivey home Friday night and joined Peter, Michael, and Savannah in their living room.

"All set," Savannah said. She kissed Michael. "See you guys later."

"Yeah, don't wait up for us," Rochelle said flippantly.

Before Savannah could leave, Michael pulled her back. "Now Craig will be involved, right?"

"Absolutely. He said he'll be with us every step of the way." She grinned. "We may even have a plant from the sheriff's office among the group. We're well covered. No worries."

"Then why are you trembling?" he asked, looking her in the eyes.

"Excitement," she lied. "I'm excited." She made brief eye contact with Rochelle as they left the house.

Several minutes later the two women pulled up in front of Iris's home. Before Savannah could step out of the car, Iris appeared through the front door. She slipped into the backseat. "Whose car?" she asked. "Yours, Rochelle?"

"Yes."

"Nice. I'd like to have one of these low, sleek numbers someday. I guess it could be soon, as the boys are both driving now. I no longer need the big clunker to chauffer them around in." Iris was quiet for a moment, then asked, "Rochelle, you know what's been going on around here, don't you—I mean, out at the seminary?"

She nodded. "Yes. I feel bad that I didn't tell Peter more about it. I'm such an advocate for couples sharing everything. But…"

"Yeah, there are some things best left either undone or unshared," Iris said chuckling. She patted Rochelle's shoulder. "We'll be okay," she said gently. "Craig will make sure of it." She laughed. "You'll have stories to tell your hubbies afterward, I imagine."

184

"I imagine so," Savannah said. "Yeah, I only let Michael in on the bare minimum and he was not happy about me doing this, although he does trust Craig." She sighed. "Iris, let's just hope your husband's little plan works."

"It will," Iris murmured.

"Here we are," Savannah said. "Turn in here." She looked around. "Not many cars."

Rochelle nodded. "Yeah, I didn't expect a big turnout. There usually isn't for things like this. They try to keep it exclusive."

"What now?" Iris asked.

"We wait in our car until we see the shuttle pull in."

Savannah pointed. "Hey, is that the shuttle?" She shivered. "I'm so nervous, I have to pee."

"Oh, you have to pee every five minutes, anyway," Iris said.

"I know. I hope there's a working bathroom out there."

"Didn't you go before you left?" Iris asked.

Savannah nodded. "Yes. Three times."

"Come on," Rochelle urged. "And no giggling."

"Okay, straight faces," Iris said, stepping out and walking with the others toward the shuttle. "There's another gal," she noticed. "And two more getting out of that blue car. Did you bring money, Savannah?"

"Yes," she hissed. "And my name's Beverly, LeeAnn."

Iris grabbed Rochelle's arm and whispered, "What's your name?"

"Rochelle." She then said, "Shhh."

Once the six women were lined up near the shuttle, they were asked to hand over the fee or a piece of fine jewelry and a note with their question for the leader. As the driver and his helper collected, another woman passenger joined them.

"Sit wherever you wish," the driver directed. He gestured toward an older man with a shock of white hair and thick, Coke-bottle glasses. "Nelson will hand out the blindfolds."

This caught Savannah's attention. She stared hard at the man. *Nelson? Could he be? No, Craig said he was dead.* She frowned, thinking, *This is just too weird.*

Once each passenger had a blindfold, the driver, a tan forty-something man with a buzz haircut instructed, "Put these on and keep them on. Nelson will ride back here with you and if you're seen lifting your blindfold at any time during the ride, you'll be dropped off the shuttle. I'll be watching through the rearview mirror, as well."

Before she put on her blindfold, Savannah strained to get another look at the man named Nelson. *Good gosh,* she thought. *I hope I'm not in over my head.* She felt an uncomfortable rush of panic and decided to bolt. But before she could make her body follow her mind's desire, the door to the van slid closed with a thud.

"Put that on and make it tight," Nelson said, indicating the blindfold.

Before she complied, she took a good look at him. *He doesn't look familiar—but I didn't see that other man's face. And this guy doesn't sound like the other Nelson. Just a coincidence*, she thought, as she adjusted the blindfold over her eyes.

"Here we are," the driver said after what seemed close to a ten-minute ride. "Keep the blindfolds on. We'll lead you in."

Once everyone had exited the shuttle, Savannah heard it drive away. Only the driver returned shortly and he helped Nelson lead the group across a dirt area, then through a door and up a long flight of stairs. Savannah was aware that they were being led down a hallway and through another door. At that point, they were told they could remove the blindfolds.

"Take that spiral staircase," the shuttle driver instructed. "Step into the room at the top and take a seat. Your leader will be with you momentarily."

It's much lighter in here, Savannah thought. *I can actually see the top of the staircase. It sure looks rickety.* Before beginning her ascent she noticed several battery-operated lanterns illuminating the area.

Once the three women had stepped off the spiral staircase, Savannah glanced around. *Ahhh, so this is the belfry room.* She noticed several candles burning and two of the black cats were wandering around. Each guest was instructed to sit in one of the mismatched chairs around a large oblong table. A chair with arms was occupied by an ornate crown atop a flowered seat cushion. Savannah, Iris, and Rochelle slipped into seats on the far side of the table, facing the chair they assumed would be the leader's. Savannah looked around at the others and wondered, *Which one is Craig's plant?* She squinted to see the faces in the dimly-lit room. *All women,* she thought. *So the plant is obviously a woman detective. Gads, I sure hope she's here. Let's see, there's a frumpy-looking woman with way too much hair. Can't even see her face. Could be her, I guess. If so, it's a darn good disguise. There's a nervous-seeming executive-type woman.* Savannah laughed inwardly at herself, thinking, *She's kind of out of place in Hammond. Looks like she belongs on Wall Street. Maybe she's the detective. Her friend looks meek and frightened.* She studied the woman sitting closest to the leader's chair. *Now that's the type of person I can imagine coming to one of these things—older, well-dressed, maybe well-to-do. She looks like someone who has lost a family member and is chasing all over the place trying to make contact with them.* She smiled inwardly at her overactive imagination, then glanced around the table at the others again. *This is crazy. I can't even believe I'm here.* She looked at Iris. *She looks excited. That's Iris. She loves this sort of thing.*

Just then, the women heard a commotion and they all turned toward the spiral staircase. *Gosh,* Savannah thought, *is it a raid? Are the sheriffs here already? I wouldn't mind getting out of here, but I'd kind of like to see what happens at one of these things. I'm curious.* She noticed that the others were also curious, because they turned in their chairs and searched the shadows for a glimpse of what was going on. Then Savannah heard a familiar voice.

"Let go of me! Let me go! I don't want to go up there. No!"

Oh my gosh, Savannah thought. *That sounds like my aunt!* She waited and watched until the two men—the shuttle driver and Nelson—entered the room holding Margaret between them.

The driver pulled out a chair next to Savannah while Nelson instructed, "Sit down and be quiet."

In shock, Savannah asked quietly, "How did you get here? What are you doing?"

"They dragged me out of the grocery store parking lot, the thugs."

"Quiet!!" Nelson hissed.

Just then the candles flickered and Nelson announced, "Aviana is here."

Everyone gazed into the shadows and glimpsed a woman who appeared to glide into the room. They watched as she practically floated around the room behind the chairs, tossing something in the vicinity of each individual.

"Fairy dust," she announced fancifully. She giggled, then removed the large crown from the armed chair, put it on, and sat down. She closed her eyes for a moment and chanted. She then looked at the guests, studying each of them before beginning to chant again. She looked straight ahead and said in a deeper voice, "I must speak to Traci."

The nervous woman with the Wall-Street look let out a whine.

"Traci, it's okay. I'm okay. You must move on. I chose to be here. I was done. You had nothing to do with it. Don't flatter yourself with guilt over my demise. Know that it was my choice."

At that, the leader slumped in her chair. Traci put her face in her hands and began to weep.

After a few minutes, Aviana sat up and spoke quietly in a slightly different voice, "Angela, I'm still with you. Don't doubt it. Don't ever doubt it. Just know that I can't direct every circumstance around you. You have free will and you have things to learn. But know that I am with you and I love you. You are safe as long as you follow the right road. You know what that is."

The younger woman gasped. She quickly asked, "Mom, is that you? Mom, should I take the job or marry Beryl? Please, Mom. What should I do?"

As everyone waited and watched, Aviana said, "She is gone, Angela. As she has told you, you need to learn how to follow the right road."

"What a rip-off," Angela said under her breath.

"And it's that attitude that has gotten you into trouble before, isn't it, Angela?" Aviana said sternly.

"How do you know?" she argued.

"Take charge, Angela, like your mother has asked you to do. You're in charge. Just know that while the joys and pleasures of your choices are yours, so are the consequences. Make good choices."

The young woman sat back in her chair and appeared to be pouting.

Just then everyone became aware of something overhead.

"Look!" shouted the well-dressed woman. "A bird. It came through that window. It's an omen. Oh God, what does it mean?"

"Damn bird," Aviana said. She shouted, "Get him out of here!" She then announced, "That's it. I'm through for tonight." She glared at Savannah, then Margaret and said, "Take them all out of here, will you Nelson and Leroy…except that one." She pointed at Savannah, then at Margaret. "And that one."

Rochelle and Iris looked at each other, then glanced at the leader and the men, not knowing what to do.

"All the rest of you go…go," Aviana said dramatically.

Savannah made eye contact with Iris, then Rochelle. Remembering what Oma had told her about not being frightened, she nodded at her friends, indicating that they should do what Aviana had asked. She watched as they followed the driver toward the spiral staircase. She then looked around the room at the others wondering, *which one is going to save us?* Her eyes rested on the older woman. *Do something,* she willed. But the woman simply stood and obediently followed the others as Nelson escorted them out. Savannah looked at the Wall-Street woman, who also filed out with the others. *It's certainly not the spoiled young girl.* When she looked at her aunt and saw fear reflected in her eyes, she grabbed her hand. Margaret squeezed it.

"Hurry back," the leader said as the men headed for the door. "I will need your help."

"Sure thing, Rita," Leroy said. He slapped his hand over his mouth and quickly said, "Aviana."

Savannah gasped. *Oh my gosh,* she thought. *Rita! That's the woman who tried to poison me. Where's Craig? God, what are we going to do? I've got to think of something!* Savannah kept her eye on the woman named Rita while trying to calm herself so she could think more clearly.

Rita walked toward the bell tower windows. She looked out into the darkness, then turned and faced Savannah. "It is such a shame that you will fall. This is an old building and I can tell you the framework up here isn't the strongest." She glared at Savannah. "It wouldn't take much for it to give way and for you to fall to your death." Her eyes wide, she said, "And of course, your friend there will try to save you. But, oh dear," she became more dramatic, "the old floor might give way and down you'll go too. Two at once." She cackled. "I love it! Two at once and no more disruptions." Just then a black cat jumped up onto the table. "And the cats," the woman said excitedly, "they can go with you on your free fall. One, two, and all of those ghastly cats."

"You know that won't do you any good," Savannah said. When Rita looked at her, she continued, "Others will come. You're not safe here from the world."

Rita stared daggers at Savannah and sneered. "But you'll be gone. That's all I'm concerned about right now." She addressed both women. "You won't demonize me from the other side will you?"

Momentarily caught off guard, Savannah froze. Then she looked sideways at the crazed woman. "Oh yes, I will. You won't have a moment of peace. If you let us go, we'll promise to leave you alone, but if you continue with your little plan, yes! I will haunt you forever. Forever!" she shouted.

The woman thought for a moment, then said, "Naw, that's not true. I know how to protect myself from your kind. Now get up, both of you." When the women didn't move, Rita rushed to them and took their arms, pulling them up from their chairs and pushing them toward the windows. She stopped and said whimsically, "Look, it's raining. Perfect." She then snarled, "You'll just lie there and rot away all night in the rain. Goodie! Goodie! This is better than I expected." She released the women and ran around the room, unfurling shades to cover all the open windows, except for one. She sneered. "This one's for you."

Meanwhile Savannah and Margaret crept back to the other side of the table and each moved to stand behind a chair. This time, when Rita came for them, Savannah lifted her chair and swung it at her, hitting her across the back. Rita fell to the floor. Margaret threw her chair on top of Rita and leaned on it to hold her down. Then they heard voices coming from the spiral stairwell. "What in the hell's going on?"

Craig, Savannah thought. However, when she turned toward the staircase, she saw Nelson and Leroy. She reached for another chair, but Leroy grabbed her before she could get a grip on it and he held her.

Nelson, in the meantime, pushed Margaret off Rita, removed the chair, and attempted to help her up.

"My clavicle is broken. My clavicle! I'm sure of it!" Rita screeched. She pointed to the open window and shouted, "Toss them out! Toss them out!"

"Out the window?" Nelson asked. "Hey, I'm no killer. No way. I just came along to help with the joke you were pulling on someone." He squinted at her. "It was a joke, wasn't it?"

"A joke?" Margaret said.

Nelson looked at her, then at Rita. He took off his glasses and removed a white wig. "Yeah, my name's not even Nelson."

"Useless piece of trash," Rita snarled. She turned to the driver. "Leroy, you toss them out."

He started to back away. "Not me. You got the wrong guy, Rita."

When Savannah saw the men step back, she shouted. "She has killed before. None of us is safe. We have to stop her."

"Not me!" the man known as Nelson said, heading for the stairs. Just then, they heard another voice. "Outta the way!"

"Craig," Savannah called, "she's trying to kill us!" When the detective entered the room and Savannah saw what he was wearing, she began to chuckle nervously. He'd removed the wig, but he still wore the frumpy, old-woman dress. He glanced at Savannah and Margaret, then approached the psychic and helped her to her feet.

She looked him up and down before snarling, "You cheated me. You're a fake. How dare you!"

He laughed. "You're calling *me* a fake?"

He started to cuff her when she shouted, "Ouch! They broke my clavicle. You can't cuff me; that's torture."

Craig stared at Rita for a moment, then pulled her arms in front of her and said, "How about this?" as he fastened the handcuffs around her wrists.

Before he could lead Rita out of the room, Margaret said, "Wait, I'd really like to know why we were targeted."

By then, two officers had ushered the driver and his sidekick back into the room. "Yeah, I'd like to know what's going on here too" the driver said.

Craig tightened his grip on Rita's arm. "Tell them," he insisted.

"Gladly," she snarled. She scowled at Margaret and then at Savannah. "You were in my

194

way. I had this good thing going here—well, once I got rid of that witch, Charmaine. I was going to take over and then you started coming around and disrupting everything. Didn't you get the hint that I don't want you here? This is my domain." She spoke more loudly, "I'm the queen."

"So you killed Charmaine?" Savannah asked.

She glared at Savannah. "This whole thing was my idea. That little witchy woman snuck in and took over. She stole my idea. When I got wind of it and confronted her, she refused to get out of my way." She suddenly looked serene. "I had to get her out of my way."

"And the man in the pond?" Margaret asked.

Flippantly, Rita said, "Oh, I hired him to do a job—wasn't sure I could trust him. He had to go." She glared again at the two women. "And you were next, you meddlers. You and that awful cat of yours." She let out a shrill laugh, then she looked at Craig and said sweetly, "Please, the cuffs are cutting off my circulation, can you loosen them?"

As Craig examined the cuffs, Rita took look that opportunity to dive through one of the windows of the bell tower to her death.

Savannah gasped.

Margaret grabbed Savannah's arm and pushed her head against her shoulder.

"Damn," Craig said under his breath. He instructed the officers to escort the men down the stairs, then he asked Margaret and Savannah, "Are you okay?"

They nodded.

"Let me help you ladies down those stairs. I have a couple of calls to make, then I'll drive you home."

Savannah nodded. "I suppose we'll have to tell our husbands what happened here tonight."

"That's up to you. But yeah, I'm sure you can't keep this from them."

"Michael will never let me out of the house again," Savannah lamented.

"Oh, come on," Margaret said, "he's not that protective."

Savannah looked at Margaret. "How did you get here, anyway?"

"Good question." She nodded toward the doorway. "Those two animals tracked me down and found me at the grocery store. I guess she really wanted to do away with both of us."

Chapter 7

The following morning while Michael, Savannah, Peter, and Rochelle enjoyed breakfast around the Iveys' kitchen table, Michael's phone chimed. He looked at the screen. "It's Aggie."

When he walked into the other room to take the call, Savannah explained to the others, "She's Michael's newly discovered grandmother."

"Oh, yes. So they're staying in touch," Rochelle stated. "That's nice."

Savannah nodded. "They sure are. They talk at least every week. I enjoy her calls too. She's an interesting woman—fun to be with."

"How old is she?"

"Ninety-two—a spry, active ninety-two. Savannah took a sip of her orange juice and chuckled. "You know, she probably would have gone with us last night on our…um…adventure. She's one game woman."

Rochelle smiled. "I hope I get to meet her sometime. Sounds like my kind of gal."

Savannah looked across the table at Rochelle, then said, "I've been thinking…" she laughed, "… probably over-thinking, actually. What causes some people who have psychic powers or who are—you know, able to read others like you do…what causes someone like that to turn bad?"

"Oh, you're talking about Aviana…I mean Rita, right? Savannah, she may have had some weak power, but she was mostly snake oil as far as I could tell. If she had any sensitivities, she was misusing them. She somehow became misguided. I hate to see that happen, but it does."

"How does that happen?" Peter asked.

"Well, sometimes when you realize you have something others apparently don't have, especially when you discover this as a child, it can become overwhelming. Some people learn to hide it. If they do so at a young enough age, it often disappears. For some, it's so strong they can't hide it and it upsets them when it raises its ugly head. When they share it, they're ridiculed. Some people begin to rely on people who have or claim to have powers." She looked at Savannah. "That can be stifling. It can be a real burden." She paused before adding, "It seems to pollute some people. They use it to control others and situations." She winced. "And sometimes it begins to control them. Some unexpectedly find themselves on a pathway to evil and they get caught up in the power of it all."

"Like Rita," Savannah said. "Rochelle, you seem to be comfortable with your gift."

Peter smiled at his wife. "She's a gracious lady."

Rochelle returned his smile, than addressed Savannah's comment. "It's a struggle at times, especially when you become aware of something that's about to happen or you see someone you love headed for disaster and there's absolutely nothing you can do about it. People have free will, you know. And some simply don't want to know or to believe. Sometimes what you see doesn't turn out as you thought it would because the individual makes a new choice. It's a real crap shoot. It's not an exact science, you see."

"Interesting."

Rochelle chuckled. "People don't usually go around talking about their gift. As I said, some even try to hide it because they find it can get them into trouble."

Savannah laughed. "It sure didn't do much for Charmaine or Rita, did it?"

"Oh, I don't know about Charmaine, but Rita was about as phony as they come."

Savannah looked at her wide-eyed. "Well, she scared the wits out of me."

"Yes, she was dangerous—one of the misguided souls I was speaking of."

Before Savannah could respond, Michael returned and handed Savannah his phone. "She wants to talk to you."

"Hi, Aggie, how are you?" Savannah said cheerfully as she excused herself from the table and walked into the other room.

"The question is how are you?" Aggie said. "I understand you had quite a fright last night."

"Oh, did Michael tell you about that?"

"Yes. He mentioned it. I hope to get the details from you the next time we meet. It sounded dreadful. I'm so sorry you got caught up in that witch's web. Why, if I'd been there, I would have…" Aggie chuckled. "But I wasn't there and it sounds as if it all came to a rightful end. Just so you and your baby boy are okay."

"Yes. We're just fine. Thank you for caring. So, Aggie, when are you coming for a visit?"

"Well, that's the second piece of business I wanted to discuss with you folks this morning. I'd like to land somewhere near you in time to witness my great-grandson's birth. Will you have room for me?"

"We sure do. Come anytime. His birthday will be around the twentieth of May—about nine weeks."

"I'm planning to make my travel arrangements today—so how about if I purchase a one-way ticket to arrive May thirteenth. From there, I'll fly to Colorado and visit my other handsome grandson and his family."

"Sounds good, Aggie. We'll look forward to it."

"Now don't go fussing over me. I'll blend in or sit out—whatever you want. I refuse to be a bother, hear?"

Savannah smiled. "You won't be a bother, Aggie."

"Will your delightful mother be there to help with the baby?"

"I'm pretty sure she will."

"And we won't be in the way?"

"No, we have plenty of room in this big house. It's like a rooming house." Savannah chuckled. "We have an intercom system to keep track of each other because it's so large."

Aggie was silent, then said, "Oh, well that sounds lovely. I'll be in touch and we'll make plans."

"Perfect."

When Savannah had ended the call and joined the others at the table, Rochelle stood and said, "If you don't mind, I'll start cleaning up the kitchen while you finish your breakfast." She glanced at her watch. "We really need to get a move on. I don't know how long it will take me to set up."

Michael motioned for Rochelle to put her plate back on the table. "I'll take care of the kitchen. Go get yourself ready."

"I'll be right behind you," Savannah said. "I'm almost finished."

***

"Ever been to this place before?" Rochelle asked as she drove along the highway watching for a sign to the event location.

"No. I've driven past it a few times."

"According to the information I received, it's an interesting place—a former stagecoach stop and a lodge of some sort during the gold-rush days," Rochelle said. "They opened it as a dance hall in the twenties."

"Oh, there's the entrance," Savannah said, pointing. "Must be a big deal. Look at all the cars."

"Uh-huh. That's why I wanted to be a part of it. It's a juried show and I was pleased to pass muster with my jewelry."

"Is it all jewelry?"

"No. A lot of jewelry, but also other forms of artwork."

"Why didn't Peter show his art?" Savannah asked.

"We decided it's best to keep our shows separate. We'll do a few together, but it's kind of nice to focus on one or the other. Usually, we attend these things together. We work as a team with his art and we plan to do so with my jewelry." She smiled at Savannah. "But I'm glad you're helping me with my first big show. I really appreciate it."

"I'm looking forward to it."

"Me too. And I think it's good for the guys to spend time together doing something recreational. Do you know what they have planned?"

Savannah giggled. "Well, they have Lily, you know. So she'll probably call the shots. I wouldn't be surprised if they end up at the playground pushing her in a swing."

"Oh, that would be something new for Peter," Rochelle said, parking the car. She became serious for a moment, "But he may need the experience."

Savannah started to get out when she turned back to Rochelle. "Wait. You said he may need the experience? Rochelle!" she exclaimed. "Are you?"

She shook her head. "Not yet. But we're hoping soon."

Savannah took her hand. "Oh, that's great. I'm happy for you."

"Don't be happy yet—it hasn't happened. We're in phase one of our attempt to have a child. We aren't young chicks and things might not work anymore."

Savannah stared at her friend and finally said, "I can so easily see you two with a child."

Rochelle let out a sigh. "You can?"

"Yes. Be patient. It will happen." She chuckled. "Hey, you're the psychic. You should know."

Rochelle shook her head. "It's way easier for me to read others than myself. Things seem to get in the way of my own readings—my emotions and desires, probably. Sometimes I foresee a potential disaster and avoid it, but other than that, I'm not very good at seeing into my own future."

***

"Gosh, this is quite an ornate old place, isn't it?" Savannah noticed as they entered the spacious building, each of the women with a rolling suitcase full of Rochelle's jewelry.

"Yes," Rochelle said, glancing around. "What a great restoration job." She looked out over the hustle-bustle in the large room. "We're in space one-oh-one. Do you see numbers posted anywhere?"

"Yes." Savannah pointed. "There's eighty-nine…ninety… I'd say you're in that next row of booths. There it is—one-oh-one. Right on the end."

"Great. I asked for an end spot so I could display my things on two sides."

"Good thinking," Savannah said, as they headed toward the booth.

Once they'd spread velvet cloths over the tables, they started to arrange the jewelry. Savannah couldn't help but stop every once in a while to admire a piece. One in particular caught her eye. "I love this," she said, rubbing her fingers over a striking necklace.

Rochelle glanced at the piece, then scrutinized Savannah's attire. "Put it on. I think what you're wearing will show it off nicely."

Savannah fastened the necklace around her neck, then looked in a mirror Rochelle had set up. "I love it." She put her hand over it and asked, "What if someone wants to buy it?"

Rochelle smiled. "If you want it, just hide it away. Consider it a gift for all your help today. Then pick out something else to wear. I want people to buy what we're wearing."

"Really?" Savannah asked, wide-eyed. "Oh gosh, look at the price. I can't take this. But I will buy it from you."

"You'll do nothing of the kind. It's yours. Your help today is worth way more than that." She waved her hand in Savannah's direction. "Wrap it in tissue and put it away in your purse. Choose something else to wear."

Savannah took the piece off, looked at it again, then hugged it to her. "Thank you, Rochelle. It is simply exquisite."

"You're welcome." Rochelle picked up another necklace and held it toward Savannah. "Here, wear this one."

Savannah took it from her. "Oh, this is beautiful."

Rochelle grinned. "Simmer down, girl… although, if you want to buy all of my stuff, we can pack up and go home."

Savannah laughed. "Yeah, I do like your style."

"Then you'll be the perfect representative for my wares." Rochelle admired the necklace Savannah had just put on. "Looks great on you with that soft aqua top you're wearing." She smiled. "Yeah, that will sell pretty quickly."

Just then a woman stepped up and began looking at the jewelry that Savannah and Rochelle had already laid out. "Lovely," she said. "Just lovely."

Rochelle smiled. "Thank you. I'm the artist." She offered her hand. "Rochelle Whitcomb."

"Hi, I'm Penelope Brownstone."

"A writer's name," Rochelle said, looking the woman in the eyes.

"Huh?"

"Your name…it's nice. I envision it across the front of a book. Are you an author?"

Penelope looked surprised. "Actually, I am… or…er…I will be. Um…" she stalled, "I'm writing my first book—a cozy mystery. I'm considering using a pen name—Penny Brown." She cocked her head and looked at Rochelle. "But you like my real name?"

"I sure do. Yes, use your real name. You'll do better with it."

When Savannah noticed the woman contemplating Rochelle's suggestion, she winked. "She knows what she's talking about. I'd listen to her."

Penelope looked from one woman to the other and said, "Okay, I'll consider it. Thank you."

As Penelope ogled Rochelle's display of jewelry, Savannah encouraged, "Tell me about your book. You say it's your first?"

"Yes, I've done a lot of technical writing and got tired of it. Well, I got tired of the subject, not the process, and I decided to try writing something light and fun." Her face lit up. "I hope to produce a novel series featuring horses. I live with a lot of animals, so some of the stories will showcase my cats, maybe my chickens and rabbits, but mostly horses."

"Way cool," Savannah said. "I'm trying to write a book myself, featuring my cat. But it will be true stories." She raised her eyebrows when she explained, "It's his memoirs."

"Oh my gosh, that's wild," Penelope said. "Has his life been that exciting…I mean to warrant having his memoirs written?"

Rochelle looked up from where she was arranging a display of earrings. She nodded. "Her cat has quite a repertoire of adventures under his belt. Right, Savannah?"

"Oh yes."

Rochelle continued, "He has his own series of children's books and he was featured in a documentary."

Penelope stepped back, her eyes wide. "Rags? Are you talking about Rags?"

Equally surprised, Savannah nodded.

Penelope stared at Savannah. "You know what? I've met you before. You're…um…I'll think of it…it's a place name…Charlotte, Havana…Savannah, right?"

Savannah nodded.

"Oh, this is crazy wild, meeting you here." She looked around inside Rochelle's booth. "Did you bring him?"

Savannah shook her head. "Oh no. Rochelle and I are hoping for a trouble-free day and, with Rags, you never know."

"Yes, I remember," Penelope said. "He was catnapped in LA, wasn't he? And he walked home to a place where he'd never been in the middle of the night. I saw him on TV."

By then Rochelle had stopped what she was doing and stared at Savannah with interest. "I didn't hear about that escapade."

"Catscapade," Penelope said, laughing. She leaned toward Savannah. "You really ought to call his book "Rags's Catscapades.""

Savannah laughed. "Good one."

Just then, Penelope glanced across the room. "Wait here, I have something to show you."

Savannah picked up a tray of bracelets. "Okay. We'll be here." She glanced at Rochelle. "Your booth is going to be so beautiful with all of your amazing jewelry." As she arranged the bracelets, she said, "I thought you were designing pieces for a company. Are you representing them here today?"

Rochelle squinted. "Just minimally. I went to work for them with the caveat that I could design and market my own stuff separate from what I do for them. I brought just a few of the company's pieces to display."

Savannah scrutinized some of the jewelry, saying, "I think I can tell the difference." She pointed. "This is the retro design you showed me before, right? This is what you're doing for the company."

Rochelle nodded as she placed a tray of rings on one of the tables.

"Your jewelry is more casual, yet elegant."

"Yeah, that's a pretty good description. I lean toward casual-modern with a Southwest flare."

"Hmmm, is that how you want me to describe it to potential customers?"

Rochelle smiled. "It's best to let them put their own twist on it, unless they ask. It seems that many people who are attracted to my work buy it because the color accents an article of clothing or it reminds them of a place they've visited—the beach, for example, or the Southwest, even New York. Sometimes they simply can't resist how good it looks or feels when they try it on."

Savannah smiled. "So I should encourage them to try it on."

Rochelle nodded, then she looked at something behind Savannah. "Oh, here comes your fellow author." She did a double take. "She has a cat."

"Hi again," Savannah said as Penelope approached. "Who's this?" she asked, reaching out and petting the Himalayan she held in her arms.

Penelope smiled. "Buffy."

"Oh!" Savannah said. "We have a part-Himalayan named Buffy."

"I guess it's not a very original name." Penelope looked at the cat. "This one came with the name and we decided not to change it."

Savannah smiled brightly. "Ours did too." She then explained, "My husband used to board her for a neighbor who traveled a lot and when Mrs. Armstrong died, he inherited sweet Buffy. We sure do love her. She's the exact opposite of Rags—she never gets into trouble."

"Same with our Buffy. She's my first purebred. We rescued her from a hoarding situation. We didn't actually know how beautiful she was until her fur grew back in and we got some weight on her."

"She's gorgeous," Savannah agreed. "And she travels well?"

"Yes. She doesn't complain about anything, actually. She's a pure delight."

"Nice," Savannah said, scratching the cat behind one ear.

"Well, we'd better get back to our booth," Penelope said. "Come visit when you get a chance. We're number seventy-five."

"I will. What do you have for sale over there?"

"Cat-hair jewelry."

Savannah raised her eyebrows. "Made of cat hair?"

Penelope nodded. She held out her arm to reveal a felted bracelet of cat hair with tiny beads sewn into it. "This is made from Buffy's fur."

"Gosh, it's stunning," Savannah said. "Rochelle, take a look at this. It's made from Buffy's fur."

"The cat?" she questioned, studying the bracelet. "That's amazing."

"Yeah, we have other things, too—toys, little kitty ears on a headband… Oh, that reminds me that I want to put one of those on. I'd better go get more organized." She smiled brightly. "It's been a pleasure, ladies."

***

Rochelle's booth had been extremely busy all morning and they'd sold several pieces when things slowed a bit and Rochelle suggested, "Savannah, why don't you take a break and look around. Get some lunch if you want. When you come back, I'll go."

"Okay, I could use a little exercise." Savannah's first stop was at the restroom. Then she decided to visit Penelope's booth. On her way to booth seventy-five, she wandered among several other booths, checking out various types of art and marveling at some of the skill and creativity put into the items. She was admiring a size-three baby dress with a crocheted bodice and hand-painted kittens playing around the hem when she heard a commotion to her right. She looked up to see a group of people gathered around Penelope's booth.

"Help!" someone called out. "Help, please!"

Savannah walked slowly in that direction and saw Penelope cradling Buffy in her arms and crying out in alarm. Savannah pushed through the crowd and approached Penelope. "What happened?" she asked.

"Oh my God," she cried, "I think she's choking on a square bead. I dropped it. She eats things." She looked down at the barely conscious cat. "I think it's choking her."

"Give her to me," Savannah said, reaching for the cat. When Penelope resisted, Savannah said, "I'm a veterinarian." Savannah gently took the cat, entered

Penelope's booth, and sat down in a chair with the cat lying across her lap. She tilted Buffy's head back, opened her mouth, and reached in for the object. "I can see it," she said. She lifted the cat, placing her in a sitting position against her chest. She then laid her hands against the cat's abdomen and performed a series of abdominal thrusts. The third one was the charm as the cat sputtered and out popped the square bead. Savannah examined the cat, making sure she was breathing normally, then hugged her, spoke softly to her, and handed her back to Penelope.

"Oh my God, Savannah. You saved my Buffy." She hugged the cat tightly and kissed her face and head, but Buffy began to squirm and push away.

"She could probably use a sip of water," Savannah said. "I'd want water after an ordeal like that. Do you have a bowl here for her?"

At that, several bystanders held out their water bottles and offered them for Buffy.

"Here's her water bowl," Penelope said, lifting it and placing it on a table in the back of the booth. She lowered the cat onto the table and smiled when she began lapping the water.

"Good girl," Savannah said, running her hand gently over Buffy's fur.

Penelope grabbed Savannah around the neck. "Thank you so much." She stepped back and looked at her, "But how did you know what to do?"

Savannah smiled. "I really am a veterinarian. I'm practicing being a mommy, more recently, but I've had experience with choking cats before." She placed her hand on Penelope's arm and said, her voice cracking a little, "I'm so glad Buffy cooperated and spit that thing out."

When Savannah returned to Rochelle's booth about thirty minutes later, Rochelle asked, "So did you see some interesting products?"

"Sure did. I may go back and buy a little dress I saw for Lily. It was handmade and had kittens on it. I had a turkey sandwich for lunch. You go if you want. I'll hold down the fort."

"Thanks, I'm ready. Oh," she said, pointing to a necklace and matching earrings, "a guy is coming back to get this. He still owes $25 on it. He went to the ATM. Name's Peterson." She started to leave, then asked, "Hey, what was all that commotion a while ago? Do you know?"

Savannah grinned. "Well, Buffy got herself into trouble. She tried to swallow a bead and it got stuck. I had to do a Heimlich maneuver."

Rochelle started to walk away, but turned back quickly and stared at Savannah. "You did what?"

"Yeah, well, it's similar to the Heimlich maneuver." When Rochelle still looked confused, Savannah explained, "It was part of my veterinary training. The cat's okay."

"I'd forgotten you're a veterinarian. Wow. Glad you were in the right place at the right time."

"Me too. She's a lovely cat. But it can be a real worry when you have one who likes to eat foreign objects. Usually they can get it down and usually it comes out. But sometimes it gets stuck in their throat or the cat needs surgery to remove it from the intestines."

Just then a few people walked up to Rochelle's booth and addressed Savannah. "You were amazing!" an elderly woman said. "I watched you save that cat's life. You were as cool as a cucumber and you knew just what to do. Did I hear you say you're a veterinarian?"

Feeling only slightly embarrassed, Savannah glanced at Rochelle, then responded. "Yes, I'm not practicing right now, but…"

A man in the group laughed. "You don't need to practice. Looks like you know exactly what you're doing."

"Oh, well, thank you. It's pretty basic. And good to know, because cats as well as dogs can get themselves into choking trouble sometimes."

A small boy said, "My dog choked on a ball once. But he coughed it up all by himself." The child looked down. "Dad said, 'don't give him small balls anymore.' Now Snickers and I play with a sponge football."

Savannah tousled his hair. "Good idea."

Another woman spoke up. "That gal said you have a famous cat." She squinted at Savannah. "Is his name Rags?"

Savannah nodded.

"I told you so, Robert. That's Savannah Ivey. I saw her in the movie with her cat, Rags."

"Well, it was a documentary," Savannah corrected. When she saw Rochelle standing back grinning, Savannah said, "Hey, have you seen my friend's jewelry? She actually has a line inspired by Rags." She pointed to a velvet-lined tray that showed off an array of silver jewelry. "See the graceful curves around the flower petals on this pendant? That's reminiscent of a cat stretching. And here's one of an actual cat on his back holding up a tiny pearl with his feet. Ever see your cats do that?"

"Yes," the sixty-something woman said. "And my Jibby, he likes to sit on his haunches with one leg out, you know, and just stare at you. We laugh every time we see that."

Savannah picked up a pendant and held it out for the woman to see. "Yes, Rochelle saw our Buffy do that once and created this one because of it. Buffy is a part-Himalayan, similar to the Buffy who just had the choking problem."

"Really?" the elderly woman said. She took the necklace from Savannah.. "I must have this one." She held it to herself as she announced, "And it has pansies on it. Pansies are my favorite flower. Now how much is it, dear?"

"One forty-nine," Rochelle said. "All of my pieces are pure silver and, except for a few, they're one of a kind. That one is an original."

"I'll take it," the woman said, pulling out her credit card. She looked down at the jewelry and said, "I'd like this ring that follows the lines of the stretching cat. May I try it on?"

"Certainly," Rochelle removed it from the tray and handed it to the woman.

"It fits. Robert, look at that." She faced her husband. "You asked what I want for my birthday." She held out her hand. "This ring."

"Okay, sold," he said, grinning as he reached into his pocket. "I'd planned to get her a new sports car, but hey, if all she wants is this ring…"

"Yeah, right," his wife said sarcastically. "It would be more like a plastic toy car."

***

An hour had passed when Savannah said, "Rochelle, you'd better take a break."

"Yeah, that was quite a flurry of activity, wasn't it? And all because of you." She giggled. "I want you to help me with all my shows."

"I'd do it. This is fun. There are really some nice people here."

"Yes, and you seem to have the ability to attract a crowd. I'm impressed. I sensed that using cat-like designs in my pieces was a good idea, but I didn't know that you…" she chuckled, "and your cat would actually sell it. Way to go, Savannah." She turned. "Okay, I'm going on break. Are you okay here on your own?"

"Sure. Oh," she said, laughing. "I called Michael a while ago. They were at the petting zoo."

"Oh, that's funny. Peter at a petting zoo? Hard to imagine."

"He said they were all having a good time. Peter was eating cotton candy."

"Cotton candy?" Rochelle smiled. "How neat. We all should visit our inner child from time to time. Good for Peter."

"Go," Savannah said. "Take a break. We'll chat more when you get back." As Rochelle walked off, Savannah called, "Take your time."

Chapter 8

Later that evening the Iveys and the Whitcombs were seated around a table at a local restaurant rehashing their day and catching up with each other. They'd dropped Lily off at Margaret's and Max's.

"Tell us about your wedding," Savannah said once the waiter had taken their order.

Rochelle and Peter looked at each other and he said, "It was nothing special—just a ceremony, is all."

Now he had Rochelle's full attention. "Nothing special?" she carped.

"Um…well…"

"How would you describe it, Rochelle?" Savannah asked, chuckling.

"It was absolutely lovely. We were married on a private dock at dusk against a magnificent sunset and we had a few of our close friends and associates standing with us."

"I don't even remember what the preacher said," Peter complained.

Michael grinned. "Does that mean you won't be following the rules?"

"Rules?" Peter repeated, feigning ignorance. "Um, there are rules?"

"Sure, the rules of marriage," Michael explained. "You know, do unto others…"

"Michael," Savannah scolded.

"Oops, I mean, for better or worse."

"Oh, I know about worse," Peter said. He leaned toward Michael as if sharing a secret. "We've lived together for a year or so, you know. I've seen her wearing that green stuff on her face, I've lived through one of her severe colds—all that coughing—ick. And then there was the time…"

Rochelle groaned. "Just never you mind, Peter."

"Green stuff?" Michael asked.

"My facial mask," Rochelle explained.

Michael looked at Savannah. "Do you have a green mask?" He asked Rochelle, "Why do you wear a mask?"

By then the two women were laughing hysterically.

"Yeah," Savannah said. "I have a mask, but I use mine when you're at work."

"Why?" Michael asked.

"It's a beautification thing," Rochelle said, still laughing.

He looked at both of the women and winked. "Seems to be working."

"Good answer," Peter said, slapping Michael on the back.

"Your wedding sounds beautiful," Savannah said. "But didn't you get married on New Year's Day? Wasn't it cold out on that dock?"

"Absolutely," Rochelle said. "As soon as the sunset and the ceremony were over, we jumped onto our friend's luxury boat and celebrated all night inside the cozy and spacious cabin."

"Yeah, here are a few pictures our friends took," Peter said, passing his phone around.

Savannah swooned. "Oh, very nice. And did you get a honeymoon?"

The couple nodded and Peter said, "Now that was something to talk about."

Rochelle put her hand on Peter's arm. "Don't you dare."

"What? Didn't you have a good time?"

"Wonderful," Rochelle said, "but you don't go into detail about your honeymoon."

"I was going to tell them about the kite-flying contest we won."

"Oh yeah, that you can talk about."

"You won a kite-flying contest?" Savannah asked.

"Sure did, with an eagle kite. And we learned how to surf." He looked at Rochelle. "Well, one of us did."

"Let me guess," Michael said. "Rochelle rode a wave and you did a belly flop."

Peter laughed. "Something like that."

"So did you go to an exotic island?" Savannah asked.

"Southern California," Rochelle said. "Remember, that's where we fell in love two years ago. And we happened to hit it when the weather was unseasonably warm. It really was a great honeymoon."

"Well, here's to the happy newlyweds," Michael said, raising his bottle of beer. Savannah raised her glass of water and the Whitcombs clinked their glasses of wine.

"Thank you," Rochelle said. "Wish you could have joined us for our wedding."

Savannah winced. "We sure wanted to, but we were dealing with some scary stuff with Rags about then, as you know, and I just couldn't leave him."

"I understand." Rochelle turned to Peter. "Babe, you have no idea how famous that cat of theirs is. We ran into more people today who know about him."

"You did?" Michael asked.

"Yes," Savannah said. "He has made an impression, that's for sure."

Suddenly Michael grabbed Savannah's right hand and looked at it. "Hey, I thought you were going to wear that ring I got you for Valentine's Day. Did you forget it?"

Savannah thinned her lips. "I can't find it."

"What? Did Rags get his paws on it?" he asked.

"No, I don't think so. I was wearing it yesterday and I took it off to rub some sunscreen on Lily. I set it on that same table where I'd put my bracelet last week. About then, after she was all greased up, Lily asked to go potty." She looked with wide eyes at Rochelle. "That's huge. Of course, I had to take her right away. When we came back, the ring was gone. Michael, someone's coming onto our property and taking things. I mean, they took Lily's play set of keys and some of your tools…"

"You have tools missing?" Peter asked. "That's no good. I mean, you like your tools as much as I like my art supplies." He looked at both Savannah and Michael. "Who do you think is taking them? Have you seen anyone around?"

Savannah shook her head. Everyone was quiet for a few minutes and Savannah asked Rochelle. "What are you thinking? You seem to be thinking about something. Do you have a vision of who it is?"

"Or what it is," Rochelle said. "A bird, perhaps. I see feathers."

"An Indian headdress?" Peter quipped. He addressed Michael and Savannah, "Do you know anyone who wears an Indian headdress?"

Savannah shook her head, then said, "I saw a neighbor the other day walking through our property toward the highway. He had a feather in his straw hat. I remember, because I thought it looked rather sharp."

"Bingo," Peter said. "Isn't my wife clever and smart and well-attuned? That must be your culprit, your neighbor."

"I sure don't like to think so," Savannah said. "He seems like a nice gentleman."

"Where does he live?" Michael asked.

"I think he's renting a room from the people who bought Kyra's family's home next door. You know, it was a young couple who bought it and I think they're renting out rooms."

"There you go," Peter said. "Keep an eye on that guy. He probably has your ring." He turned to Michael. "…and your tools."

***

Two mornings later after seeing the Whitcombs off, Savannah kissed Michael goodbye and wished him a good day at work, then she stepped back into the house, put Lily down for a nap, and went into the office where she'd been making notes for Rags's memoir. "Oh, hello there, Rags," she crooned when she saw him saunter into the room. "Did you come to help?"

Rags rubbed against her legs and she reached down and ruffled his fur.

"I could use some inspiration, boy, if you have any to spare." She watched as he stepped into one of the cat beds, rolled over, and went to sleep on his back.

***

Later that evening over dinner, Savannah shared her progress on her writing project. "Michael, today I talked to a few of my friends and co-volunteers who knew Rags when we were still in Los Angeles, and they brought up things I'd totally forgotten about. I still have email addresses for some of my former neighbors there and I contacted them as well. I've heard back from one of them. One woman—Nancy—thinks it's hilarious that I'm writing a book about him and she wants a copy hot off the press."

"Cool. That's one sold," Michael said.

"Oh, and I talked to the pet store clerk at the place where I adopted him. He was surprised that we're still together—Rags and I. He said the original owner had some stories to tell. I asked him if he could put me in touch with her. Turns out it's a guy and he emailed me this afternoon. He's a kick. I've decided to quote some of the people who have stories about Rags—with their permission, of course. I also talked to Rob, and he's thrilled with my progress so far."

"Well good. I suppose you'll want to interview me."

"You? Why?"

"For my perspective. Remember, not only do I live with him, I'm his veterinarian."

"Oh, that reminds me," Savannah said, "I had him groomed once and the grooming staff had quite a time with him that day."

"Why did you have him groomed?"

"Long story short, he must have rolled in something dead. It was when I used to let him roam the neighborhood, so I don't know exactly what happened, but he came home stinking all to heck. I knew a groomer who worked with us at the shelter where I volunteered and she agreed to clean him up. What a fiasco. That's a whole chapter—his experience at the groomer."

Michael smiled at his wife, then asked, "So how many pages do you expect the book to be? Has the publisher requested a certain number?"

"From what Rob said, he just wants me to go with the flow and write a cogent story with a lot of anecdotes and see what we end up with. Rob suggests around a hundred-and-fifty manuscript pages."

"So have you started the actual writing?"

"No. I met a writer at Rochelle's show over the weekend and I've been in touch with her. She's writing a cozy mystery featuring horses. I told her I'd give her some ideas for stories from Peaches's life. She used to write nonfiction and she suggests I organize my material and sort of outline my chapter topics before actually writing anything. That makes sense to me, so that's what I'm doing now—organizing it as I collect it."

He looked at her over his glass of iced tea and said, "I'm proud of you, hon."

"Thank you. But maybe you'd better wait until you see if I can actually do this."

"Oh, I have no doubt that you can."

"Thanks for the vote of confidence!"

Michael smiled at her, then said, "Hey, did you find your ring?"

"No, did you find your tools?"

He shook his head. "And your aunt hasn't seen any of our stuff over at her place either, huh?" Before Savannah could respond, he asked, "Have they been missing anything over there?"

"Not that I know of."

Just then Savannah's phone rang. "It's my aunt," she announced after picking it up and looking at the screen. "Hi, Auntie, what's up?"

"Hi. Sorry if I'm interrupting your supper, but we have an emergency."

Savannah sat up straight. "What happened?"

"Max cut his hand and I need to get him to the hospital for stitches, but I can't find my keys."

"Your car keys?"

"Yes. Did they fall out of my purse in your car when we took Lily to the park this afternoon?"

"I don't know. I'll go check." As Savannah walked outside with the phone, she asked, "How did he get cut?"

"Filleting a fish. Darn it, the knife slipped and boy, does he keep sharp knives. I won't even use his knives. Too sharp for me."

"Awww. Poor Max. I'm so sorry," Savannah said. After looking around in her car for several seconds, she said, "Auntie, I don't see your keys in my car. When's the last time you drove your car? Anyway, don't you have an extra key?"

"Yes, as a matter of fact. Would you believe I lost my original set of keys and I've been using the spare? Now that's gone, too."

"How did you do that?" Savannah asked. "I mean, lose your keys?"

"I'm not sure. But what is, is, and I need that key. Otherwise, I'll have to drive Max's truck and I hate that thing."

"I can drive you guys to the hospital," Savannah suggested. "We can look for your keys later."

Margaret thought about the offer. "No. I don't want you to do that. I need to find my keys," she whined.

"Okay, when's the last time you had your keys—I mean your original set of keys?"

"Yesterday. I dropped them when I was coming into the house with a load of groceries and when I went back to get them I couldn't find them. That's when I got out the spare key and put it in my purse."

"So what happened to the spare key?"

Margaret huffed. "Vannie, if I knew that, I wouldn't be calling you."

Savannah was silent, then asked, "Auntie, did you see the old guy with the straw hat around here yesterday?"

"Huh? Oh him? Yes, I did. Why?"

"Rochelle thinks maybe he's the one who's taking our things."

"Why would he take my car keys?"

"To rob you when you're gone, maybe, or to steal that snazzy red car of yours? I don't know. Want to borrow my car?"

"I want my keys." Before Margaret could continue, she said, "Oh wait, Max found them. Where were they, Max?"

Savannah waited, then asked, "Where were they, Auntie?"

"Well, it's just too strange to say."

"What? What do you mean?"

"He said they were out behind the house in a box of bulbs I was planning to plant next week."

"Oh, so you must have dropped them out there, huh?"

"Absolutely not. I have not been out in the backyard for days." She paused. "Vannie, maybe that old guy did take them and had duplicates made, then brought them back."

"I can't imagine him doing that, can you? However, Rochelle does seem to think he's the one taking our things."

"Why? How does she know that?"

Savannah backpedaled. "Well, I guess she didn't actually say that. But she saw feathers and he does have a feather in his hat—and around the band. Have you seen that? Pheasant feathers, I think."

"Well, I need to get Max to the emergency room. I'm sure he'll need stitches. Let's talk later about this. I'd sure like to catch that scoundrel in the act. Maybe we can set a trap."

Savannah rolled her eyes. "Oh dear. Just when I thought I could relax." She then added, "Tell Max we're thinking about him, poor guy."

"Yeah, poor me. I'll have to do his chores if his hand is out of commission for a while—you know, bathe kittens, wash dishes…anyway, see you later."

"Your aunt found her keys?" Michael asked after Savannah had ended the call.

"Yes, at least one set of keys, and pretty far from where she remembers leaving them. Strange."

"Sure is."

Chapter 9

It was nearly two months later, a week from Savannah's due date—May thirteenth, to be exact. The Ivey family had just arrived home with Michael's grandmother, Aggie.

"What a lovely home," the ninety-two-year-old woman said as they pulled into the driveway. "You're right, it is large. What a wonderful place to raise a family. I enjoyed bringing up my boys on our estate there in Connecticut. They could play croquet, romp with our Jack Russell Terriers, play badminton, swim… it was an ideal home for active boys."

"I imagine so," Michael said.

"Oh yes, your father loved sports. He was active—played tennis, soccer, squash…"

Michael looked at Aggie as he helped her out of the car. "Which one was my father? You never really answered that question."

She cringed. "I guess you won't get the answer to that question unless you do a test." She raised her voice. "I believe firmly that it was Scott. But there's a chance I could be wrong, I guess." She raised her eyes to the sky. "Only God in heaven knows for sure."

As Savannah and Aggie walked arm-in-arm across the gravel driveway, Michael released Lily from her seat. "Come help Daddy get the luggage, punkin," he said, opening the back of the SUV. He handed her a small tote. "Here, Lily, can you carry GranGran's bag?"

"Handle it with care," Aggie called out. "There's something very important inside."

As the four of them made their way toward the front door of the house, Michael suddenly let out a yell. "Watch it!" He ducked and began looking around overhead. "That dang bird nearly scalped me."

"A bird?" Savannah repeated. "What kind of a bird?" she asked, glancing overhead "A raven pulled my hair a few months ago—you know, out at the seminary."

"He was probably using your pretty blond hair to build a nest," Aggie suggested.

Savannah chuckled. "Oh, I didn't think of that. I've heard of them using horse hair, but human hair? That's kind of carrying things a little far."

"I guess animals have prerogatives, too," Aggie stated matter-of-factly.

Michael continued looking around for the bird, when Lily chirped. "Bird, Daddy. Bird."

When he saw where she was pointing, he said, "Oh, there he is on the corral fence in the shadows, watching us."

"Oh, I see him," Savannah said.

Michael rubbed the top of his head. "That's eerie, isn't it? I feel like I'm in an Alfred Hitchcock movie or something." He addressed the bird. "What do you want Mr. Crow?" He paused. "Or is it Mrs. Crow? Hey, there's horsehair on the ground out there. Take what you need."

"It's a raven," Savannah said quietly.

"Raven?" Aggie repeated. "Aren't crows and ravens the same thing?"

"Evidently not. The raven is larger and has a greater range of sounds," Savannah explained.

"Since when did you become a crow and raven expert?" Michael joked.

Just then they heard a shrill call as the raven swooped over their heads and flew off toward the highway.

"That was a raven!" Savannah exclaimed.

Michael looked at her. "That's what you just said."

"I mean, that sound he made, that's the sound we heard a couple of times while we were inside the seminary, just before we'd see the raven."

Aggie focused on Savannah. "What were you doing in a seminary, might I ask?"

"Long story," Savannah said. "Let's get you and your belongings safely inside, then we'll catch up with one another."

"Sounds good. I'm eager to sit where the seat isn't moving at a high rate of speed in the air or on the highway."

Savannah and Michael laughed.

A little while later Savannah poured everyone a glass of lemonade and they made themselves comfortable on the porch in time to watch the sun go down. Savannah had put a pan of lasagna in the oven and a salad was mixed and ready to serve. The trio and the toddler had been visiting on the wraparound porch for several minutes when Aggie said, "Oh, Lily, GranGran brought you something." She motioned, "Can you go get that little bag you carried in? I think we dropped it in the kitchen."

Michael helped Lily open the door and watched as she ran into the kitchen. "There it is on the table, punkin," he said. "Bring it to GranGran."

Lily ran back to the porch with the bag and handed it to Aggie.

Aggie smiled. "Good girl." She put her hand on Lily's and said, "You open it. It's for you."

At that, Lily sat down and dug into the small bag, promptly pulling out a colorful spinning top. When she looked confused, Aggie explained, "It's a top, Lily. It spins. Haven't you ever seen a top before?" She motioned with one hand. "Show her how it works, will you, Michael?"

Once Michael had it spinning to Lily's delight, Aggie said, "That was one of my boys' favorite toys—a spinning top. They spent hours playing with them." She chuckled. "Of course, we didn't have such sophisticated toys in those days—all those electronic automated toys that do everything but clean the child's room." She shook her head. "Basics. We should go back to the basics with our children. Just look at how much she's enjoying that toy."

Just then, everyone heard a trill of musical notes and Aggie pulled her cell phone out of her pocket. She looked sheepishly at the others before answering it, saying, "Dang modern gadgets—they're a bother and a bane when you're busy enjoying life." Into the phone, she said, "Hazel dear, how wonderful to hear from you!"

After a brief but lively conversation, Aggie ended the call and reported, "That was the elderly mother of my friend, Corinna."

"Elderly?" Savannah questioned.

"Yeah, Hazel just turned eighty-five and lives in a nursing home. Corinna and I go to the same church and she picks me up sometimes for Bible study." Aggie's eyes lit up. "We celebrated Hazel's birthday last month at a Greek restaurant." She raised her hands up in the air and laughed. "What fun that was—women doing belly dancing and men dancing around with the table in their teeth. I've never seen such carryings on."

"You have a lot of fun, don't you, Aggie?" Michael said.

"Oh yes. That's what life's all about." Aggie looked at Michael, then Savannah. "You must make time for fun and laughter. If life's too serious, you become dull. So keep it lively, kids. Keep it lively."

"Good advice," Savannah said. "Have you always had this attitude?"

"Heavens no, child. I wasn't exactly miserable in my younger years, but you might say rather intense. I don't think I began to loosen up and see things from a more…um…lighthearted perspective until my forties or fifties." She laughed. "And I just keep finding new ways to have fun."

"I hope we can amuse you while you're here," Savannah said.

Aggie rested her hand on Savannah's arm. "No problem. Just being in the company of your little family makes me feel good. You are exactly the kind of people I want to be with. There's no stress in your relationship. You don't sit around worrying about everything." She smiled at Lily. "And your little one radiates happiness and love." She shook her head. "Oh, no, don't you worry about me while I'm here. This is just the sort of atmosphere I crave."

Michael grinned. "Well good. Glad to hear it. We're happy to have you here."

"Yeah," Savannah said, "talk about someone who's fun to be around…"

Aggie smiled at her, then asked, "Will your charming mother be here for the big event?"

"For when the baby comes?" Savannah said. "Yes, she's driving up Monday or Tuesday. She was here just last month for the baby shower. I wish you could have been there, Aggie. It was so much fun. Colbi and Iris threw us a couples shower." She giggled. "You should have seen Michael trying to mold a baby out of bubble gum." When Aggie looked confused, she explained, "Yeah, we played baby shower games, can you believe it?"

Michael grinned at Savannah. "Tell her who won the tape-measuring contest."

"Yeah, everyone thought that was rigged since you're more familiar with the size of my baby bump."

"I was right on the mark," Michael boasted.

"You guessed how big around she is?" Aggie asked. "Yeah, I'd say you should have been disqualified from that game."

"Disqualified from what game?" Margaret asked, as she and Max appeared.

"Well hi, guys," Michael greeted.

"Come on up. Want lemonade?" Savannah asked.

"Sure," Max said, stepping up onto the wraparound porch. He approached Aggie. "Hello, Mrs. Harmon. Nice to see you again."

"And you folks too," she said, "Maggie and Max, am I right? We met at the library on that cold, wintery day months ago."

Max smiled. "And we partied at the condo afterward."

"Oh, that's right," Aggie said. "What a perfect evening that was—with all of my little grandchildren and new friends."

Margaret approached Aggie and hugged her. "You look well. Did you have a good flight?"

"Wonderful. I met the nicest gentleman and his wife. I always seem to meet wonderful people during my travels. His wife has a quilt shop in San Francisco and he's a merchant for health food, I think it is. They were in Connecticut celebrating their fiftieth anniversary with family. Turns out I knew his aunt, rest her soul. We were in a club together a long time ago. Small world. The longer I live, the smaller it becomes."

"Because you know more people?" Margaret suggested.

"Could be." Aggie leaned toward the Sheridans, who both sat across from her at a small table. "Now how are you two? Is the world treating you well?"

They looked at each other, then Margaret said, "Yes. I have no complaints." She reached out for Lily as she walked past. "Unless it's that this one didn't come give Auntie a hug. Where's my hug?"

"Bird," Lily said with big eyes. "Bird bite Daddy."

Margaret looked at Michael. "Did one of your patients nip your finger?" she joked.

"No, it was a wild bird," Savannah said. "It swooped down and pulled his hair." She laughed. "You should have seen Michael's quick athletic move."

"Oh, I would like to see that," Max said, chuckling.

"Go ahead—show them, hon," Savannah urged.

Aggie laughed.

"What kind of bird?" Max asked.

"My wife tells me it's a raven," Michael explained.

"Oh my gosh," Margaret said, looking at Savannah. "Remember when that raven pulled your hair out?"

"Yes. I was telling Michael and Aggie about that."

"Do you think it's the same raven?"

Savannah laughed. "How would I know that, Auntie? He didn't introduce himself."

"Are you sure it's a raven and not a crow?" Max asked.

"According to our research, it's a raven—larger body, bigger bill—you know." She looked at her aunt. "I think that one at the seminary was Charmaine's pet."

"Well, Charmaine's dead, so maybe he's adopted us—followed us home or something. I've seen him around our place lately too." Margaret said.

"You have?" Max asked. "I haven't."

"You don't get out as much as I do. I run most of the errands and do the yard work."

Max thought for a moment, then said, "I spoke with the preacher yesterday and he said…"

"What preacher? Do you mean Sheila?" Margaret asked.

"No. Ned Kline, our neighbor."

"The older man with the feather in his hat?" Savannah asked. "He's a preacher?"

Max shook his head. "He used to be. Well, he said someone's been looking for a lost pet raven. He saw a poster over there in that tract and he asked me if I'd seen one. I told him no. I wonder if the raven you've been seeing is the missing one."

"Someone was keeping him as a pet?" Aggie asked.

"I guess so," Max said. He made a face. "That would be one messy pet to have. I wouldn't want to clean his cage."

"Well, this could sure be the one they're looking for," Savannah said. "I've never noticed it around here before. He just showed up in the last few months."

Just then they heard a faint meow. Margaret looked toward the house. "Rags wants out. He's on his window perch, crying."

Savannah frowned. "He hasn't enjoyed his outings much lately."

"He hasn't?" Michael asked.

"No. In fact a couple of times I saw him at the window acting like he wanted to go out. But when I picked up his harness, he ran the other way."

"That's strange for him," Michael said.

"Yes, and once Lily and I were out here with him and all of a sudden he slunk to the door and wanted in. Something in the yard has him freaked out and I don't know what it is."

Max gazed at the cat in the window. "Do you think he's afraid he'll encounter someone with a knife again? He was hurt pretty severely when that guy stabbed him, and animals do remember."

"Could be, I guess," Savannah said. "But he seemed fairly relaxed when we were traveling."

"Yes, he did." Michael agreed. "So whatever has him upset is new."

234

"It's the bird," Aggie said quietly. "He's watching us now, you know."

"The raven?" Margaret asked, glancing around the property. "Where is he?"

"I don't know. He doesn't want to be seen. But he's out there and he's aware of us." Aggie smiled. "He's a playful devil." When Savannah looked quizzically at her, Aggie said, "I don't know that for sure, but that's what I'm sensing. Sometimes I sense things, you know."

Chapter 10

A few days later Savannah and Aggie were walking with Lily and a slightly reluctant Rags through the orchard, checking the fruit on the trees, when Aggie swooned. "Oh, this reminds me of my childhood on the family farm. We had so many different types of fruit and I was expected to help with preserving it, canning it, drying it. We did it all." Aggie glanced up. "Oh, who's that?"

Savannah looked. "I don't know." The women watched as a man in his thirties or early forties approached them. "Hello," she said.

"Good morning. Beautiful day, isn't it? And your fruit trees look healthy and happy. You'll be busy putting up fruit before too long, won't you?" He leaned toward Lily. "Will you help Mommy and Grandma with that chore?"

Lily stepped behind Savannah and held onto her leg.

Savannah put her hand out. "I'm Savannah Ivey. This is Aggie Harmon, visiting from Connecticut." She shook her head, saying, "…actually Rhode Island."

Aggie waved her hand in the air. "Yeah, same difference. You can drive through several of those tiny states in a matter of hours like you do your counties here in California."

He laughed and offered his hand. "I'm Clay Dawson. I used to live in that tract over there. We moved a couple of months ago, but one of our family members didn't make the move with us and I've been on the lookout for him ever since."

"What?" Savannah said. "A family member is lost?"

"Yes." He chuckled. "Well, he's not of the human kind. It's a bird—you know, a raven to be exact. I keep coming back here, hoping he'll see me and land on my shoulder like he used to do. But I haven't even caught a glimpse of him. Oh, he's still around. Our house is vacant and I've been going back there and leaving treats for Jonathan…"

"Jonathan?"

"Yes, that's his name. And he answers to it too. Well, I see evidence that he's still around here, but doggone if I can get him to perch. He must like his new-found freedom." He gazed at Rags as the cat sniffed around a patch of weeds. "Maybe I should have kept him on a leash when I gave him outdoor time." He looked at Savannah, then Aggie. "So have you seen him?"

"Probably," Savannah said. "We have seen a big black bird that we think is a raven. He tried to pull my husband's hair out."

"Oh no. I'm so sorry. Yes, I'm afraid that's Jonathan, all right." He began looking around the yard, in the trees, on the ground, in the shadows. He chuckled. "He also likes trinkets."

"Trinkets?" Savannah asked. She tilted her head and squinted. "Do you mean like jewelry, keys, and small tools?"

Clay Dawson nodded. "Anything shiny that he can carry, yes." He glanced around the area again. "So you *have* met my best friend, have you?" He winced. "What has he taken from you?"

Savannah grinned. "Jewelry, car keys, and small tools."

Clay let out a sigh of frustration. "How am I ever going to get him back?"

"Have you tried trapping him like we do cats?" Savannah asked. "...I mean, in a humane trap?"

"No. He's too smart for that."

"He won't just come to you?" Aggie asked.

Clay shook his head.

Suddenly Savannah noticed Rags pulling on his leash. He hunkered down and behaved as if he wanted to make a run for the house. "Rags, what are you doing?" she asked. Suddenly, it occurred to her. "Hey, I'll bet your bird is watching us right now. Do you have any of his treats?"

The man nodded. He looked around the yard again.

Savannah crouched next to the cat and asked, "Where is he, Rags?"

"The cat is going to find my bird?" he asked, tilting his head suspiciously.

"Don't worry, he won't hurt him."

"I'm sure of that. Jonathan's pretty ornery where cats are concerned. We have a cat and that poor thing stays hidden whenever Jonathan is out of his cage."

"You let your bird fly around inside your house?"

"Yes, he's house-trained. He belonged to a guy who trained animals for the movies."

"So where is he?" Savannah asked the cat. When she saw Rags look sideways toward the corral and tug toward the house, she said, "I'll bet he's in that tree behind the corral or on the corral fence in the shadows."

Savannah tried to lead Rags in that direction, but he planted his paws and refused to walk. Suddenly, Aggie called, "Watch out!"

Savannah looked up in time to see a black streak flying toward Rags. She quickly picked up the cat and turned her back to the bird, who skimmed the top of her ponytail as he flew into one of the apricot trees.

"Jonathan," the man said. He then instructed, "If you ladies will stand back I think I can lure him."

"Do you want a cat carrier or something?" Savannah asked as she and Aggie scrambled to get themselves and Lily out of the way.

He shook his head and spoke quietly and calmly. "Once I can get him to come to me, he should become obedient. I have his cage over at the old house. I'm pretty sure he'll let me walk him over there." He looked up at the bird, then moved closer, talking to him quietly. Finally, Jonathan hopped from the tree onto Clay's shoulder and began accepting treats from his hand. "We're going to walk home now," he said, still calmly and quietly. "Listen, you said you're missing things. I found some jewelry and other items lying around the place over there, if you'd like to come over and take a look. Maybe some of it's yours." He put his hand up. "Give me a few minutes to get him settled in his cage, then come over, okay? It's 212 Baker."

"Yes. Thank you."

***

"So you found your ring?" Michael asked Savannah later that day as they sat at the kitchen table.

She nodded.

"Bird take ring, Daddy," Lily explained. "Bad bird," she said, shaking her finger. "Bird take GranGran pen."

"Isn't she just the cutest thing?" Aggie said. She confirmed what Lily had said. "Yes, it seems the raven is the culprit who took my sparkle pen when I set it down to walk into the orchard with Savannah. But I got it back." She leaned forward and grinned at Michael. "Your cat helped that man capture his bird."

Michael shook his head. "This is just too much, having a klepto bird and a klepto cat in the same community, let alone the same neighborhood."

Aggie began to giggle. "You know, I'm an on-the-go gal and I do like to keep busy. But I don't know if I can survive being here with you people and your clever cat. My goodness, there's never a dull moment, is there? In Connecticut it was the cat finding someone's passport. Here, the cat finds the bird that's been taking everyone's belongings." She turned to Savannah. "You started to tell me about the feral cats. Have you located and rescued all of them?"

Before Savannah could respond, Gladys walked into the kitchen. "Hi, Mom. Did you have a nice nap?"

"Sure did. I don't know why I was so tired when I got here this afternoon. Maybe it was the traffic. It was the worst I've seen. Well, those two accidents didn't help." She hugged her daughter. "But I feel much better now." She reached out and squeezed Aggie's hand, then asked, "Can I help with anything?"

"We're just waiting for the potatoes to cook. Come sit with us. Want a glass of tea, water, lemonade?"

"Water sounds good." Gladys motioned for Savannah to stay seated. "I'll get it." She turned to the others. "Can I get you something?"

Savannah shook her head, then said, "To answer your question, Aggie, yes, we think we got all of the feral cats. At least we hope so."

"Now, you say they were living in an old seminary?" Aggie asked.

"Yes, mostly under the building, but some of them were inside." Savannah shuddered. "It's a spooky old place. I had hoped we'd visited it for the last time several weeks ago, but my aunt, who's more experienced with colony rescues, says it's important to check back every once in a while just to make sure. I think she suspects there are more cats. If so, they may have recently found their way there. We've been leaving food and someone's eating it."

"I'd like to see the place next time you go out there," Aggie said.

"Sure, I think Auntie wants to do a check tomorrow, actually. I'll ask if we can ride along with her."

"Why don't you take your cat?" Michael suggested. "He's not getting much exercise, since he's still so cautious about that bird having been in his yard. And he might be able to help you find any cats that have wandered in."

After thinking about it, Savannah said, "Good idea. Okay, we'll make it a family affair out at the seminary tomorrow." She turned to Gladys. "Mom, want to go with us?"

"I think I'll pass. How about if I entertain Lily while you gals go do your exploring?"

The three women and Rags arrived at the feral-cat-colony site around ten the following morning. While Savannah and Aggie scanned the building and the grounds, Margaret prepared two small carriers. "Just in case we need them," she said.

"So this is a former seminary," Aggie said. "Hasn't been loved in a very long time, has it?"

"It appears that way," Margaret agreed.

"Auntie, you rescued all of the black cats, didn't you?"

Margaret nodded. "At least I hope so. It was a total of three adults and all those cute babies. But I always like to do a follow-up for as long as we have access, just in case we've left one behind or new cats have found their way here. Some feral cats can be awfully slippery and even invisible."

"Invisible?" Aggie questioned.

Savannah looped her arm in Aggie's. "If a cat doesn't want to be caught or even seen, she can be mighty cunning, right Auntie?"

"Right," Margaret agreed. "Sometimes you find the stragglers—those that are most expert at staying hidden—simply from what they leave or take from the environment." When Aggie looked confused, she explained, "Is someone eating the food we leave? Is there evidence of cats using the little beds we've placed here and there? Are the toys disturbed?"

"So you operate as if cats still live here, do you?" Aggie asked.

Margaret nodded. "For a little while." She smiled. "But sometimes it's raccoons or squirrels messing with things. We sometimes have to do some mighty slick detective work in order to determine what sort of critter we're dealing with."

"Can't you set one of those have-a-heart traps?"

"Sure. We generally do that too. But, as Vannie said, some cats are just more clever than others." Margaret walked toward the feeding station and examined the area around it. "Not much activity here. Looks more like birds have been nibbling on the food, than cats." She chuckled. "And maybe taking a bath in the water bowl." She looked at the building. "Let's go inside, shall we?"

"Yes," Aggie said. "I've always been fascinated by historic buildings, especially before they're restored." When she noticed the others looking at her, she added, "You get a more genuine feel for the history of the place when it's still in the raw—when the past hasn't been washed and painted away."

Savannah tilted her head. "Oh, I never thought about that before." She glanced at her aunt. "I think the two of us have had more than enough reality where this place is concerned, right Auntie?"

"You got that right. I've never been so glad to finish a rescue operation." Margaret gazed at the building. "I hope this is the last time I have to come out here." She let out a deep sigh. "Well, let's go in and see what we find, shall we?" Before walking in that direction, however, Margaret trotted back toward the car and pulled a small blanket out of the backseat.

The women entered through the small door under the belfry and walked into the original reception area when Aggie gasped. "Oh my. Conflict. I sense awful conflict within these walls." When she noticed the others staring at her, she said, "I can't help it. It's something I was born with, I guess. Walls of old places tend to talk to me." She grinned. "Or else I have a big imagination." She continued. "I had to leave the Alamo when I visited there in Texas as a child because of the tension I felt. I didn't know what it was, but my parents couldn't get me to stop crying until after we'd left the place. Later in life I realized that I get these strong feelings when I enter an old building or even a site where the building no longer stands." She looked at Savannah, then Margaret. "Sometimes it's light and happy feelings." She frowned. "Other times…" she shuddered.

"What do you sense?" Savannah asked. "Certainly not a war zone."

"Oh no, it's not so much violence," she cocked her head, "although, there's some of that. It's a conflict of values and beliefs. Now that's rather odd for a place like this, don't you think so?"

Suddenly, Margaret looked at the storage area under the staircase. "The occult stuff," she said, pointing.

"Occult?" Savannah repeated.

"Yes. Remember, we found all that stuff in the storage area under the stairs. I took some of the photographs home." She winced when she looked at Savannah. "I guess I never showed those to you."

"No, you didn't. What did you find?"

"Well, do you remember all that voodoo and other weird ritual stuff Iris was talking about?"

"Yes," Savannah said. "But I didn't take it too seriously."

"Well, it was serious, Vannie. Those photos showed things that I'd consider completely against

244

what a religious seminary would or should stand for. Know what I mean?" She hesitated and asked, "Do you remember Iris telling us about the robes those people out in the forest wore and the shiny belts?"

Savannah nodded. "Yeah."

"Well, some of the pictures I found show people wearing that garb—shiny silver belts and all. Max and I wonder if she was right—that there were people secretly practicing some sort of witchcraft right here under the noses of the seminary leaders."

"Well, that could explain what I sense in this room—" Aggie said, "—a conflict of convictions or principles." She raised her eyebrows. "When people are at odds over something as personal and strong as religious or spiritual beliefs, things can get ugly. Isn't that what many of this world's wars are about?"

Savannah wrapped her arms around herself and shivered. "Well, let's finish our search and get back to a house with nice walls, shall we?"

Aggie smiled at her. When she noticed that Rags had walked to the end of his leash toward the staircase, she addressed the cat. "You want to go upstairs? What's up there, huh, boy?"

"Yes, let's go up there," Margaret said. "I want to check the food I left." She turned to Aggie. "We found a whole family of black cats living in here. We think we rescued them all, but just to be sure, I left food in here and we propped the door open." As they approached the indoor feeding station at the top of the staircase, Margaret exclaimed, "Oh!"

"Looks like someone's been eating here," Savannah said, shining her flashlight into the hallway.

"Yes," Margaret agreed. "Darn, we did leave someone behind." Under her breath, she said, "Now, where are you? Gosh, I hope he'll let us take him. I sure don't want to come out here again."

Just then Savannah put up her hand. "Shhh. Did you hear that?" she whispered.

"No. What?" Margaret asked.

"Listen." Savannah pointed toward the end of the hall. "That way."

"Oh, I hear it." Margaret walked swiftly in the direction Savannah indicated, muttering, "Oh my gosh, it's a cat in trouble." She stepped into the last room on the right. "Where is it? I hear it, but I don't see it."

Meanwhile, Rags pulled toward the back of the room and Savannah did her best to keep up with him. When he stopped and began meowing and pawing at the wall, she said, "Isn't that where we found the secret room? I think there's a cat in there. Kitty-kitty," she trilled.

The women listened and heard nothing.

"Well, do you remember how we opened that hidden door, Vannie?"

"Yeah, I sort of fell into it." She ran one hand over the wall. "Come help me, Auntie. We're bound to find the release. If not, I'll get Michael out here with a sledgehammer."

"Wait," Margaret said. "I heard a click. Now, we don't want the cat to run out past us. We need a strategy. Vannie, why don't you see if you can get this wall to open and I'll block the doorway. I can toss this blanket over the cat if he's wily. Aggie, why don't you stand over to the right there? Vannie, give Aggie the cat's leash." Once everyone was in place Margaret said, "Okay, see if you can move the wall."

Margaret was right. The click she'd heard had disengaged the secret door. When Savannah put her hands on it, it began to move.

"Slowly, Vannie," Margaret coached. "We don't want him to get away."

However, when Savannah opened the door, a cat did not appear. She shined her light around the room. "Oh no. Auntie, you're not going to believe this."

"Good God, what now?" Margaret asked.

"Come look," Savannah encouraged.

Margaret and Aggie quickly joined Savannah at the opening and looked in the direction of the light.

"Uh-oh," Aggie said when Rags began to tug.

Savannah quickly took the leash from her and struggled to hold him back. "I think that cat's caught in the closet door! Oh my gosh, look how fat she is— lumpy fat. She's expecting, like any minute."

When Savannah started to move toward the cat, Margaret said, "No, Vannie. Don't open it yet. We don't want to lose her. Hold Rags back. Let me get my hands on her. Easy, little one," Margaret crooned as she approached the very pregnant cat. After a few moments, she whispered, "Okay, Vannie, slide that pocket door aside…slowly now. I don't think she has a limb or a tail caught."

"No, it's just her belly," Savannah said, stifling a chuckle.

"Poor kitty," Aggie said. "She must have tried to come out of there to eat or get a drink of water and found she no longer fit through that opening."

"Yeah, and the kittens rolled and tumbled, making her considerably wider, and she got wedged in there." When the cat was free, Margaret gently lifted her, wrapped the blanket around her and held her close.

"I've never seen anything like that," Savannah said. She reached out and petted the black-and-white cat. "Poor thing. She looks exhausted."

"Yes, I imagine she is." Margaret peered into the closet. "Looks like she found some old tablecloths or blankets or something here in this closet and made a bed for her kittens."

"How long do you think she's been stuck like that?" Aggie asked.

Savannah shined the flashlight around on the floor. "Uh-oh, it's been at least several hours, I'd say. See the puddle there on the floor?"

"Even several days," Margaret said. She told Rags, "Good job, boy. You may have saved this little girl and her babies." She looked around. "Now how do you suppose she got locked up in here like this?"

After thinking about it, Savannah squinted. "I'll bet the cats know how to open that secret door. Do you remember when we first saw the black cats up here? They kept disappearing right before our eyes. Yeah, they must be able to trigger the latch on that secret door and get in and out."

"Or there's another way in," Aggie said, glancing around the room.

Suddenly Margaret yelped. "Uh-oh, I think we're about to welcome a new family of kittens into the world. We'd better make her comfortable. Grab another blanket from that closet, will you, Vannie?" As an afterthought, she said, "And don't you get stuck in there with your big belly."

Savannah smirked at her aunt's attempt at humor. She pulled a piece of fabric from the closet and handed it to her. Then the three women made their way back down the staircase and out to the car with the cat. As Margaret carefully placed her in the larger of the two carriers, she said, "Ohhh, here they come. Vannie, why don't you take over? This is your expertise."

"Sure," she said, handing Rags's leash to Aggie, "but I doubt she'll need help. I'd like to offer her a little water. We don't want her to dehydrate."

"I'll get it," Margaret offered.

"No food right now," Savannah suggested. She then said, "You know, if she's been without food for a while, it might be a good idea to let her eat if she wants to."

"Coming right up."

Aggie approached Savannah. "Good job," she said.

Before either of them could stop him, Rags leaped into the back of the car and the female cat began to hiss and growl.

"Oh no you don't, Ragsy. This little girl does not want company right now—especially from a male," Savannah said easing him back down to the ground.

"Oops, my fault," Aggie said, taking up the slack on his leash.

Just then, Savannah leaned over and grabbed her belly.

"What is it, Vannie?" Margaret asked as she returned with a dollop of canned cat food and a bowl of water.

Aggie quickly supported Savannah and said excitedly, "She's about to have my grandson, that's what."

"Really, Vannie?" Margaret asked.

"I'm afraid so. I've been having small contractions all day." She took a deep breath and stood tall. "Yeah, I think it's time. We'd better get us home." She smiled at Aggie and took Rags's leash from her. "Are you ready to welcome your newest grandson?"

Aggie nodded. "Yes. Yes. Oh, Savannah, I'm so happy. This is a magical moment."

"Aggie, you're crying," Savannah said, hugging her.

"We've got a kitten," Margaret announced as she latched the carrier. "Looks like she'll do okay." She spoke to the cat. "Sorry girl, you'll have to push the others out while we're on the road." She glanced at Savannah. "You hold yours in until you get to the hospital."

"Yeah, I think I can do that. Just get us home. Michael will take it from there," Savannah said as she slipped gingerly into the car with Rags."

"Michael's going to deliver this one?" Margaret asked.

"No. He's going to drive us to the hospital."

"Oh this is going to be the best day of my life all week," Aggie said.

Chapter 11

At one fifteen in the afternoon on Tuesday, May sixteenth, little Theodore Michael Ivey was born.

"He's beautiful," Aggie said, dabbing at her eyes. "Just beautiful."

"Isn't he?" Gladys agreed. She hugged her daughter. "What a lovely gesture, Vannie, to name him after your father." She glanced toward the heavens. "He would be so pleased. Will you call him Ted?"

"Probably eventually," Savannah said. She looked into her baby boy's face and smiled. "For now, he's our little Teddy."

After several minutes spent admiring her new grandson Gladys said, "Your aunt is down in the lobby with Lily. I'm sure she's eager to come meet her new great-nephew." She patted Savannah's hand. "I'll send her up, then you should get some rest while he's sleeping."

"Okay, Mom. Thank you for taking care of things at home. We really appreciate it." She turned to Aggie. "And you too. I understand you made a coffee cake this morning."

"Yes, she did," Gladys confirmed. "And it was wonderful." She took Aggie's arm and the two of them walked toward the door. "Where did you learn your culinary skills?" Gladys asked.

Savannah smiled while watching them leave the room, then looked up at Michael. "We're so blessed."

He leaned down and kissed her, then softly kissed the baby's head. "Yes, we are."

"Where's my nephew?" Margaret asked as she stepped into the room. "I want to meet this robust little boy."

"Right here, Auntie," Savannah said, smiling down at the infant she held in her arms.

"Awww, Vannie, he's adorable. Oh my gosh, I thought Lily was the most beautiful baby I'd ever seen. But look at this guy. He's…he's…oh, Vannie, he's gorgeous," she said, her eyes filling with happy tears.

"Handsome," Michael corrected.

"Yes, that too," Margaret agreed.

"How's Lily?" Savannah asked.

"She's fine. She misses her mommy and she's eager to meet her baby." She laughed. "Not her baby brother, but her baby. Vannie, I think she plans to take him over…maybe keep him in her toy box, push him around in her doll stroller. I do believe she thinks you're bringing home a new dolly for her to play with." She looked at Savannah, then Michael. "When are you bringing him home—I mean, so we can hold him and all?"

Savannah glanced at Michael. "I think tomorrow."

He nodded. "That's what they told us."

"Good. Well, I have things to do and you need your rest. I'd better go." Margaret sighed deeply. "I must talk to that sister of yours and see if I can straighten her out."

Savannah frowned. "What's going on with Brianna?"

"Well, she wants my blessing for something I'm not too sure is a good idea."

"Like what?" Savannah pushed.

Margaret thinned her lips, then said, "Oh, I don't want to burden you with it."

"What, Auntie?" Savannah urged. "She isn't leaving Bud, is she?"

"Is that why he's been so preoccupied at work?" Michael asked, thinking out loud. When both women looked at him, he said, "He just seems a little grumpy—sort of in a funk. I've wondered if it has anything to do with Brianna. What's she up to, Maggie?"

When Margaret realized that she probably wouldn't get out of there without an explanation, she said, "Well, she wants my permission…um…or approval…to go on one of those adventures I used to suggest when she was a younger woman— you know, to learn something about life and to sow some of her wild oats." She winced. "But that was then—when the world was a gentler place. Now, I'm not so sure I'd suggest such a thing and I'm not sure the timing is right for Brianna to be doing this."

"She wants to travel? What about her practice?" Savannah asked.

"Yeah, and Bud…" Michael persisted.

"That's what I hope to talk to her about." Margaret gestured widely with her arms. "But she has this grandiose idea of traveling to places she's never been before and experiencing things she's never experienced. She figures it will give her time and space to consider her future, with or without Bud."

Savannah shook her head. "That sister of mine. I should have known she wouldn't settle down for long. She's one adventurous gal. I guess if Bud wants her, he might have to open up his horizons, if you know what I mean."

"Yeah. Bud is set in his ways—comfortable in his world," Michael offered. "I think he'd be better off with a woman who shares his love of the farm life."

Savannah looked into his face and said rather defiantly, "Or he could change."

Michael thought about her comment for a moment. "I think we all have limits as to how much we're willing to change, don't you?" When she didn't respond, he said, "I wouldn't quit being a veterinarian for any reason. And I'd hope that you wouldn't give up something you love to please someone else. We have to be true to ourselves, Savannah."

"Ohhh, this is a deep subject to be having in front of our brand-new arrival," Margaret said, running her fingers over Teddy's little head.

Everyone laughed when he scrunched up his face.

"You're right," Michael said. "Good luck with Brianna. I hope she does follow her heart and if it doesn't include Bud, it's best that they find that out before they start bringing little farmer boys and girls into the mix."

***

A couple of days later Brianna entered the Iveys' living room and announced, "I've been dying to see my new nephew. Where is he? Where is he?"

"Hi, Sis," Savannah said, hugging her.

When Lily saw her aunt, she ran to her shouting, "Baby, Auntie Bri!" She grabbed Brianna's hand and pulled her toward the portable crib, which was set up in the living room. "Baby, Auntie Bri."

"Awww, he's so cute," Brianna cooed.

"Yes, and I think it's about feeding time," Savannah said. "I'll change him and that'll wake him up enough to eat."

Once Savannah began nursing Teddy, Brianna looked around and asked, "Where are Mom and Michael's grandmother?"

"Out picking apricots. They want to make a cobbler and if we have enough, maybe a batch of jam."

"At ninety-two, the woman is still climbing trees and making jam?"

"Yes, well, Michael's helping them. We don't want either of the grandmothers on a ladder." She studied Brianna for a moment. "Sooo?"

Brianna avoided making eye contact. "So what?" she asked flippantly.

"So what's this I hear about you wanting to make some lifestyle changes just when it seems you have everything a woman could want—a nice career, a nice young man in your life…"

Brianna slouched a little. "Oh, Vannie, I don't know. I just don't know what to do. What I feel like doing is traveling—seeing people and places I haven't seen and helping along the way if I can—you know, sharing my medical skills."

"But you haven't decided for sure?"

"No. And I don't want to know what you think."

Savannah's eyes flashed rather mischievously. "Oh, you don't?"

"No. We're too different. You can't understand my needs any more than…um…than I guess I can understand yours. You've never had the wanderlust— the sense of adventure that I have. Vannie, I crave it like

255

I guess you have always craved being tied down to a family."

Savannah stared at her sister for a few moments. "Bri, are you running away from something? Bud, maybe? Your relationship? Are you feeling pressured…trapped?"

"Yeah, kind of. Sure. Wouldn't you? I mean really—me on a farm, feeding chickens?"

After thinking about what her sister had said, Savannah asked, "So what are your plans? Will you just distance yourself from Bud for a trial run? You aren't thinking about closing your practice, are you?"

"Maybe."

"That's a big step."

"Hey, I started a practice once, I can do it again, if I so desire. Anyway, I have someone to take it over for now while I'm on a…sort of a sabbatical."

"So you've put some thought into this, have you? Do you know where you're going?"

"Not really."

"Brianna," Savannah said sternly.

"Wait. It's not what you think. I joined a group. It's an adventure group. The leaders, Nancy and Bart, plan the itinerary and we just go along with it, adjusting to what may come. Vannie, I'm convinced this will be good for me—having to go along with someone else's agenda. You've told me before I should be more flexible—more open-minded."

Savannah rolled her eyes. "I think I said you might benefit from a more conventional lifestyle—that maybe you should consider settling down."

"I have settled down—maybe too much. I practice medicine all week and hang out with Bud and his parents most weekends." Brianna shook her head. "It's stifling, Vannie. I sometimes feel like I'm dying a slow death."

Savannah took a deep breath. "So you don't know if you'll be canoeing the rapids, wrestling alligators, or going on a safari?"

"That's right," Brianna said, smiling. "Maybe all of the above." She grimaced. "Packing will be a bear."

"Does Bud know about this?" Savannah asked quietly.

"He knows I've been thinking about it. That's all."

"When is all this happening? I'm guessing you're past the thinking stage. You've already signed up, haven't you?"

"Yup. I'm leaving tomorrow."

"Bri, I don't know what to say, except are you sure about this? Can you get out of it if you want to? You don't know what you'll encounter out there."

Brianna's face lit up. "Exactamundo!"

"And you're still game, huh?"

"Sure am. Sis, I need more excitement in my life than…well, than what I can get here in my practice and on Bud's farm." She peered into Savannah's eyes. "Can't you understand that?"

Savannah smiled at her sister. "No. I can't understand it. But…" she let out a sigh. "I wish you all the best. Stay safe. Will you write?"

Brianna walked to Savannah, who was now burping Teddy. She ran her fingers over his head. "Yeah, I'll write, as often as I can. I don't know about the rules on that yet. I had email conversations with a couple of people who've gone on these excursions and I guess they can be rather challenging. I'm actually eager to test and maybe strengthen my resolve."

Savannah sighed. "Well, I can think of better ways to do that, but hey, whatever works for you, I guess."

Brianna wrapped one arm around her sister, giving her an awkward hug. "Hey, I wish you could go with me. We'd have such a good time."

"I think my resolve will be tested enough this summer with two babies, a ninety-two-year-old, and Mom, not to mention an orchard that's starting to ripen."

Brianna rolled her eyes. "Dull. That's what I'd call it—dull." She reached out for Lily as the child walked past with her dolly in a blanket. "...except for this one. She's a laugh a minute." She kissed the top of the toddler's head. "I'll sure miss you, little one."

"Are you going someplace?" Michael asked, entering the room.

"Um...oh...yeah, I might be. But Michael, Bud doesn't know about it, yet. So mum's the word, okay? I'll probably talk to him...um...tonight."

"You aren't going to break his heart, are you?" he asked.

"Well, it's all in the perspective, I guess. I hope not. But what I have to do just might make him very happy in the long run." When she noticed Michael and Savannah staring at her, she said, "I'll know more about that when I return." Just then she heard her mother and Aggie chatting in the kitchen. She picked up her purse and rushed to the front door. "Gotta go," she said, quickly stepping out.

"Was that Brianna?" Gladys asked when she entered the room. "Where's she off to so fast?"

"Um…I guess she had an appointment, Mom."

"It's Thursday. Why isn't she working?" Gladys asked.

"She has taken some time off. You know she's going on a trip, don't you?"

"Yes, she told me. But I still don't know where she's going."

"Neither does she."

Michael looks confused.

"It's an adventure. She's going on one of those lifetime adventures before she settles down and starts a family."

"Oh, is that what the young women do these days?" Aggie asked.

"Well, I've never heard of such a thing," Gladys complained. "But then, I married young and my adventure was raising my daughters."

***

Later that evening as Michael got Lily ready for bed and Aggie was rocking baby Teddy, Gladys and Savannah chatted over tea in the kitchen.

"I'm thinking about selling my house, Vannie. What do you think?"

"And go where, Mom?"

"Well…" she hesitated.

"Here?" Savannah asked excitedly. "Are you thinking about moving back up here with me and Auntie?"

Gladys smiled. "Actually, yes. I know you've suggested it before, and I believe the timing might be right. I really do want to be closer to my grandchildren and you and Brianna, when she isn't off gallivanting. It just makes sense to live out my twilight years near family, before I'm too old to enjoy the little ones."

Savannah scoffed. "Twilight years? Mom, you're barely sixty?"

"Yeah and counting…"

"I'd love it if you'd move up here. I suppose you'll want a place of your own and you'll be eager to establish a life of your own."

"To an extent, Vannie." She leaned forward. "But what I'd love even more is to be involved with the kids."

"Sure, that's what being a grandmother is."

Gladys studied her daughter for a moment, then said, "I was thinking about being a sort of nanny-grammy. I could help you with the children and this big house and your canning duties…why, you could even go back to work, if you wanted to, or have more time to work on Rags's book. What do you think?"

"You mean move in here?" Savannah asked, her eyes wide. "I'd love it! Yes, that would be great. As you said, I can certainly use the help and I love having you here. Oh, I can't wait to tell Michael!"

"Good, because I've rented my house out for the rest of the year. I have a few things left to do like put my things into storage. Then I'm free to come back to Hammond."

Savannah asked quietly. "What about Bob, Mom?"

"We've kind of gone our separate ways. I think he knew I was ready to make a move and we just stopped seeing so much of each other."

"Oh this is great. I'm so excited."

"What are you excited about?" Michael asked when he walked into the room with Teddy in his arms.

"Michael," Savannah said, "Mom's going to move in with us and become our nanny."

Obviously startled, Michael looked at Gladys, then smiled and said, "Well, that's great. We'll be glad to have you...and your help...for as long as you can handle all the pandemonium here."

Just then the baby began to fuss and Gladys said, "It's music to my ears, believe me."

Michael gave his mother-in-law a one-armed hug. "Well good, then. It's settled. You're our new nanny and most welcome guest."

Chapter 12

Teddy was two weeks old when his Grammy Gladys arrived along with some of her belongings, which came in a small moving van. Michael and Damon moved her things into the master bedroom upstairs and Savannah helped her decorate it to her liking. By then, Aggie had left for Colorado to spend some time with Michael's twin brother, Keith, and his family. That evening Max and Margaret joined the Iveys and Gladys for dinner.

"What do you hear from Brianna?" Margaret asked, as they sat down to eat.

Savannah glanced at her mother before responding. "Not much. I guess she's not allowed to communicate with the outside world anytime she wants to."

"Yeah, or she's just having too much fun and doesn't want to write letters. She's never been a very good letter-writer, has she?" Margaret asked. "I got more phone calls from her than letters when she was in college."

"That's right," Gladys said, chuckling. "She isn't much for writing." She looked at Savannah. "Unlike my oldest girl. But I did get a note from her a couple of days ago."

"Where did it come from?" Savannah asked. "New York?"

Gladys nodded. "Yes, all of her letters come from New York. She said she was in South America, but I'm not clear as to where." She thinned her lips and complained, "That girl's penmanship is atrocious."

"That's 'cause she's a doctor," Margaret said, grinning. "I've never met one with decent handwriting."

She looked across the table at her sister. "South America, huh?"

"Yes, she was actually packing up and getting ready to leave the jungle or rain forest or whatever it was." She furrowed her brow. "She seemed a little concerned about their next stop."

"Did she know where they were going next?" Max asked.

Savannah shook her head. "They don't tell her anything ahead of time. She seems to be completely in the dark until they arrive someplace. Then everyone has to scramble around to gather the supplies and clothing they'll need."

"How much longer does she have to stay with the group?" Michael asked.

"That seems to be part of the adventure—not knowing the agenda," Savannah explained. "We don't know when to expect her home." She turned to Gladys. "Mom, has she given you any idea about that?"

She shook her head. "No. That's the part that's hard on the family."

Margaret was quiet for a moment, then asked, "So how does she seem to you, Gladys? Is this what she expected? Has she started to miss the life she'd begun to establish here?"

Savannah and Gladys looked at each other questioningly. Savannah spoke first. "When reading between the lines, I think the stress of the trip is kicking her you-know-what."

Gladys winced. "I agree. Oh, she's putting up a tough exterior…" She laughed. "She doesn't want to hear, 'I told you so,' but I get the impression that she's ready to come home."

"Yeah, I don't think she's a happy camper," Savannah added.

Gladys turned to her sister. "Maggie, have you heard from her at all?"

"Yeah, I got a couple of postcards. She seemed rather excited. But that was early on. I haven't received anything from her in a week or more." She looked at Gladys. "So a South American jungle, huh? I used to have a hankering to go there—you know, when I was younger."

"Not now?" Max asked.

"No. Too many mosquitoes and snakes." She shuddered, then asked, "So you think Bri is having second thoughts about this?"

Gladys winced. "I don't know if you'd say that. It sounds like the travels have been kind of hard on her—harder than she expected. She said they'd been living in a jungle for a few days—in cabins, but more remote and primitive than she likes."

Savannah nodded and added, "She told me it's been hard, but she's glad she's challenging herself."

Just then they heard a sound coming from the dining room. Savannah looked at Michael. "What was that?"

He laid his fork on his plate and stood up. "Probably your cat," he said, heading in the direction of the commotion. When he returned, he had a handful of envelopes in his hand. "Rags was getting into the mail. Didn't you have time to open it this afternoon?"

"Actually, no," Savannah said. She frowned. "But what does he want with the mail?"

Margaret chuckled. "Maybe he's expecting a letter or a sample from his favorite cat-food company."

Michael grinned at her, then handed Savannah one of the envelopes. "He was most interested in this one. He had it on the floor and was rolling around on it."

"Oh, from Bri," Savannah said, taking it. After looking it over, however, she said, "But this isn't her handwriting. It says it's from Brianna Jordan at the generic address she gave us to use if we needed to reach her—the one in New York. I guess that's the headquarters for the group she's traveling with." She paused. "Wait! It was postmarked in Los Angeles." She smiled at the others. "Maybe she's back."

"Open it, Vannie," Gladys urged. "What does she say?"

Before Savannah could tear into the envelope, however, Rags reached up with his paws on her lap and began pawing at it."

"I think he knows it's from her," Savannah said. She squeezed the envelope. "It's fat. Maybe she sent him some treats."

"Open it," Margaret insisted.

"Well, this is odd," Savannah said seconds later, while holding up a piece of cloth.

"What is that?" Gladys asked.

Savannah frowned. "I'm not sure—it looks familiar, though."

"Is there a note?" Michael asked.

Savannah looked into the envelope again. "Oh, yes. Let's see, it says, 'Twenty-thousand dollars and she's yours.'"

"What?" he said, reaching for the note. "What is this?"

Savannah shook her head. "I don't know, but I sure don't like the sounds of it."

Suddenly, Gladys slapped her hand over her mouth. "Oh nooo," she wailed.

"What, Mom? Do you know what this means?"

"That's a swatch from Brianna's carpet bag." When the others looked confused, she said, "You know, that funky overnight bag she wanted so badly when she had the wanderlust before she enrolled in college." Gladys took the piece of fabric from Savannah and fondled it. "She had to have this black-and-red paisley print bag." She looked up at Michael and Savannah. "What does this mean? She stared down at the fabric, her words lost in her emotion. "Has someone snatched Brianna? Oh my God, where is she? Where's my little girl?"

Made in the USA
Middletown, DE
16 October 2017